THE AUTHOR

Philip Callow, who was born in Birmingham in 1924, is the distinguished and highly praised writer of fourteen novels, as well as books of poetry. He is also the author of three biographies: *Son and Lover: The Young DH Lawrence*, *Van Gogh: A Life* and *Walt Whitman: From Noon to Starry Night* which was short-listed for the Yorkshire Post Book of the Year Award, 1992.

ALSO BY PHILIP CALLOW

NOVELS
The Hosanna Man
Common People
A Pledge for the Earth
Clipped Wings
Going to the Moon
The Bliss Body
Flesh of Morning
Yours
The Story of My Desire
Janine
The Subway to New York
The Painter's Confessions
Some Love

SHORT STORIES
Native Ground
Woman with a Poet

AUTOBIOGRAPHY
In My Own Land

POETRY
Turning Point
The Real Life
Bare Wires
Cave Light
New York Insomnia
Icons
Soliloquies of an Eye
Notes Over a Chasm

BIOGRAPHY
Son and Lover: The Young D. H. Lawrence
Van Gogh: A Life
Walt Whitman: From Noon to Starry Night

THE
MAGNOLIA

Philip Callow

a&b

This edition first published in Great Britain in 1994 by
Allison & Busby
an imprint of Wilson & Day Ltd
5 The Lodge
Richmond Way
London W12 8LW

A catalogue record for this book is available from the British
Library

ISBN 0 74900 168 2

Typeset by TW Typesetting, Plymouth, Devon
Printed and bound in Great Britain by
Cox & Wyman, Reading, Berks

TO PETER DAY

It's February. Weeping, take ink.
Find words in a sobbing rush
For February, while black spring
Burns through the rumbling slush. . . .

BORIS PASTERNAK, *February*

Ashes of one world
crumble
upon the colours
of another one . . .

JAAN KAPLINSKI,
The Same Sea in us All

PART ONE

BLACK
OF
SPRING

1

Daniel Marron opened his eyes. He had been dreaming violently. He had heard or read somewhere that life itself is a dream, but had never managed to make sense of this notion. Now, at the age of forty-six, he understood it perfectly – or rather, accepting it was no problem. *Hamlet*, apparently, is a dream play, and therefore a dream within a dream. He accepted this too. Shakespeare was lost on him anyway. At school he had been unable to follow the impossibly rich and complex language. Now he wouldn't even try. The very name Shakespeare had a punitive ring to it for him. Moreover, he suspected that his plays were beyond many people who were secretly ashamed of the fact. It was like being unskilled in the art of reading and writing – you learnt various stratagems in order to hide the disgrace.

The moment Daniel opened his eyes he felt relieved. It was a Sunday morning. In his last dream before waking – the one he believed to be his last, since he remembered it so vividly – he wandered down a long corridor which twisted and turned. He must have been in a hotel. There were doors everywhere. He went on searching in a mounting panic for the door to his room. Each one was identical with the one before. Why weren't they numbered? The corridor was on different levels, up two steps, down three, turning suddenly at right angles, curving in a circle. In real life, new surroundings would often confuse him. He would enter a large house and become bewildered at once by the landings and doors.

He was thankful for an instant, when he opened his eyes and found himself safe and sound in his own bed, a single divan. His wife's bed was empty, separated from his by a bedside locker. The bedroom door opened and Cora came in with the morning tea. Normally this was his task, because his wife slept late. She put the tray down on the locker. Instead of getting back in, she sat on the edge of her bed in her flowered kimono.

Daniel sat up. A slight man, his pyjama coat fell open to reveal his narrow chest. Always thin, his thinness was even more pronounced than usual; he had lost weight he could ill afford to lose. Stripped to the waist, his ribs showed. No longer bright-eyed, his habitual expression was a haggard look.

'You're early,' he said.

'Aren't I,' his wife said. 'I couldn't sleep. I had something on my mind.' She poured the tea, handing him his porcelain cup and saucer.

'I didn't hear you get up.'

Cora smiled enigmatically. 'Who's Margaret?' she asked, so brightly that a chill gripped his heart.

'Who?'

'You know – Margaret. An old friend, isn't she?'

'I'm trying to think.'

'Yes, think.'

'You tell me – you know my friends as well as I do.'

'Evidently not!'

'No?'

'I was hoping you'd remember.'

'No, I can't remember,' Daniel said with a slight tremor in his voice, angered by the feebleness of his words and the agitation they caused in him.

'Isn't that amazing!'

'Is it?'

'It's in your handwriting, too.'

'What is? What are you talking about?'

'Daniel, don't be obtuse. I'm not a fool, though I'm sure

3

you take me for one. I know something's going on. It is, isn't it? Why not be honest and say so?'

'All right, I'll be honest. Nothing's going on.'

'So who's Margaret?'

'Suppose you tell me. Margaret who?'

'I've been looking through the old diary in your desk drawer. Because I know, you see, I *know* something's going on.'

'You've no right to look in there!'

'And there it was. Margaret Sewell. Who is she, Daniel?'

'Ah, Sewell.'

'An old friend, is she?'

'She's not anybody. She's left now. That's right, she was doing a post-graduate year, and now she's teaching I suppose. Why didn't you say Sewell in the first place?'

'And you don't see her any more?'

'Even if I wanted to, which I don't, I couldn't. I don't know where she is. Exeter, probably. That's right, she wanted to teach in Exeter. She's the nun, the ex-nun I told you about.'

'You didn't tell me about any nun.'

'Ex-nun. Yes, I did. I told you. She climbed over the convent wall, metaphorically speaking. They kicked up a stink because they'd sent her to university and then she wouldn't go back inside again.'

Cora's eyes shone with derision. Still smiling, she said, 'Is that the truth?'

'It's the truth.'

'You're such a liar. There isn't any nun.'

'There is. There was. I told you all about her, for God's sake.'

'Why is she in your diary?'

'I can't remember. Maybe I had to see her about something.'

'I bet you did. Trust you to pick a bloody nun. Ironic, isn't it? I'm living with a monk and he's seducing a nun.'

'Cora, stop it. I told you, I haven't the faintest idea

4

where she is. She was unhappy, she was hopelessly in love with some man from Dawlish, a mature student like me, who didn't even notice.'

'Really? How do you know?'

'She told me. One day in the Common Room. At great length. Why am I saying all this when you don't believe me and it's none of your business anyway?'

'Because you're a liar. I don't hate you or anything, but I do loathe being taken for an idiot. That's what your lies do to me, you see, make me into an imbecile. You do see that, don't you?'

'Yes, all right. I'm having an affair with Margaret Sewell.'

'Who then? And there's a number under her name, a phone number probably. Why is it scribbled through?'

'Am I supposed to answer that? To destroy the evidence, what else!'

'You're such a liar.'

'Please keep your nose out of my desk and my diaries.'

'I'll find out who it is, and then look out, you liar.'

'Is that all for now?'

'You humiliate me with your dishonesty. Mother was right, she told me right at the start I was a fool to trust you. You have a viper's mouth, she said.'

'Well, there you are. A discerning woman.'

Walking away, she said, 'Give my love to Margaret when you see her.'

It was true that Margaret Sewell had left the college and disappeared from his life, and true that nothing had been going on, though God knows Margaret had wanted it. So did he – with someone, not with her. There was an element of subjugation in his relationships with women, and Margaret's forlorn passivity defeated him. He was desperate for something to happen which would save his foundering life, and who was he given? Margaret Sewell! She was foundering herself, God help her. So they had foundered together for a while, and it was sad, in a muted

5

way even terrible, and he was painfully conscious of the effect on Cora, who in spite of his miserable attempts at infidelity still lived with him, but alone now because, as she put it, he was 'somewhere else'.

Cora's retaliation, when it came, took various bizarre forms, each one more unexpected than the last. Her mother would purse her lips and bend her head, pretending that it was just another symptom of her daughter's unhappiness, but no doubt as dismayed as Daniel by its manifestations. First came the unmanageable hound she produced one day, all legs and exuberant jaws, a huge Afghan which became rapidly neurotic, in fact impossible to get out of the front door or even down the basement steps and into the garden. Next came the portrait, a large fantasy oil of Cora herself, in an Indian palace setting with arches, trellis and crenellated wall, wearing the pink and silvery green of a tightly swathed sari, bracelets hung on her wrists – a proud maharanee who displayed like a bullet hole dead centre on her forehead the red caste mark of her supposed rank. Her expression could only be described as a kind of triumphant bliss. Daniel gazed disbelievingly at this vision hanging over the bookshelves in its thick gilt frame – the whole thing accomplished while he was away for a few days visiting a friend in Wales – which had been paid for out of the remains of their joint account.

'Who did it?' he asked, like someone asking after a crime.

'Abner Yankel. I commissioned it.'

Yankel was the Jewish artist, down on the Barbican, who sketched tourists and their children and pets throughout the summer as a means of financing his one-man shows. They knew him slightly.

'How much?'

'Is that all you can say? Sixty pounds, if you must know.'

Then one evening Primrose called. This was a local char-

6

acter, his nickname famous, an effeminate elderly gentleman, accosted from time to time by sailors rolling down through the town towards the naval barracks. Still handsome at sixty, the wings of his snowy hair bushing out and lacquered, he had a measured and somnambulistic stride. The fine head and wincing nostrils, held well back, bore witness to an unspoken distaste. Cora had announced that she had spotted him with his hold-all on the concourse of the GPO. Rushing over on an impulse she invited him round for that evening, or any evening he cared to name, and he mustn't be alarmed but she had often admired him from afar and hoped to make his acquaintance one day.

'Please don't be offended, will you?'

'On the contrary,' he said, with perfect good grace, 'I shall be delighted to call on you, madam. What is your address?'

Hurrying home, Cora was – no doubt – naively eager to tell her mother. As she explained to Daniel, she burst in and said, 'Mother, I've seen Primrose! He's going to call in. You'll like him, I know you will, he's an absolutely charming man. Well, person,' she had laughed. 'You don't mind, do you?'

'Why should I mind?'

'Well, some mothers certainly would, I can tell you.'

'I'm not as narrow-minded as you might think.'

'Oh no, you're not, of course not. How could you be, with me for a daughter!'

When Primrose arrived, and had been formally introduced, they sat down to tea and conversation. Primrose's talk was more likely a stately dance, revolving prettily and getting nowhere. Things only livened up when he asked politely if he might get out his knitting.

'Why, of course you can! You hear that, Mother? Are you going to knit as well?'

'I don't see why not,' the old lady said tightly, with her best accent. 'I always do, don't I?'

'Oh good. You'll be able to compare notes, I mean patterns – is that what you do? I'm absolutely hopeless at knitting and sewing, aren't I, Mother – so I'll feel quite out of it. But I don't mind, not at all.'

Primrose smiled discreetly to himself, lifted his bag on to the sofa beside him and unzipped it with care. The knitting he drew out was a rich purple.

'What a lovely colour!' Cora cried. 'What's it going to be?'

'A cardigan,' Primrose said gently.

'A cardigan, I say. Aren't you clever. Don't you think he's clever, Mother?'

'Quite a few men can knit. Your father could. He learnt in the navy.'

Daniel slipped away upstairs.

Meanwhile, he was seeing Margaret from time to time, walking about with her despondently whenever he could on the college campus, sinking into bogs of silence with her and thrown into tongue-tied confusion by her adolescent shyness, for which she would try desperately to apologise. 'It's my fault . . . it's the convent you know . . . all those years. Talking was vanity, they said. Yes, really! Oh I'm hopeless, I don't know what to say, how to act . . . I – I can't *think* of anything . . .'

She had a first-class English degree and was speaking, he told himself, to a half-educated ex-clerk of forty-four. They both blamed the convent – where she had been locked up since the age of eighteen – for her underdevelopment. She would still be there now, she said, shaking her head in disbelief at her escape, if they hadn't seen her as teacher material and sent her to university. Once there she promptly fell in love with all and sundry, including a homosexual tutor and a drug-addicted student. At college it was the same story. The mature student in her group whom she had told Daniel about was a married man unaware of her existence. She widened her gentle brown eyes and invited Daniel to laugh at her. Her doleful dark looks and old-fashioned hair-do seemed curiously Victorian, her clothes drably woollen no matter what the season. He would find her on a bench near the rose beds, her head bowed over a copy of *Villette*.

She was thirty-three and looked sometimes like a disappointed woman of fifty. In spite of this he was drawn to her. Often he was shamed by her sad dignity. They would meet sometimes at Totnes Station, halfway between his home and the college. That was him in those days, he thought later – halfway to nowhere. He remembered that she was fond of Edwin Muir, and carried his autobiography about with her. Another bad sign! Here was a writer whom, with his wife Willa, Daniel connected with Kafka. At that time he had an aversion almost amounting to loathing for this Czech genius whose enormous tubercular eyes spoke to him of denial, fear, rejection of life, all of which would soon engulf him horribly and rush him straight to the brink. Was it a premonition, was that why he shrank back and made excuses when Margaret urged him timidly to read Muir? They walked the steep streets, sat speechlessly in cafes, sharing a banquette if nothing else, admiring nature down by the river and in the grounds of Dartington Hall, and he would glance surreptitiously at his watch and long for his joyless home.

And here was another irony. He had developed a horror of home, according to Baudelaire the 'great malady' of modern times, and yet when he tried to desert it he was petrified. His legs froze where he stood, his feet were nailed to the boards. How could he survive without walls and a roof for shelter – by which he probably meant without love? Yet in his house now there was only simmering hate, created by him and his deceptions. With his own two hands he had demolished hearth and home until not one brick stood on another. He sat in the ruins – or rather on the bed in his room. Below him were his two deadly enemies, Cora and her mother, both, it seemed, monsters of his creation. Each time he attempted to eat, it hurt. He got steadily thinner, with a lust for sugar, stealing marzipan from the pantry in the small hours. One evening, slinking downstairs to stand pressed to the closed sitting-room door, convinced that they were plotting against him, he was surprised by Cora coming up from the kitchen.

'What are you doing?'

'Nothing,' he mumbled. He stepped hastily to one side.

She stared at him with her face blank. 'You're a fucking nutcase,' she said. 'Or I should say a non-fucking one.' She went in and shut the door.

Soon he was almost a skeleton, jabbering aloud to himself that it was all a mistake, he had a 'problem' and if only he could remember what it was he would solve it – except that he had long ago forgotten it, or it had got mislaid somehow, so that this mislaid 'problem' was now the problem, he must locate it as a matter of urgency.

Before long, though it seemed a lifetime, they came for him in a car. He begged to be allowed to go to his mother instead of to the place where they had booked a bed for him. 'Later on, old man, not now,' the doctor said, his smile conciliatory but his arteries iron. 'You may find this hard to believe, Mr Marron, but after a month or two you'll see the world through different eyes.' How could the man have known?

On the motorway he tried to make himself open the car door and jump out. They swept into the curve. His arm wouldn't move, his brain was seized in his skull. Behind him, Cora was chattering to the driver about the fourteen-hour gale. It was still blowing. The Mini rocked and sped along.

2

It was at the hospital that he saw the black girl, and in the south-west such a sight was still unusual. Daniel found it startling here, a raw dusky note to confuse the anxious pallor. An ancillary worker, she came wafting in and out daily, and for all he knew that was the sum total of what she did. What Daniel appreciated was the frivolity, and her high bottom, high heels. She was long-legged. She looked happy. He saw her one day prance down the corridor like a giraffe, trot round the corner, and as she went she peeped back over her shoulder and let out her silly laugh. Was it for his benefit?

Once he was near enough to smell her – the sweet, heavy and thick patchouli oil. One of the male nurses would come over. He would hang around her. She squeaked and giggled, she'd flap her long loose-jointed fingers over his arm and say, 'Get away, let me by!' Watching her in admiration, Daniel would mutter the word 'Odiferous' under his breath, laughing at the word and at her. He used to ask himself what it must be like with someone like that, no question of a relationship, no thoughts in common, just touch and appetite. All you could do with laughing flesh was live peaceably with it. So he told himself, though he felt nothing. Not a thing. He was simply curious. 'It would be like living with yourself in a kind of happy mud,' he thought.

And in a way that was how it was, he felt, as he left that terrible first week behind and found himself set free, liberated from his past self as never before. He thought his character must have been transfigured, changed drastically overnight. Instead of his usual watchfulness he was unguarded, and he wanted to go on in that fashion, that direction. Expanding. The smile on his face was new, coming up from his feet, out of the ground – a fountain of smiles.

It had been so long since he'd actually smiled. And such an age since he'd laughed that he was forced to manufacture something resembling a laugh. When he tried it out it sounded phoney, he thought. He stopped doing it and smiled instead. Endless smiles, from the groundswell. Spring. It invaded him in a single wave and went on, out through the smiles, snaking around trees and people like lassoes. Could it have been the drugs? Hypomania? And if so, why weren't the others feeling as he did? They could have been. They didn't look as if they were. Idly musing, becoming interested in things again, enjoying the joke on himself, he preferred to think it was a combination of ingredients. Take Ruby, the big girl in the wheelchair, and Stan the Brummie in the room next door – surely they must have played a part in it. Why not? Weren't they somehow always with him in the day and in his thoughts at night? Didn't they share the only reality which now meant anything to him? He wandered about with time deliciously on his hands and considered this. Whatever he did or didn't do, it felt good. Being stupid and vague was so pleasant. Sometimes he could scarcely keep from laughing, even though he didn't possess a laugh. Here I am in middle age, he would think, shaking his head and chuckling in a kind of snuffle, a mystery to myself.

Ruby was an adept. She would make it her business to find out things. She soon wormed his story out of him. What she didn't worm out by devious means she just asked for, direct. She was easy to oblige, and her own story was there for the asking, and she was that rare

12

person, a good listener. Her long years incarcerated in hospitals had given her lots of practice. Clearly she was sane as an animal, so Daniel asked her first what she was doing here, and in a wheelchair.

'They can't think of anywhere else to put me,' she said cheerfully.

He was soon glad of that. He would sit talking to her, and liked to push her up and down in her chair now and then. What was nice about her was her availability, and the spontaneous welcome she gave you. She was the same with everyone. She was a young woman in her late twenties with a broad, open face. Big shoulders, big hands. She was from the country around there.

Her story was simple enough. As a young kid she kept falling over for no apparent reason and in general acting clumsily, and her father, a farm worker, used to belt her for it. Eventually they found out she had polio. She was one of a large family, so they were glad to dump her in hospital for a while. Then they split up: she had no home to go back to. She had landed up in this place and was supposed to be on a waiting list for a home for the handicapped that wasn't even built yet.

'How long is it going to be?'

'Well, they started it four years ago, and stopped.'

'What happened?'

'I think they ran out of money.'

Naturally, he was glad of that – though he expressed sympathy, and even a mild disgust. Selfish though this seemed, it was the way he felt. Ruby was nice to catch sight of in the mornings, even in his happy mud state. 'Hallo,' she'd call. 'Come here, I've got something to tell you. Something interesting.' She soon sized him up: she saw possibilities in him. He would go over obediently, with a gleam in his eye. If she was heading for the Day Room he would start pushing her chariot. Usually she had some harmless titbit of gossip to trot out. Sometimes she didn't want a pusher. 'It's all right, I can do it with my hands.'

'I enjoy it,' he told her once.

'Go on, then. Are you used to prams, is that it?'

'Prams, no – not any more. How old d'you think I am?'

She ignored this. 'Listen,' she said urgently, and she lowered her voice. 'Clifford's been telling me about his two women.'

'Who's Clifford?'

'Ssshh – not so loud. Over there, by the door. Is he looking this way? Talk about something else.'

She loved these little games, and he was amused at first. Then it dawned on him that they were the spice of life for her. She would swing round her head, her eyes sparkling. She had a wide, frank grin. Her eyes dived straight into him. Once upon a time this would have made him clam up. Now he was changed, broken wide open to everything, and yet strangely tranquil, like an old man without ambition and with no more desire. He imagined he felt like an old Jew, full of ancient sorrow, all sly peppery humour. Walking around in this funny state, in this safe place, he remained essentially solitary, yet here he was enjoying his first experience of communal living. At the same time he was every man who had fallen down howling.

One morning, after collecting his breakfast from the serving hatch, sitting at one of the small tables with a group of fuddled men, saying one or two stupid things about the weather, grinning at them, feeling pretty chirpy, opening a letter or two and swallowing his pill ration, he wandered out to the kitchen with his tray of empties and Ruby was there, in the corridor on her wheels, waiting for him. This wasn't normal, not so early. Women were segregated in the other wing of the building, fraternising only in the evenings.

'Good morning,' she said brightly.

'You're out of bounds,' he told her, and took his stuff into the kitchen. He wasn't on the washing-up rota for this breakfast. A towering dog-rough man with ginger hair

14

stood violently over the sink, crashing plates and cutlery around. It made a fearful din. Steam billowed up. Water was everywhere. His two helpers were hanging back timidly, clutching teacloths.

'The rules don't apply to me,' Ruby told him proudly, when he got back to her. 'I'm exempt. I go where I like.'

'So you're a trusty.'

'Something like that.'

'Where are you going this early?'

'Well, I know it's drizzling and cold and horrible outside, but I want to go and look at it. I want to smell it.'

'Is that all?'

She gave me a look. 'Yes,' she said.

He got behind her and steered her down to the far end of the short-stay block and came to the door opening on to the panoramic view, where the ground fell away and you could see clumps of trees in the distance and beyond them a glimpse of wild moor. She leaned forward confidently and shoved the door open, telling him by her action that she had done this dozens of times before. And she was right: a bleak wet morning in early March lay there; no colour, nothing to see. Yet it excited her. She sat sniffing it up, wedged in the doorway staring hard at nothing.

'Last night I could hardly sleep,' she said. 'My side hurt, but it wasn't that. It was a full moon, I think. Was it one?'

'Couldn't say.'

'Perhaps it was that. And it's the spring coming. Can't smell it?'

'No,' he admitted. He could feel it, though. If you craned your neck far enough you could see, outside the library building next to the mouth of the tunnel leading to the innards of the main hospital block, a magnolia in a circular bed that was urging itself into new life almost visibly as you watched, its thick juicy buds sticking up for everyone to admire.

Once, late at night, when he was pushing Ruby back through the corridor on the way to her wing, she said, 'Turn right here.'

Up in that direction it was a dead end, leading to the X-ray equipment and nothing else. Naturally he assumed that she wanted to make a phone call. They went trundling towards the call box used by patients. He parked the chair so that when he took the phone off the hook she could use it, just about, by leaning sideways with her head in the doorway.

'Tell me the number and I'll dial it for you. Give me some change, will you?' Saying that, it struck Daniel suddenly that she wasn't carrying a purse or a handbag. Her face exuded the wickedness of some secret.

'What number?' she said.

'Aren't you going to ring someone up?'

'What for? Who the hell have I got to call?'

'I don't get it.' He stood perplexed, like an idiot. There was a switch on the wall to the right of the phone box. 'Why are we up here?'

'Turn off the light,' she said. It was an order.

He did as he was told. 'I thought you were going to bed?'

'I am,' she whispered, in the half-dark. 'Say goodnight to me first.'

'Goodnight, Ruby.'

'With a kiss.'

When he obeyed, she sucked at his lips hungrily and stuck her tongue into his mouth as far as it would reach. Her arm grappled him to her in a headlock, but even without that he'd have been powerless to stop her; he liked her too much. It was a matter of acting and hanging on. With one eye he was watching nervously for any sign of life along the lighted main corridor.

'Okay,' he muttered, breaking free at last. It wasn't the kissing, it was what it signified. 'That was a wicked goodnight.' Hopefully he reached for the light switch.

'Not yet,' she whispered, her eyes glistening, and he heard in her voice something that was hard and yearning at the same time. She made herself the dream actress to his bad actor. 'Daniel, quick – give us another wicked one!'

16

This time she didn't hook her arm around him. He decided that she had seen through him. Her wet pulpy mouth tasted sad. They went on to her room without another word. She didn't twist around to grin at him as she usually did.

She shared a room with an older woman whose bed was empty.

'Where's your friend?' he asked. It came out as a croak. He could hear the shame in it.

'Oh, gone to a social. Sit down a minute. It's all right – I told you I'm a special case. The rules don't apply to me. They don't regard me as an able-bodied woman.' She laughed.

'Little do they know.'

'Would you like to hear some music?' She had a record player by her bed. She rummaged around and put on a disc: Simon and Garfunkel's *Bridge Over Troubled Water*. The music played. 'Isn't it beautiful?'

'Very nice.' Daniel had always detested that syrupy rendering. After a few minutes the other woman came in and he got out of there.

3

Back in his room, thinking his own thoughts, Daniel made up his mind to steer clear of Ruby for a while. She was getting too fond of him. Soon she would start demanding to know what he felt about her. Surely, though, with her long experience of broken men passing through this place in an endless procession, she could see how it was with him? What an empty vessel he was? Well, maybe he didn't resemble the others in her eyes. He had no way of telling. It didn't bother him one jot. He saw himself as a person of no importance, so the whole question was irrelevant. His hold on life was tenuous, frail, growing stronger every day. Even now he could hardly believe what was happening to him. Since it was the first time in his life that he'd fallen ill, recovery was a kind of miracle. So was life itself. He wondered how it was that he could see so much clearer now that he was lower than the grasses.

Even as he swore to himself that he would keep away from Ruby, he knew he would postpone the decision next time he saw her. She was no beauty but she magnetised him, like the sky endlessly changing, the muddy ground registering footprints, the pallid shine of the sogged grass. His feet would start walking in the direction of that sturdy grin. Sex had nothing to do with it: in fact he wondered if he still possessed any. Had it been consumed utterly by his illness along with everything else? He could no longer remember what lust felt like. What a privileged person he was, lapping up the licentiousness of the new milk in the magnolia tree, the first wet flowers, the whistling of birds, wading around in it blithely without having to pay the price of his freedom for any of it. He was going to enjoy the condition for as long as it lasted. It seemed permanent, absolutely natural and normal. He was quite dazed with his good fortune. Even the word 'enjoy' had a dream quality. In the so-called sane world he came from it had seemed empty of meaning.

First of all he had found himself in a large ward of anonymous wrecks, then a smaller dormitory where he was able to put names to people. Soon, when it became clear that he was on the mend and no longer a problem, he was given a room of his own. It was only necessary to apply for it. It baffled him when they seemed pleased, until he saw that they interpreted his request for privacy as a sign of real progress. It meant that he was acting freely once again, in other words like everyone else. Clever fellow! He was curious to see what their records said. He didn't ask. Things were going along so beautifully, swimmingly. The word 'contentment' would rise up and nearly choke him.

It was like a continuous dream that was both strange and curiously familiar. In the late evening he would enter his neatly furnished cubicle, stare around with pleasure, then take the few steps to the other end. There was nothing in this tiny room to admire, but when he fastened the door behind him it was his own domain, the space filled by the narrow bed, a rudimentary dressing table with two shallow drawers, and even a matchboard wardrobe in which to hang his jacket and top coat. Scrambled moss and decaying leaves in lurid colours exploded under his feet, a carpet designed by a lunatic who was no doubt a respected member of his community – unless, that is, he had slaughtered his wife and family with a sawn-off shotgun before leaping from a suspension bridge. Daniel liked to stretch out on his bed and let his fancy roam free. French windows, narrow, with corroded steel frames, let in the murky daylight.

19

He would yank over the curtains and shut out the dark. Not any more out of terror. If he found himself lying awake but sleepless in the hours after midnight he wandered down to the night nurse, a soft-voiced boy threading plastic beads into bracelets and necklaces in order to kill time, and sat with him for a while. If he stayed too long, the boy's eyes would turn a little sneaky and his hand would reach out for a beaker and some medication to knock out his visitor. Daniel, to humour the lad, was quite happy to drink it down. What difference did it make? At the first crack of light through the curtains, or even earlier, at the first sounds of life, he would leap out and dress, eager for another serving of day, buzzing to live. It was a shame to waste a minute. Maybe he had become afflicted with another classifiable sickness, namely elation. Why complain, if it felt so good? It was like dwelling in heaven without experiencing a moment of boredom.

In the room to his right, Daniel could hear Stan moving about, soft and insistent, like a moth banging against the walls and then colliding with the light bulb, a creature who was always active, never at rest, and this was doubtless why he had landed up here. Everything had become too much. He smiled and smiled to disguise his habit of incessant worrying. 'Like I once was,' Daniel thought, 'but worse. And without my cynicism.' An innocent. In this place you were always recognising yourself in the mirror and feeling relief, usually at the expense of some poor mutt whose comical or sad traits had got out of hand. You laughed and pitied and you congratulated yourself on a near escape, all in the one breath.

Stan was desperate to be liked, to be of service. On the outside he was a steward in an army officers' mess, as well as working at two or three other jobs besides, to make ends meet. He was a small neat man, with tiny feet, his voice sing-song, but bright and chirrupy, not the customary Brummie whine. Now and then Daniel was reminded of the childishness of his own father. 'He's a bird,' Daniel

20

thought, and then at night he would imagine a lost soul circling and banging, a moth-man. The daytime Stan had a warm and yet pouncing manner, a combination to be found in cities but hardly ever in the country. And this was the close, secretive south-west.

Daniel had to admit that Stan knew: he knew what was wrong with him. 'I'm a terrible worrier, you see,' he told Daniel, smiling.

'Aren't we all, Stan.'

'Ah yes, well, that may be, that's interesting, you mean people, some people, cover it up?'

'They do, yes. Like a lot of things.'

'Yet take you, my friend – you don't strike me as a worrier. You're relaxed.'

Daniel had to smile. 'Now I am.'

'Well, yes, I don't really know you I suppose, do I?'

'I'm in the dark myself.'

A chance remark, but Stan pounced; he was uneasy with it. One more thing to worry about. What was Daniel getting at? Why did he grin? Because Daniel was grinning, Stan laughed.

After living next door to Daniel for a week, Stan presented him one morning with a gouache he'd painted in the art-therapy room: a spray of daffodils floating in thin air, the stems stiff as if they were starched. Each bloom was naively bright, wide open to the world, defenceless. Each one reminded him of Stan. In the bottom right-hand corner he had scrawled a laborious inscription: 'To Daniel, from Stan.'

'I want you to have this.'

'Thanks, Stan.' Daniel was waiting for the apology he could see brimming up.

'It's not very good,' Stan said. 'It's the first picture I've ever painted as a matter of fact.'

'That's amazing. Are you going to do some more?'

'Oh no, I doubt it. I think I'm leaving next week.'

'Then you ought to keep it. A memento.'

Stan shook his head. 'No, no, I painted it for you. You're my china.' He grabbed Daniel's hand. 'I want you to know that,' he said. His eyes were shining with devotion. 'Fancy a cup of tea?'

'I wouldn't mind.'

Stan hurried ahead to the Day Room as if he were on a tight schedule. Turning right into the kitchen he called, 'Daniel, how many sugars?'

'Two.'

'You go and sit down.'

The big room was for men only, except at visiting time, which seemed to stretch throughout the afternoon. Several middle-aged men sat dopily on easy chairs against the walls. Daniel nodded to one or two.

Stan came fussing in with the tray. As well as the tea he had brought a plate of biscuits and the sugar bowl. 'Listen, you won't believe this,' he said worriedly, 'I forget how many sugars you said.'

'Never mind,' Daniel told him. 'One.'

Stan sugared his friend's tea, then his own – the eager steward whose memory slipped occasionally. He sat like a man who would welcome a complaint, simply for the pleasure of putting it right. Daniel leaned back and sighed, enveloped in warm kindness, and crossed his legs, and tried to feel like an army officer.

4

Daniel regularly received a cheque from the Department of Health, and that same morning he took it to the village post office and cashed it. As he hadn't realised he was entitled to benefit, he would experience first a little shock of surprise as he tore open the envelope, then an illicit thrill, before laughing for no apparent reason at the breakfast table. The others were in receipt of theirs, no doubt. He never noticed.

Money in this haven was superfluous. All he ever used it for was to buy peanuts and chocolate bars and the occasional beer in the evenings, but to have it arrive out of the blue and so smoothly was beautiful, like a joke but also a miracle, and he only cashed it in order to enjoy the feel of the money in his hand. On his admission day, as they were leading him round like a drunk who was liable to fall over at any moment, an official came up and asked if he knew his National Insurance number. He could only shake his head dumbly. Even his own name had become meaningless to him.

Ruby caught him one morning as he was making for the craft-therapy workshop. They had a bulky worn-out office typewriter in there for general use. He liked tinkering with it. Or he would sit doodling on a sheet of typing paper with a ball pen. Also there was a great deal of lively chatter, men and women conversing, some sawing and banging, and one of the women would make tea at the sink for them all and start dishing it out. People were busy

23

with different tasks: raffia and basket work, simple carpentry. Daniel messed about with the typewriter as a cover, so that he could remain idle. The delight of idleness was for him a new discovery. And he could watch the others in peace. The instructor would come by, ask if he needed anything, and that was his job finished – he could concentrate on the ones with problems. The truth was that Daniel had no desire to make anything. To do absolutely nothing without guilt was wonderful. When he got bored with that he wandered out again.

He was moving quite fast this morning, going in, when Ruby came round the corner and caught him – swung her chair deftly so that it was slewed against the corridor wall and his path blocked. Obviously she had succeeded with the same trick dozens of times. She glowed with triumph. Daniel saw again what a paradox it was, her strong thick body and beefy shoulders denied properly working legs to carry her over those fields where she belonged. Even so, the force of life in her made the chair somehow part of her, and her movements glittering and undeniable.

'That was neat.'

'You're in a hurry, aren't you? Where's the fire?' She spoke with her usual pugnacious good humour.

'I'm just going in here.'

'Why, what are you making?'

Whatever you made you paid for, materials only, at a special rate. 'Nothing,' he told her. 'I can't think of anything I need.'

'Then why go in?'

'Sometimes I like the company.'

'Mind if I join you?'

As he held the swing doors apart and she wheeled herself through, she said over her shoulder, 'Listen, have you been avoiding me lately?'

He frowned. Stuck for an answer, he scratched his head clownishly.

'Come over here where it's quieter,' she said. 'I want to ask you a personal question.'

They backed into a quiet corner. Daniel had begun darting about inside himself, guessing at her question – he was right – and preparing an answer that would leave him room to manoeuvre. Then, before she lifted her head and dived in, he surrendered. 'Ask away.' Why be on his guard, he thought, against Ruby. Besides, he trusted her. There wasn't a crumb of malice in her.

Because he had offered no resistance she blushed, looked contrite and began fidgeting with her hands. 'I'm not being nosey,' she stammered, 'it's not that.'

She was hungry for information, that was all. People confided in her, the mother hen, the fixture. If they didn't she coaxed and wheedled the details out of them. In Daniel's case, she bullied. She was young and zestful, unable to stay passively quiet, so she had appointed herself general adviser to all and sundry. What had begun as a pastime, to combat boredom, was now an addiction. Under the guise of doing good she was hooked. Daniel had watched her watching everyone else. 'I might as well succumb,' he thought.

'When are you going to tell me about yourself?' she cried impulsively. It was nearly a wail. 'We're friends, aren't we?'

'What shall I tell you?'

'Anything you like.'

'My problem is that I don't have any problems.'

'Liar!'

Daniel shut his eyes for a second. He thought of Cora as he heard this word. But hers had dripped with vitriol, while Ruby's couldn't have been friendlier. 'It's true, really,' he said.

'Not one single problem?'

'What's the matter, do you want me to manufacture a few?'

'No. Just talk to me.'

'My story would bore you.'

'No, it wouldn't – I love stories!'

'I'm a bit shy.'

'I know you are. You needn't be, not with me.'

Her eyes shone with childish fascination, staring directly into his face. Their session was under way.

As he trotted out a few details from his recent past he kept one eye on Jim Oates, over by the door, who sat chainsmoking and glaring round at the scene with furious disgust. Daniel was a secret admirer of this foul-mouth. For one thing, he was without a mask. What you saw was the truth, ugly or not. Oates was an alcoholic who kept trying to kill himself, but so far had always bungled it. 'Perhaps, like me,' Daniel thought, 'he lacks the courage.' Ruby dealt with him in short order. She called him a souse. 'He's particularly abusive on the subject of women.' There was plenty of covering noise but she still lowered her voice discreetly. 'I've spoken to lots of souses here. It's nearly always woman trouble.'

What Daniel appreciated was the man's deadpan violence in the mornings, gazing down at the wrecked bed, confronting the mirror over the washbasin in the communal toilets, rubbing his electric razor around his sunken cheeks in the dormitory. He could load the sum total of his disgust into a single outburst and somehow it came out comic as well as savage. 'You fucking abomination, you mistake,' he'd say to his own face as he shaved.

Daniel said, 'He must have a first name. What is it, do you know?'

It was the only time he had seen Ruby stumped for information. 'I think it's Jim,' she said uncertainly. 'He's vile, I have to say it. He's never once said a friendly word to me. Has he to you?'

Daniel shook his head, smiling in spite of himself. 'And I was in the next bed to him.'

'Typical. I can believe it.'

'What's made him like it?'

'God knows. He's a horrible specimen of a man. Isn't it terrible, saying that? I can't help it, he is. Men are all the same, all egotists, but some are charming with it. Like children, you know? Oh Daniel, you're a man, but you're different.'

'Are you sure?'

'Yes. Oates, he's a particularly nasty specimen, that's what I think. He's too close, I'm not saying any more. Ask me another time.'

When Oates spoke to anyone, which was rare, he left off the person's name. Names were probably too personal, and therefore disgusting. One morning he was called in to see Mr Quinn, one of the visiting consultants. So little happened that this was big news among the others. It was also a puzzler. Who would want to waste time interviewing such a lost cause as Oates, a man only interested in killing himself? The Day Room buzzed. Mixed in with the excitement was a certain envy. Nearly everyone dreamed of a personal chat with the consultant; for a brief moment you became important, considered seriously as an individual, plucked out of the crowd. It meant status, too. When you emerged, no matter how futile the exchange might have been, you kept the futility to yourself because of all the jealous eyes fixed on you, and because of the rarity of the event. Quinn was in fact a funny old dodderer who waved his rolled umbrella at you in the corridor from twenty paces and went off cackling to himself. You found yourself asking who *his* consultant was.

Oates had been in for at least half an hour. He came out. In the Day Room, Daniel saw him through the glass, approaching. Entering the room, he crashed down in the first available chair, next to Daniel. He said nothing, which was perfectly normal. His dead gaze was fixed on the blank wall opposite. Screwing up his nerve, Daniel asked, 'What's he like?'

'Who?'

'Quinn.'

'A prize cunt.'

End of conversation.

Ruby was saying gratefully, 'I'm glad you confided in me, Daniel. We *are* friends, aren't we? You don't mind me asking these things?'

Daniel smiled, telling her that yes, they were friends and no, he didn't mind. If you trusted Ruby with a few scraps, that was sufficient, she tucked you into her womb without more ado. What he had told her, in half a dozen disjointed sentences, were just bald facts which made little sense to him now. She was welcome to them, though they made no attempt to answer the fundamental questions. For instance, where did he get on the downward spiral, when did it start? Was it when he ran off with Cora, someone else's wife? Or with the death of his father? When he went to college and became infected with the common restlessness? His wife's mother moving in with them? His daughter's metamorphosis, an adult of eighteen who was still his child? 'Dadda, I want to get married.' Was it then?

Ruby clutched urgently at his sleeve and held on for a second. 'Look at that basket Doris is making – isn't it fantastic? Wouldn't you like to make something like that with your hands?'

'Wouldn't you?' he retaliated, and then felt mean.

'I have. I've made so many, I've lost count.'

'Where are they, then?' he joked. 'Under your bed?'

'I usually give them away. To friends. You could do that.'

'My friends have nearly all been women,' he found himself saying. 'In other words, I don't have any.'

'Not even one?'

He said he would think about it.

'Love has to ripen into friendship,' she said naively. Though it sounded like one of her records, somehow she made it ring true.

'I've been bad at that.'

'You'll get better. Don't be so hard on yourself. Give yourself a chance. Hey, I'm going over there, I want to ask Doris something about last night.'

'Why, what happened?'

'That's what I want to find out.'

'I see.'

'Don't think I'm deserting you!'

'I won't.'

She thrust at the chrome rims of her wheels, steering smooth and oiled between the work tables. After years of practice she was able to give the operation an air of grace and sophistication.

Daniel sat down at the ugly typewriter and messed about with it, tapping out one-liners, 'It's not bad being mad' and suchlike nonsense. Then he got hold of a pencil and did a crude sketch of Ruby's head as she sat talking to Doris. After a few minutes his drawing began to resemble a massive chunk of stone, with chisel marks. This led him to wonder whether he should find a large lump of clay in the art-therapy room and try modelling her head life-size. He had seen them at it in there. You did whatever you liked; no one was turned away. A woman artist came in a couple of times a week, but if you were quiet and seemed occupied she left you alone. The thought of that dollop of clay excited him, the sensations were already there in his fingers, filthy with the grey mud, the slime. That was as far as it went. Later he did a few more sketches of Ruby's big squarish head with the broad nose squashing out into nostrils, the long, incongruously happy mouth. He told her in confidence about his vague project. She showed little enthusiasm but she humoured him. Once or twice he sat sketching away by the side of her bed in her room. She had no vanity, no illusions about her thick plain features, so she found it hard to sit still.

'All right, move,' Daniel would say.

'Let me see.'

'It's the shapes I'm drawing, not your expression.'

'Why not that?'

'What's the point? You have hundreds of expressions.'

She lost interest then. The only art which meant anything to her was soulful art.

Daniel's urge to model clay on a big scale, and with no experience whatsoever, could have been his exhilaration wanting to manifest itself, or it could have merely been the result of all the vitamins they were pumping into him. The first week he had been skin and bone, ordered to stay put in bed. What a fool he felt – he was the only inmate in such a woeful physical condition. He lay, and sat up if anyone was around, ashamed of his difference, imagining that he looked a freak. One morning a businesslike, ratty little man in a dark suit arrived with a syringe.

'Roll up your pyjama sleeve.'

He did as he was told. 'What is it?' he mumbled.

'Vitamins.' To make sure he wasn't wasting the stuff, the man checked Daniel's name a second time. 'Marron?'

'Yes.'

Then he had trouble finding a vein in the stringy, dead-white arm. 'Not a lot of you, is there?' he complained. The needle, when he pulled it out, reminded Daniel of a six-inch nail.

'These shots,' the man said, 'cost five pounds each.'

They gave him four altogether, followed by insulin jabs each morning after his shave, to liven up the pancreas and induce a raging appetite. Soon he was gobbling up everything in sight and looking round for more. Each mealtime his loaded plate was the envy of the whole table. He would go up to the hatch in the queue with the others and the kitchen hand would call out his name. 'Yours is a special,' they told him.

Soon he was putting on weight rapidly, his eyes brightening and his legs carrying him off strongly on walks, and down to the cafetaria between meals, where he reached out for snacks as if his fingers had developed appetites of their own.

Also he was noticing the weather again, particularly at night, hearing the wind battering at the window as it came streaking off the moor on this exposed site where there was nothing to stop it, a noise which had put the fear of

God into him when he was demented, frightened of everything and everybody, cowering under the blanket in his room at home. He thought 'they' were coming for him (they were). He was about to be punished and locked away behind bars for all the deceptions he'd practised, the crimes he'd committed. Now, though it was hardly a lullaby, it was the opposite of fearful. It had the sound of shouldering power, it was packed with muscle, *his* growing muscle – and he could hear the spring. Things were reversing, he was getting younger instead of older. In between the sheets, listening, his ears seemed to be sharpening, while the crisply laundered hospital sheets resting on his skin made him feel newly born. The twitching of his legs wasn't nerves, it was impatience; or maybe it was something goatish. The resilience outside seemed to be a power supply he had got himself hooked into. He wanted to laugh, to shout. He felt drunk.

Each day the food came up from the main block on trolleys in the heated metal boxes, to the low modern buildings that were now his home. One day, queuing for his dinner, ravenous as ever, Daniel peered in through the serving hatch and saw a new woman strolling around, carrying hot trays, her hands in shapeless kitchen gloves. She was tall, hefty, and looked mature, but could he supposed have been any age between twenty-five and thirty. She came up the hillside every day for a week from the main kitchens and then was missing for another week.

Her mouth looked a little mean, her eyes close together under dark thick eyebrows. You could see black hair curling on her legs underneath her tights. It must have been her walk, her regal stance, which made him think of a queen. Once, a special treat, he saw her cross the floor of the kitchen in slow motion and then return. If he'd had the nerve he would have applauded. 'Look at how she holds herself,' he was thinking – her shoulders back like that, her torso's weight settled down over her heavy hips. Heavy and yet young. A young matron.

31

Such indolence! And yet she did her work efficiently, he would have said, her hands moving pretty fast. He thought that surely she must be pregnant, walking with that kind of deliberation, as though taking care not to jolt anything. She was thick-waisted. Her smallish breasts bounced. He imagined her whole body squelching lazily like an axle in its grease.

The older woman would serve up the plates. Daniel carried his off and tucked in with relish, whatever it was, sitting afterwards with his elbows on the red-checked tablecloth in a euphoria entirely new to him. He was without frustration, yet he stirred like a plant with sappy life. And not a fantasy in his head. In some peculiar way he was emptied of desire, and yet felt gratified like a well-nourished baby. Maybe it was the spring coming, or the drugs. Or the new flesh he was acquiring daily, without the slightest effort. It wasn't only the woman he had been watching so intently who was luscious – the lusciousness was in him, too. And not only that. It ran into other shapes. And it was something he had become immersed in, a sexual juice oiling his eyes and getting inside his clothes, everywhere. Yet nothing had been asked of him.

He hadn't heard the kitchen woman utter a word. As she didn't serve, there was no need. If someone had told him that her sheer physicality rendered her dumb he would have believed them. Then one day at noon she opened her mouth. Her accent was town Devon, probably Plymouth, and she was yammering away at top speed to the counter hand. Daniel stood listening to the sound of her voice, so stupid and petty, winding on in an endless monotony, then took his tray and his knife, fork and spoon, shaking his head and laughing at himself. From that moment he stopped admiring her body from afar. All he could think of was that voice, that din, locked up inside her but ready at a moment's notice to come running out and spoil everything.

5

As the strength returned to the veins and sinews of his legs he found it hard to sit still. Apparently he wasn't to be sedated like so many of the others. If he mentioned going out for a stroll, Connor, the nurse in charge, would be all encouragement. That's to say, he stuck his fists in the pockets of his white coat, drew back his head like a wary tortoise and nodded moodily. He was swarthy. He slitted his eyes, looking anywhere but at you. Daniel knew of course that he had to get permission, they had told him often enough. Presumably this was it. He began walking away.

'Cold out there,' Connor called after him, smiling the faintest of smiles.

'Yes.'

'Got a top coat?'

'I've got a duffle.'

'Put it on, there's a good chap.'

'That's where I'm going now,' Daniel said, though he hadn't been, and he turned into the locker room.

Dragging on his old duffle coat, which smelled musty and felt strange, bulky as a blanket, nothing to do with him any more, he realised that he was annoyed at being treated like a child. Connor looked a good ten years his junior. 'Clearly I'm getting better,' he thought. He had started to recover his normal edgy self. The difference was, he kept stopping in his tracks, gaping round in amazement and wanting to pinch himself, to make sure it was no dream. Once he even said aloud, 'I'm alive!' as he headed downhill on the gravel drive, making for the six-storey Victorian granite barracks where the permanent insane were housed. On the far side of this immense grim block lay the cafeteria, another world, where you emerged as if from hell and sat on a terrace overlooking beautiful sunken lawns, tall trees, hopping birds, the crocuses and daffodils of a paradise on earth. To get there you entered the lit tunnel which burrowed under all the storeys and took you straight into the catacombs, down a long concrete ramp and past sewer-like holes to the right and left, leading to underground kitchens and other hell-holes, before the floor lifted and fetched up in the lobby.

Going through there always made him shiver. What if someone broke loose and came lurching out of the shadows with a carving knife? Daniel had to force himself not to hurry. Yet it didn't occur to him to skirt the place, out in the open. There was fear swirling in him but also a kind of zest. This was the worst there was! He popped in and out of the tunnel like a rabbit, his throat dry, his heart pumping. The trick was to keep moving: that was how you stayed alive.

In the lobby he would skip around Betty, a filthy old crone who was a fixture by the door, her hand out as she cadged for cigarettes. 'Any fags?' She was tanned, deeply wrinkled, her toothless mouth folding in like an old boot. He didn't feel bad about her – she seemed happy in whatever world she was in. Adjacent to the lobby was a hall where they showed vintage films once a week. Betty would be there cadging cigarettes, hobbling out in front of the screen and casting a shadow. A chorus of catcalls would go up, but only Ruby seemed able to get her settled. 'Betty, sit down and shut up,' she'd shout above the parrot cries, and the burnt-out wreck would immediately shuffle to a seat. 'You have to remember she's a child,' Ruby told him. 'When she knows what she's supposed to do she's as good as gold.'

34

'That was my trouble.'

'What?'

'I forgot what I was supposed to do.'

'Tell me later,' Ruby whispered, eyes gleaming.

In the cafeteria, a long room raised up on brick piles and swimming with light, with furniture of pale yellow wood and pale blue tablecloths, Daniel sat over his coffee and chewed at peanuts, asking himself lazily what he was doing here. Though it didn't bother him in the slightest, he was beginning to feel a fraud. What did he do except stare at the view and congratulate himself? As far as he could see he was perfectly well, in fact crazy with health, able to sit patiently and soak up the sights, studying the sly looks of harmless lunatics, noticing the vague ones and wondering if he resembled them. If he lived all alone for a long spell, would he begin to look like that? He spent a lot of time merely thinking, as he had always done, but now without any torment, purely speculative. Perhaps they were all at it, even those who looked totally gaga, slobbering over their institutional teacups. 'It could well be that there's no real difference between us,' he reflected. 'There are disabled maniacs and there are those with the luck, like me, who happen to be flourishing at the moment. The sick help to support the well, who go about oblivious, full of complacency, unaware of their privileges.' He sat around in his healthy new skin, quietly bursting with good fortune, each day feeling more and more Jewish. Every survivor was a kind of Jew.

One Tuesday evening he was about to take a bath, and then dab out a shirt and some briefs. In one hand he carried a packet of soap flakes, which he deposited carefully on the window sill. Cleanliness was another of the new joys in his life. There was no lock on the bathhouse door and for that reason he didn't intend to lie soaking. He did everything quickly as usual, ran the water, unfastened his belt and was stepping out of his trousers when Alf, a

35

scrawny old man, came in without so much as a knock. His eyes popped. 'Hey, what you doin' in here?'

'Taking a bath.'

'Not now you ain't.'

'Why's that?'

'Why? Because it's my time, that's why. What time is it?'

Daniel looked at his watch. 'Half past eight.'

'That's my reg'lar time. Ask anybody. Anybody'll tell you that. Alf's time.'

'You go ahead, I'll wait.'

'Tuesday, half past eight. That's me.'

'I didn't know you had a time.'

'Everybody knows.'

'Not me. I'm new here.'

He stood glaring, eyes popping. It was true that Daniel didn't know about Alf's time, but he knew about Alf. He was a miserable old cuss.

'When should I come back?' he asked.

'Suit yourself. It won't make no difference. I ain't hurrying for nobody.'

On the way down the corridor he went past Connor, who was going home. He wore a blue mac, and was carrying his bicycle pump. He said, 'What's Alf raising a rumpus about?'

'I was getting into his bath.'

'Oh God, you can't do that.'

'So he tells me.'

'Take no notice. He's a funny old sod.'

Daniel said, 'Does he bath every Tuesday?'

'No, he does his washing. I doubt if he has more than one bath a year. But don't tell him I said so.'

Daniel would hear a voice warning him that he was getting a little too smug. He went about feeling well-liked. He was even becoming gregarious. But Alf was one failure, and then came another.

Short-term patients were encouraged to manage their

own social activities, form a ward committee and so forth. At one meeting, Daniel was proposed for the job of organising the purchase of the tea and sugar which they served up for visitors. The voting would have been unanimous but for one man, Foley. This was a gangling black-haired giant with morose eyes and a fleshy twisted mouth, who put Daniel in mind of photographs of Mayakovsky.

'I object,' Foley said.

'On what grounds?' Daniel asked, since no one else did, and he was curious.

'I object,' Foley repeated, glowering at the floor between his feet. He was wearing his enormous black boots again. One eccentricity he had become known for was his habit of climbing into bed at night with his boots still on. Also, if asked to contribute a few pence to something, or fork out for his tea money, he was invariably broke. But it was his refusal to explain his actions which made him so unpopular. It didn't bother Daniel, but most of the others were incensed. Someone has to be the scapegoat.

To get around the problem of Foley's objection it was suggested that Daniel should organise the social evening instead. Hearing this threw him into a panic. What did he know about such things? He had been antisocial for as long as he could remember. They took another vote.

'I object,' Foley said. Daniel was delighted.

'On what grounds?' asked Davis, a clock-repairer, and meticulous in everything he did – obviously the compulsive type. Whenever he opened his bedside locker you saw how beautifully the interior was ordered, like the inside of a watch.

'I object to him doing anything!' Foley said, and went on staring at the carpet.

They all sat there, stymied. Waiting for an explanation from Foley was useless, since he had never been known to give any. Finally they over-ruled him. Daniel was given the first job he had been proposed for.

After that he went down to the cafeteria with a sense of purpose, now and then buying a few packets of tea and a bag or two of sugar, before settling down to ruminate, chew peanuts and gaze dreamily at the view. Sipping his coffee, he would continue thinking, but stupidly, indolently, for pleasure. Some of these people would have been Hitler's degenerates, he mused: like gypsies, and certain artists. Like him, for instance, sitting there absorbed in watching, of no use to anyone.

He was no longer the same person. How could this be? It was astonishing to find that one's outlook of a lifetime could change so drastically in a matter of weeks. How had this happened, what was the substance of it? Passing a pane of glass he would glance sideways at his reflection to see if his walk had altered. No, nothing so obvious. He saw an image of himself as he had always been, a thin fellow with a springy step, head nervous like a cat. But he was surely different. Where was the timid boy who longed – like his mother – to be invisible, and then the sickly worrier and tongue-tied neurotic burning to live, afraid to act, part of his brain paralysed, scared of his own shadow? His mother would say of a total stranger, 'I don't trust him, he's a twister,' her mouth clamped as tightly shut as her mind, and his father would twitch at his trousers because this was altogether too extreme and fearful for him. His instinct was to befriend people first and ask questions later. They were opposites. They both lived in Daniel, only now it seemed he had jumped out and got beyond them, his own person at last.

He was carefree, irresponsible, with no duties whatsoever. He was being kept, a charge of the State, strolling about like a lord and feeling marvellous. Was this, he wondered, how a kept woman felt? It was definitely voluptuous. Painters of voluptuous women had always impressed him, and in the beginning it was why he had wanted to be a painter. It was no more than an excuse, a longing to drown in those sensations, burn and drown at one and the same time.

He saw now that what made his mother so suspicious and afraid was her terror in the face of life itself, and the pain she suffered as a girl because of her lack of a skin. Later she managed to overcome these handicaps after a fashion by being good, a perfectly legitimate trick which enables you to feel somebody while pretending to be nobody. Sitting in the cafeteria it occurred to him that he was pulling the same trick, acting the benign spectator who imagines he has escaped his own nature. Well, illusion or not, it felt wonderful, sublime. So did the most menial of tasks, pushing the tea trolley around in the dark mornings before dawn, snapping on the lights in the dormitory and wheeling up the brown pot-bellied teapot, the biggest he'd seen, asking how many sugars. Mostly they said two. Another strange thing: they nearly all struggled to sit up, in their various stages of deathliness.

Oates, though, was one who failed to appreciate the morning tea treatment. 'Turn the fucking light off,' he would snarl into the pillow, before yanking the sheet over his head. Others who had been made compliant by lifetimes of wage slavery mumbled their thanks, and anyway they didn't want to miss their breakfast. Soon they were dragging on their trousers and blundering out to the washroom while they gulped down the dregs of their cups, exactly as if they had buses and trains to catch. Daniel could never get over this. Something in him laughed, but he was saddened to see it. Breakfast was an hour away. Such crazy haste belonged outside, not here.

6

Under the spell of this heaven, floating delightfully, he was snatched up one night by a nightmare. Afterwards he couldn't remember anything, and was thankful. He woke up gasping for air, heart pounding like runaway machinery. Still disturbed after half an hour, he got up and went in to the night nurse. It was the same youth on duty, placidly at work with his nylon thread and a bag of coloured plastic beads under the pool of light. His young fingers sorted smartly through the various shapes and sizes.

Daniel's legs were buckling. He felt absurdly weak. 'Mind if I sit down?'

'Help yourself.' The youngster's bored eyes examined his visitor for signs of trouble. 'What's up?'

'Oh, just a bad dream.'

The youth went on threading. Daniel felt an urge to share his feelings, but an instinct told him it would be a mistake. Nurses were trained to be wary of patients in the small hours. He became alert, wondering if this young cunning mind was regarding him suspiciously. Daniel saw him as bland and easy and impervious, like his beads.

He asked, 'What time is it?'

'Coming up to midnight.'

Daniel was astounded. It felt halfway through the night to him. 'Are you sure? Your watch hasn't stopped?'

These were dubious questions, he could see. The boy did examine the watch on his wrist, then brought the watch up to his ear. Daniel got up with as much dignity as he could muster and ambled back shakily to his room. How he loved its door – *his* door, sealing him in so snugly, leading him out again to the conduit of the passageway, so that he was thrilled time and again by his mastery over these simple choices, once so terrible to perform.

The next evening he sat talking to Ruby at the rear of the Day Room. Although she clearly enjoyed joining the men, she took care not to overdo this privilege, parking her chair just inside the door, by a table, where she could put down her cup of chocolate.

Men kept arriving, visitors, dressed as if for a night out, macs over their arms. They passed by in ones and twos, in a discreet silence, making for a small room leading off from the Day Room at the far end. Daniel asked. 'Who are these characters? Ever seen them before?'

Ruby waited, her face expressionless, until another stranger had slipped past and disappeared through the inner door. 'Of course I have,' she hissed. 'It's Alcoholics Anonymous. They hold a meeting here once a month.'

'Why trail out here?' The hospital was fifteen miles from the city.

'I told you, we have a lot of souses here.'

'So that's it.'

'Probably, yes.'

'Where are ours? Have you seen any you recognise?'

'No. They'll come, when the coast is clear.'

At first Daniel didn't understand. 'You mean they're waiting for us to go?'

'Could be,' she said mysteriously. 'Wouldn't you?'

He thought she was guessing, and that often she wasn't as much in the know as she pretended. After all, she had established herself as something of an authority and would lose face if she failed to come up with an answer each time. He was happy to accept that. Didn't we all need to be good at something? Occasionally she seemed gloomy, maybe in pain, but tonight she was her usual self, curious, plenty of appetite and mischief, laughing a lot. She asked suddenly if he had any brothers and sisters.

'One brother.'

'Older or younger?'

'He's a little younger.'

She looked closely at him, then considered a moment. 'Is he anything like you?'

'Yes and no. His set-up is very conventional. You could say he's hung on to the rule book. Though there's a side to him no one knows anything about.'

'Isn't there to all of us?'

The sharpness of this surprised him. 'True.'

He stopped talking. Sudden changes of mood worried Ruby, and she studied his face carefully. 'Now what's wrong?'

'Why should there be anything wrong?'

'You've gone very quiet.'

'I can't talk for talking's sake. I'm a quiet person – you must have noticed,' he said gently, teasing a little.

Daniel's brother belonged to a past which was hard now for him to believe in. Somehow it had been sheered off, clean as a whistle. He thought of his brother as he thought of his mother, his wife and his daughter, as strange ghosts. Mostly he didn't think of them. At his one and only interview with a consultant – it was Quinn – the man did a rapid calculation based on his total years, divided them up in a sort of mumbo-jumbo and threw in sibling rivalry for good measure. What was that? Daniel hadn't even heard of it. How could the man attach so much importance to his brother when they rarely saw one another? This of course could be called naive, he realised. On the last occasion, Anthony had called in as an emissary of their mother, to find out what was wrong with Daniel and report back. They hadn't seen each other in years. Sunk in a black world, staring at the ground like a beast, Daniel struggled to register what his brother was saying, mesmerised by his highly polished black shoes. Once, at home, they had

42

shared the same room, even the same bed. Where was that closeness now? He was being interrogated by a stranger whose face gave nothing away and who seemed to be asking the same question again and again. Why didn't Daniel write to their mother any more? What was he thinking of? Cowed now by any show of firmness, Daniel stood hating his brother, standing there dull and hopeless while his cheesy preoccupied mind tried to compose an answer which would get rid of him.

'I don't want you to be sad,' Ruby was saying.

'I'm not.'

In fact he was mildly irritated for no reason. A perverse imp whispered in his ear. He thought how funny it was that no one mentioned insanity in an insane asylum. These words were the new obscenities. Even funnier, he told himself, you soon found that you were conspiring to maintain the tone of the place, especially with your fellow inmates. Naturally this didn't apply to the main block rearing its bulk below them down the hillside, with its locked wards. He reflected on it, wondering whether there was ill-treatment or neglect, the kind of thing one read about in the papers. Out in the grounds you saw them, weeding, sweeping, standing around in peculiar attitudes, their faces dead with indifference, dead to their surroundings. Gone were the days when crazed escapees charged from the bushes like demented goats. These were heavily sedated, so they shambled, and slumped harmlessly on benches. Now and then you heard rumours of suicides, of a man found face down in the goldfish pond. Daniel would hurry through the tunnel with eyes peeled, his heart scampering while his legs marched in a dignified manner. There was never anything to see. If there was any delirium it was driven underground, submerged, leaving the inmates robbed of meaning and danger, like stalled empty vehicles.

He was still delirious himself as the spring took hold of him, crocuses exploding on all sides, in his mind too, even

43

in the soles of his feet. There was no need any more to sit around quietly in the mornings while the insulin took effect, after swallowing a tumbler of glucose – they had abandoned the treatment. He was ambulatory whenever possible, as if he was intent on catching up with the world's news, which included the world of nature. He caught himself acting like an inquisitive old man, though not yet a garrulous one. His recent brush with death prevented him from chattering too much. He stood soberly to one side, as it were. He had a view of himself now. It was an extraordinary business. He saw himself in a tender light, as one does the newborn.

Somewhere or other he had read that to kill yourself it was necessary to sink to an infantile level. He considered this. Hadn't he exhibited all the infantile symptoms, moaning aloud for his mother, stealing marzipan from his own pantry? He had desperately wanted to disappear, as orphan children sometimes do. Towards the end he had thought incessantly of death, which beckoned to him like a mother. Afterwards he thought that what had stayed his hand was the horrible self-assault involved, his living flesh and blood beaten to the ground in a degradation so inextricable. He had always loathed the trampling confusion and the horror of violence. If only there was a single pill he could take, one little knock-out drop, he remembered mumbling to himself. The ghost of what his body had been, its superb health, kept haunting the room, and finally that was why he couldn't do it. 'I was healthy, I was so healthy!' he wept aloud, in the bitter freezing air.

Ruby's attitude to the hospital, which Daniel regarded as her absurd loyalty, irritated him at times, and this was another sign of his growing normality. She was a free agent, set apart, yet he never once heard her speak disrespectfully of the place. Maybe she was superstitious. She was a country girl after all. He had met unbelievers, women, who didn't like it if you ridiculed the existence of God. They started to glance uneasily at the ceiling.

A devil would rise up in him and say things. 'These places have all sorts of names,' he remarked once.

'How do you mean?'

'Laughing academy. Funny farm. Nuthouse. Loony bin.'

'I don't like them.'

'I didn't think you would.'

'I mean I don't see it like that.'

'Well, on the inside, it's not easy to see how funny it is.'

'What's funny about it?'

'It's all funny. Everything. The whole catastrophe.'

'Everybody in here – is that what you think?'

'No, all of us, everywhere.'

She could be very stubborn. He was equally pig-headed, to use a favourite expression of his mother, herself an impossibly pig-headed person at times.

Once Ruby accused him directly, in a rare flash of rage: 'You think I'm ignorant, don't you?'

'No.'

'You do, you do!'

'No, never. Well, hardly ever.'

She calmed down, even smiling at herself for being upset. 'Let's go to the library, can we?'

'Fine.'

'Are you a cynic?' she asked naively.

'Sometimes, yes.' Then he remembered something. 'I used to cycle home from work with a friend, Pete – this was when I was young – and he egged me on to make cynical remarks that he found amusing. I was a real clever-dick in those days. Insufferable, probably. I suppose what I am now is a pessimist who can't stop hoping. That's pretty stupid, you must admit.'

'You're still nice.'

'Not really. But it's nice of you to think so.'

Embarrassed suddenly, he was glad of an excuse to push her down to the library. She said, 'See if you can find a Catherine Cookson for me, will you? There's one of hers I haven't read yet. I'll remember the title in a minute.'

'Catherine Cookson, right.'

7

Raised up as they were on this vantage point, exposed, wild, it was difficult to ignore the weather. The moor up above their heads somewhere delivered it, slapped it into their faces. An icy wind blew, then it sleeted, shot a few arrows of white sun, then for a change every hour or so the cold rain emptied down. The sky would go black in the face and start flexing its muscles.

As a city man he wasn't usually aware of the sky. Looking back, Daniel seemed to have spent his days either on the way to work, freezing and cursing, or coming back, the same, or getting drenched, or with his back itching and sweaty. Or if the weather wasn't something to wade through then it would be flaunting itself on the wrong side of an office window, giving winks and smiles, blue flashes, tantalising with warmth and distance.

Daniel lay on his back with his hands underneath his head. Through the french windows he watched the rain falling steadily in the gathering darkness. Glancing over at his gimcrack dressing-table mirror he found he was smiling faintly. People in this world were half mad with loneliness and he was sighing contentedly, congratulating himself on his taste for solitude. After half an hour it began to pall a little and he would sit up and pull on his shoes. The evening meal was at six, a convenient excuse. He walked out to satisfy his appetite and seek some company at the same time.

Entering the dining room he would often pause and

look around, marvelling to think that he was on easy terms with most of the inmates. They were such a weird assortment, all different from one another, none of them remotely like him, yet with this one thing in common – they had all been shipwrecked. Some clung to the wreckage, others seemed about to sink. One or two looked old enough to be pensioners, and there was Paul, the baby, a good-looking blurry-eyed boy of sixteen, heavily dosed with Largactil, whose voice surfaced in soft gluey bubbles. He was black-haired, white in the face. Walking up and down he gave the impression of someone wading under water. Paul was desperate to be understood, but it was hard to unravel what he was saying. Apparently his old man heaved logs at him when he went in through the door on his weekend visits home. Paul would sit droopily on his bed all day studying for 'A' Levels. Now and then he sat in the Day Room.

If Daniel stopped to talk to him it would make Paul nervous. If instead he tried to pass by with just a friendly nod, the boy was immediately worried.

'You went by the other day without stopping. I wondered if you still liked me.'

'Yes I do, of course, yes. I must have been in a hurry. Wanted a pee or something. How are you, Paul?'

'All right I suppose. Am I speaking distinctly?'

'Sort of.'

'I'm not, am I?'

'Don't worry about it.'

'It's this muck I keep swallowing.'

'Don't worry.'

'It's all right though. It calms me down.'

'I expect so.'

'So I don't mind.'

'That's right.'

'Aren't I calm now?'

'Yes, yes, you are.'

'It's working, then?'

47

'I'd say so, definitely.'

'Stops me going on about my dad all the time.'

'Why shouldn't you?'

'People get sick of hearing about it.'

'Not me, Paul.'

'Really?'

'It doesn't bother me, no.'

'Am I still speaking distinctly?'

'Yes, you are. Not bad at all.'

'How is it you don't have any trouble understanding me? Most people do.'

'It's just a matter of getting used to it.'

'And patience.'

'Possibly.'

'You're a patient bloke. Not like my dad.'

'Good, I'm glad.'

'Did you know you were patient?'

He was too anxious a person to joke. Daniel laughed anyway. 'No,' he said. 'It's certainly news to me.'

'Without this beaker of muck they give me to swallow every morning I talk faster and faster. Hell of a pace. I can hear it. You'd never understand me then.'

'Probably not.'

Feeling restless, Daniel was walking down the corridor when the charge nurse poked his head out of his little cubicle and called him in. 'Mr Marron, sit down, will you? You're making excellent progress. I thought you might like to know that.'

Daniel opened his mouth to say how happy he was, then shut it again. Best keep my elation to myself, it might be certifiable, he decided. The nurses here were friendly, but in the way primary-school teachers were friendly. He wasn't sure how far it went. Suddenly he became aware of his loyalty to a group, a totally new sensation which took him completely by surprise. We were all behaving ourselves, he told himself, apart from Foley of course, who still climbed into bed wearing his great boots whenever the mood took him.

'How do you feel about going home at weekends?'

Daniel knew then that he didn't trust the man. Connor watched him clinically while pretending to be bored, studying his fingernails. 'How do you feel?' he repeated, with a studied laziness. He even half closed his eyes and turned to the window, away from Daniel.

Daniel wasn't sure that he felt anything, but he answered, 'Fine.'

'You'd like that?'

'Yes,' he said, irritated at being given the child routine again.

'Excellent. Come in for a pass and your medication on Friday before you leave, there's a good fellow.' He scrawled something in a file, nodded, and Daniel went out feeling ridiculous, as if awarded a good grade.

As soon as he saw Ruby he told her his news. 'Are you pleased?' she asked at once, sharply for her. 'You don't sound exactly over the moon. Not like some people.'

'Perhaps it's different for me.' He still felt nothing, except that like a boy he had begun to anticipate climbing aboard one of the special hospital buses and sailing through the gates as though on a 'mystery' trip.

Ruby could have asked something blundering and tactless, such as whether he was missing his home, but she was well practised in these matters. She only asked him, delicately, 'What were you doing before ... before you came here?'

'Doing?'

'Yes, what job.'

'Oh, this and that.'

'Stop teasing. I've tried to guess. Daniel, give me a clue. You don't seem to fit any of the things I've thought of.'

'That ought to tell you what a misfit I am.'

'Oh, very clever. Seriously, what were you?'

'A student.' She looked dubious, so he went on. 'A

mature student. Training to be a teacher, God help me. I finished the course, then instead of taking a job I got ill.'

'I bet you'd have been good.'

'No, rotten.'

She shook her head in disbelief. 'You like children, surely?'

Daniel stared blankly at her and couldn't answer. What kind of question was that? Did he like children? Come to that, did he like people in general? He still had no answer. Certainly he wasn't fond of children when he was one himself. When a well-meaning friend suggested teaching, somehow he didn't think of kids. He thought of short hours, long holidays – and time to live. Being a teacher is often the last refuge of a misfit, he nearly said but didn't. Ruby would have called him cynical. The truth was worse: his problem was that he detested schools, everything about them. They had a special smell. As soon as you stuck in your nose, there it was, frightening – and too late. The memory rushed through him like a wave as he was going in, on his way to his first practice, a student of forty-four. How could he have blotted out the reality of schools?

He told Ruby lamely, 'I liked my daughter very much when she was small.'

'Only then?'

'No, of course not. More then.'

'I wonder why?'

He thought seriously about this. Really it was laughable. 'Don't laugh.' She said solemnly, 'I wouldn't dream of laughing at you.'

'I was important to her, that's why. She didn't argue. No opinions. And I liked the way she went to sleep. Bird-like, she was.'

Ruby, pressing home her advantage, wanted to hear all about his brief teaching experience. 'Why was it a fiasco?'

'I don't know where to start.'

'Start anywhere. At the beginning!'

He began by describing the dingy ghetto school where

he spent three months learning how to cope. It took him less than a week to discover he was wasting his time, he couldn't do it. Only his grizzled looks and a specially cultivated scowl saved him. All he ever learnt was the grim lesson of survival: how to survive a forty-minute period, how to hang on for the bell, how to sit as if calmly in the staff room and quake invisibly, then walk out of the dirty building at four, over the asphalt yard into the council estate and down the grey road, past the grey cement houses and splintered fences, catching his toe on the uneven paving slabs, feeling blasted but triumphant, as only a survivor is triumphant, shaking his head at the grand lunacy of education.

'Was it really as bad as that?'

'Worse.'

'Carry on.'

He thought Ruby would interrupt him as he got into his stride, but no, she heard him out to the last word. The Head of this secondary modern, he told her, was in his fifties, with wide shoulders and the face of a bull mastiff. His coarse appearance was matched by his mind. He regarded himself as an iron man. Mr Binns was a physics and maths specialist.

Daniel felt at once that what made this man dangerous was his cunning brain. He thought fast, with the instincts of a thug. Ushered into his office, Daniel felt trapped, the instant he went through the door. He rose mentally on his toes, and stayed that way, the whole three months he was there.

Mr Binns' eyes gleamed with intent, yet they were swallowed up by the bulk of him, like a pig's. He seemed to watch with his body rather than his head. Daniel would observe the flushed skin and feel the power. A frightened boy inside him ran off, as he stood telling himself he was immune, temporary, merely a visitor.

That first morning, wandering about made of water, he saw a row of urchins with pasty scared faces lined up outside the Head's door for the cane, and kept noticing stained walls and cracked plaster, smelling the smell he hated. A messenger had come up: 'Mr Binns is waiting.'

Mr Binns wore a three-piece suit, dark grey with a loud chalk stripe. 'Well, well, you've come then. Have a look at us. Give us a hand.'

'Morning, Mr Binns.'

'Ah, have you. Sit down, sit down. You might regret it but you never know.'

'I beg your pardon?'

'A rough district, this. I'm telling you now for your own good. English is it, and a bit of drawing and painting. You won't get far with English here. Try it and see. In one ear and out the other. Here's a bit of advice for nothing. Whatever it is you're saying, say it six times. Right? Then another six. Got that? They might remember it then. If you're lucky. Doubt it. They doze off a lot. Can't concentrate. Any trouble, straight in to me.'

'Yes.'

'A piece of general advice on teaching, if you want the benefits of my experience, and I've had plenty. Keep your tongue in your cheek, know what I'm getting at?'

'I think so.'

Someone knocked timidly at the door. Daniel glanced over. Mr Binns was staring down at a file which had appeared on his desk. His red meaty hands, resting on the file, seemed to be sleeping. The black hairs sprouting thickly around the knuckles were full of brutal life, and so were the squarish horny nails. A spidery thin girl came in silently with a tin tray. There was a squat plated teapot with a hinged lid, a thick jug of milk, a bowl of sugar, two cups and saucers. The girl placed the tray down on the desk and left without looking at either of them.

'You'll have some of this?'

'Thank you.'

'Is that yes?'

'Yes, it is.'

'Sugar and milk?'

'Please.'

'They were rioting here when I took over. At weekends they'd come up from the estate and smash half the windows, next week the other half. Protection rackets in the playground, all that. In a month, Mister, I stamped it out. I said to my staff, right, we'll give it a month. I took a month exactly. Now you can hear a pin drop, can't you?'

'Yes,' Daniel said, out of a dry throat, as if humouring a madman.

'As I said, if the police want to know who the law-breakers are they come to me.'

'I'm sure they do.'

'They do, yes. I'm shocking you, am I?'

'No, not at all.'

'You can't teach in unruly conditions. Contradiction in terms.'

'Absolutely.'

'Tell them that at the college you come from. The Binns method works.'

'I will.'

The ugly man laughed, showed his teeth. Daniel smiled politely. Gulping down the tea he stood up, itching to escape with his guilty thoughts which he felt sure were about to be detected at any moment. Then it dawned on him that Mr Binns was hanging on to him, prolonging the interview for reasons of his own – out of loneliness probably. Daniel thanked him, obeying some instinct to placate a natural enemy, and left the room.

Lonely or not, he now saw Binns as a bulky spider who sat at the dead centre of things with his hairy knuckles poised, waiting. Pin-pointing errors, eliminating disorder, rooting out petty crime, these were his passions. He was fanatical on points of order. Being a spider was his fate, his one and only purpose.

Telling bits of all this to Ruby, Daniel came to what he now saw as the hilarious part, though it seemed sickeningly unfunny at the time. He had been at the school a fort-night, and already he loathed the man with every fibre of his being. One morning he was reading to a first-year class. Searching through the storeroom for something dif-ferent he had found a story called *Walkabout*. Two white children, brother and sister, wander about in the Austra-lian outback after a plane crash. There had been sniggers from the class already, and he hadn't yet reached the point where the girl strips off her clothes and goes native. When he did, the result was uproar. The whole class erupted in embarrassed laughter. He nearly lost his temper and yel-led, 'Who's got a sister? Hands up! You mean to say you've never seen her naked?' Just in time he controlled himself. He had been recalling his own childhood, with tin baths in front of the fire, forgetting that these children's houses were all equipped with bathrooms. Other than that, what had changed? Old inhibitions were still intact, people communicated by means of grunts and silences, blows, outbursts of hysteria, exactly as in his own childhood.

Suddenly the class stood up. Bewildered, he glanced over his shoulder. Binns was there. He said, 'Good morn-ing,' and the class shouted in unison, 'Good morning, sir!' He waved his hand and they sat down again.

'Reading a story to 'em. They like stories.' He was ad-dressing Daniel and yet ignoring him, not even looking in his direction. 'Do you like stories?' he asked the class.

They were all nodding vigorously and smiling. He leered back.

'This one,' Daniel said, and tried to hand the Head a copy. Again Binns ignored him.

'What's it about, you?' he said, pointing a finger at a boy in front.

The boy scrambled to his feet. 'The desert, sir!'

'Where, Africa?'

'Australia, sir!'

'What's it about?' he said again, pointing to an excited-looking girl near the back.

'How to survive!' the girl cried eagerly.

'Looking for water, are they?' Binns said. He leered at them all.

'Yes, sir!'

'So it's about survival, then. What's it about?' he asked, prodding the air with his finger aimed at another boy, who leapt up as though spring-loaded.

'Survival, sir!'

Binns nodded. Heading suddenly for the door, he advised Daniel over his shoulder threateningly, 'Make sure they know what's going on. Check up on it, Mister.'

Daniel assured him that he did, so pleased to see him leaving that he hopped to the door ahead of him and yanked it open like a lackey. Coming back, he consoled himself with the thought that he had kept his vow never to 'sir' this boor. And he was too old in the tooth to be a sycophant. He had heard members of staff calling him 'Headmaster', so he avoided that, too.

Why then was he feeling guilty? Why? Guilt was always waiting to jump into his guts. So it was with every job he had tackled. For the first week or two he went around feeling certain he was about to be unmasked, convinced that he would be seen through, exposed for the imposter he really was. When nothing happened, old frustrations began to plague him. Why was he wasting his time doing this? Surely life amounted to more than this senseless round of activities and duties? He would present an innocuous expression, a meekly smiling face, an agreeable manner, behind which he seethed, furious at his acceptance of a world in bondage, yearning for something else, dreaming of escape.

8

Ruby was looking puzzled.

'What's wrong?' he asked.

'You seem to make friends easily enough here,' she said thoughtfully, 'and yet you haven't mentioned a single person you liked at this school. Wasn't there even one?'

'Yes, one.'

'Who was that? A colleague?'

'No, it was Helen. Would you like to hear about her?'

'Of course, tell me.'

It was hardly an equal friendship, he told Ruby, turning over in his mind the best way to begin. Helen was eleven years of age, and she was a little clinger. Yes, clinger – that was the word. In the staff room it was explained to him: someone at a poor school like theirs, of either sex but usually female, would hang on to a teacher. Often there would be a broken home or a bad marriage in the background. The father may have deserted the family.

Once or twice he had been asked to look after a backward class for one man he did happen to like, Freddy Titterton, a fatherly old teacher who fussed over the illiterate scrawls of his charges and listened patiently to them labouring to pronounce simple sentences aloud from the board. For a few minutes Daniel watched him at work, wagging his finger helpfully, telling his pupils how well they were doing and making excruciating little jokes. His homespun techniques, evolved through years of experience, certainly worked. Clearly he was devoted to his job.

His class loved him. Daniel was quite envious. Titterton wore a thick tweed jacket. His glasses slipped down his nose, which was drippy, liver-coloured. His cuffs, always smothered in chalk dust, were a reminder of how teachers had been thirty years ago. He had a happy aura which Daniel admired. Before leaving his substitute in charge he explained how to mark the arithmetic exercises – Daniel could hardly grasp it – and then he hurried from the room on a personal errand. 'I'll be back before the end of the period,' he promised, 'but they're good, they're really very good, you won't have any trouble.'

Helen wasted no time. Out she came with her work. Though it was execrable, she was unabashed. She introduced herself and began at once making demands. Her brown hair was chopped short. She wore a clean dress, poppy red, which needed ironing.

'Helen Crout is my name,' she announced. 'That's what it says there.' She flipped over the cover of her mauled and stained exercise book to show Daniel, jabbing her finger confidently at it. 'Helen,' she said.

'Yes, I see.'

'Can I collect the rulers please?'

'What, now?'

She giggled. 'At the end of the lesson!'

'I don't see why not.'

'Can I have a new book?'

'What's wrong with this one?'

'It's full up.'

'There are three pages left, look.'

Helen fidgeted impatiently as Daniel marked her sums, then she darted back to her friend. 'I'm collecting the rulers!' he heard her exclaim, loud enough for the whole class to hear.

A fortnight later he had to be a stand-in for this class again. This time they were instructed to come up to the library where he sometimes had to teach. He had asked Titterton what he should do with them. 'Read them a story. They love it when you read to them – it takes them so long on their own and there's never enough time.'

It was an afternoon period, straight after lunch. In they came like a wave, frothing with excitement, flowing everywhere. This was their first-ever time upstairs. There was a sudden crash, some loud squeals of laughter. A little runt of a boy with a snotty nose, elbows out of his jersey, had slid or been shoved off a chair.

'Now settle down!' Daniel yelled; that was the phrase. 'If you can't be quiet, it's back down to your own room. It's up to you.'

The empty threat worked like a charm. In the stunned silence, Helen walked up to his table. 'I'm Helen Crout.' She looked radiant. Her eyes were fastened on his face.

'Yes, I remember. What is it, Helen?'

'Which story are we going to read?'

'Just go and sit down and I'll tell everybody.'

'Can't you tell me?'

He couldn't see why not. '*The Silver Sword*.'

'Is it good?'

'Helen, go and sit down.'

'Can I give out the books?'

'All right.'

'Now? Can I do it now?'

'Yes, now.'

'And can I collect them after?'

'One thing at a time.'

'I don't understand.'

'Give out the books – just give them out!'

Helen rushed with her ecstatic smile at the piles of dirty grey books. 'Doreen, come and help me!' she cried, her chin wedged on a wobbly tower. Her friend grabbed what was left.

The story was easy to follow, with short words, and the narrative at least had a grip. The class listened in such a rapt silence as Daniel read that he imagined them all holding their breath like a single person. He suspected that they would have been just as enthralled if he had been reading out the instructions on the fire extinguisher. They were ravenous for language, for the spoken word: they wanted to be put under and so they were. It was mass hypnosis. When his voice became a hoarse croak he called for a volunteer to carry on where he had left off. Helen's was the first arm to shoot up. Daniel saw it, but he ignored her. Part of him had already succumbed to her and he feared his total enslavement. A freckled boy with the knot of his tie lost under his tattered collar was reaching up so hard with his hand that his eyes were popping. 'You,' Daniel said.

The boy fought desperate battles with every other word. Nobody laughed; his struggle was also theirs. They were all in the same boat. He choked, gobbled, spat his way through one small sentence and fell on the next. After half a paragraph of this agony Daniel called a halt, thanked the boy, then went on with the passage himself.

Before the bell, he felt obliged to let Helen read a few lines. Her eyes were burning holes in the side of his face. Near the bottom of a page he stopped. 'Helen, carry on.'

At the mention of her name she sprang to her feet, gleaming with pride. She began tussling and floundering, almost as bad as the boy, but showing no signs of distress. It was an honourable defeat and not her fault if the language she used daily was made to look unrecognisable when printed in a book. Touched by her efforts, Daniel groaned under his breath. Helen chewed away on the final sentence, mangling it out of all recognition and completely ruining the effect. Somehow Daniel managed to keep his mouth shut.

'That's very good,' he said, nodding and smiling. 'Right, collect up the books.' Bells exploded on both floors, to his left and right and underneath his feet. By now he had these sessions timed to perfection.

Ruby said meaningfully, 'She was lucky to have you.'

'No, not me. Mr Titterton. He had faith, I lacked it. I see him now as a kind of saint, but really he just loved his work. If his pay had been cut by half, he'd have kept going on sheer joy. He's what I'd call a fortunate man.'

'Helen was ESN?'

'Yes, they all were.'

'Any more about her?'

'There's always more about anyone.'

'So can I hear it?'

'You'll be bored. It's boring.'

'Let me be the judge of that.'

He had never encountered such an avid listener who was also an adult. She absorbed every syllable. With such an audience it was easy to go on.

He had taken to hanging around for a while in the staff room at the end of each day. Most of the others did this, sunk in shabby upholstered chairs with the self-absorption of psychotics. Sometimes it was fatigue, one or two had genuine tasks, and there were those – Daniel was one – who had little desire to go home. One afternoon, sitting in a heap like a casualty, he told himself several times that he ought to get going, yet seemed incapable of moving. He sat for ten minutes more, until the room's atmosphere of squalor and despondency began to claim him.

Waiting outside the staff-room door was Helen. Daniel knew that pupils in a backward class weren't given detention.

'Hello, sir,' she said brightly.

She walked along the corridor to the exit with him. He asked whether she was looking for someone.

'Yes, you,' she said, not hesitating for a second. 'You go past my house.'

'I do?'

'Yes.'

'How do you know?'

'I've seen you, haven't I?'

'When was that?'

'Oh, lots of times. I can always tell it's you.'

'You can?'

'Yes. You've got a funny walk.'

Daniel assumed a stern expression. 'Show me.'

The girl giggled, and put her hand over her mouth. 'Are you sure you want me to?'

'I've just said so.'

'Why?'

'Why d'you think? I want to see what I look like.'

They were heading downhill, council houses on either side, drearily identical. Helen looked up at him, suddenly suspicious. 'Are you really a teacher?'

This was so penetrating and so unexpected, it caught him on the hop. This was what females did. If he admitted he was a student she would pester him with more questions. 'I'm not the caretaker,' he joked.

'I know that,' she said scornfully.

'Show me how I walk.'

'Like this.' She bounced up and down on her heels springily in a fair imitation.

'Never,' he gasped, as if shocked and astounded.

'Yeah, you do, honest!' Helen cried, nodding violently. Her face was jubilant.

They had reached a dirt path winding up through some waste ground to the left of the pavement. Helen pointed to the top of the barren slope. 'That's where I live, up there.'

'Off you go, then.'

Pleased, she strolled away between rusted junk half submerged in the lolling ropes of brambles, kicked at an ice-cream paper, glanced once over her shoulder and then ran, as if carrying a secret which wouldn't keep.

From that day onward she would be there waiting every afternoon at the end of school. Daniel didn't hurry himself. Maybe he was testing her, but for what reason? If he delayed leaving for an hour, two hours, would she materialise? Once she was missing, and the stab of regret he felt alarmed him. One day a woman who taught French, a dry stick and a busybody, remarked sarcastically that his 'clinger' was outside the staff-room door.

'My what?' It was the first time he had heard the expression.

Heading through the gates with Helen, he suggested that in future this would be a better place for her to wait. Or down the road a little. Helen skipped along, playing imaginary hopscotch, her face red with effort, and he thought she hadn't heard him. The next day there was no sign of her in the corridor, or outside on the playground. The pavement outside the gateway was deserted too. Feeling relieved of an obscure responsibility he walked through the gates, turned right and started down the hill in the direction of his home.

'Mr Marron! Mr Marron!' Helen came charging up behind him, her satchel banging, eyes shining with triumph.

'Where did you spring from?'

'I was hiding,' was all she'd say.

A bitter north wind was blowing. The road up there was as bald and exposed as an airstrip. Somebody had made him a mug of coffee, so he was warmed through. 'You must be freezing.'

'No, I'm not. I've been playing.'

'Who with? I can't see anybody.'

'They've gone home now.'

He didn't believe her. 'Who was it?'

'Doreen Buncle. She's got a bad knee, she fell over.'

'Where are your gloves?'

'My mum says she won't buy me any more.'

'Why not?'

'I keep losing one.'

As they approached the dirt path leading to her house she began to talk earnestly, putting pressure on him to join her in the building where they served up the school dinners. There was nothing flirtatious about her: she cocked her head, looking him straight in the eye, and demanded to know why not. He kept shaking his head and laughing defensively. Nothing was going to drag him into that place at midday, he valued his peace and quiet too much. It was bedlam in there, and the food was terrible. Either he brought sandwiches or he went off alone to the local pub. Estate pubs were a kind of slow death. Old women, with the grim wrinkled faces of those who have lost all illusions, sat by the vending machines sucking at their stout. The cessation of life, settling on him like a curse, was as bad as anything he would have suffered by submitting to Helen's request, but he needed to make his gesture of independence. There was also his male pride to consider.

This time she was more than usually insistent. Feeling bad, he trotted out threadbare excuses, then came out with the truth as he saw it. 'I'm sorry, no. I can't stand the racket.'

'I *want* you to come,' she said fiercely. 'Promise!'

He shook his head.

'Yes – yes, you will!' Helen punched his upper arm with her fist. All her vehemence went into it.

'Hey, that hurt!'

'Come tomorrow. Say you will.'

'I'm late, I've got to get home,' he said, breaking into a trot.

'Remember!' she called after him.

He went on shaking his head. Out of sight he slowed down, tramping along quickly and nervously. He crossed over several junctions without noticing, then told himself how stupid, not watching what he was doing. One of these days he'd be so engrossed in thoughts he'd walk under a lorry.

'That's it,' he thought, 'I'm becoming engrossed in her.' From her chatter on various days he had learnt that her mother worked in a fruit and vegetable shop somewhere on the estate. He asked, 'How d'you get in the house if it's raining?' Oh, she had a big brother, Frankie, who was allowed to carry a latch key. 'I'm not old enough yet.'

63

Whatever he wanted to know she told him innocently, in a series of blunt answers which seemed to have no particular interest or importance for her. There was nothing in the least pathetic about her, nothing to be concerned about, he assured himself. She seemed well able to take care of herself. How about her father, what did he do for a living? 'He's gone away.' Where? She shrugged. 'My uncle lives with us.' Had he been there long? Helen shook her head: clearly the question made no sense to her.

'He's going to buy me a bike!' she cried – this was the vitally important bit. So Daniel dropped his detective act, imagining a steady stream of 'uncles' and a tough mother who at any rate kept her daughter clean, and apparently didn't abuse her out of misery or vindictiveness. Of course he was only guessing. Not once did he think of his own daughter, now a teenager and engaged to be married.

He was later than usual getting in. His wife Cora was upstairs; he could hear her banging about, perhaps shifting the furniture around yet again. Certainly not cleaning – her elderly mother did that.

Nellie was in her late sixties, recently a widow, and she disliked Daniel for being the cause of her only daughter's unhappiness. That was understandable. In fact she had always found him unacceptable. She had sensed at once, or so he believed, that he was a malcontent. Grinding away at a job with prospects like Cora's first husband wasn't for him, though as it turned out he had done exactly that for years, seeing no way out. Nellie regarded him as suspect, untrustworthy from her point of view. For his part, Daniel admired her, this bony, courageous lady who had known much grief. She was aloof with strangers, secretly snobbish, and she had the old instinct to serve a man. Her rigidly held opinions infuriated him whenever she voiced them, though mostly she kept her thoughts to herself. For her the age of the common man was demonstrably vile and could only end badly, after destroying all the old values and lowering standards of decent conduct.

64

She believed in 'proper' speech, no swearing. As it happened, her own background was lowly: no parents she could remember, brought up by an ignorant, sour grandmother – but she revered what she liked to call breeding. Radicals were a kind of regrettable scum. Any mention of sex was unnecessary. Daniel's own upbringing made it inevitable that he should oppose all this, yet something about her forced respect from him. Also, he went a little in fear of her unswerving nature. Facing her with his endless ambivalence, he was at a loss. The old woman knew exactly where she stood. He never did.

Before she came to live with them he had tried to ingratiate himself with her on visits over the years. Finally he gave up and accepted her scorn. Now that she was living with them her disillusioned northern eyes would fix him palely in a withering stare as she asked in a demure voice how his day had been. Inside the bitter widow with her petrified flesh, stiff joints and sagging skin was a gentle girl, intact and trembling like a virgin. That was how he saw her, and the vision tore at him.

He could hear her now in the kitchen. As well as cleaning through the large old house, everything except their bedroom, she had taken over most of the cooking. Cora and he, both egotists, rushed down to the shops under protest and dragged back the provisions. If Cora went alone, she would come in muttering that she was a beast of burden. The truth is that she cared for animals rather than people. Of course she denied this absolutely, seeing herself as a warm outgoing personality, and Daniel as calculating, cold and selfish, entirely without spontaneity. Whenever she made these pronouncements, with such total conviction, he always wondered if they were true. Like her mother, she never wavered.

Cora came down the stairs. She was on a diet, looked younger, and was flushed from her exertions. Dismayed by her swelling forms, she preferred to dwell on her peaches-and-cream complexion, still undimmed at forty-five. Her large hectic eyes fixed on him as accusingly as did her mother's. 'You're late,' she said.

'I know.'

'Not that it matters.'

'I stayed for a cup of coffee.'

'For an hour?'

'People sit around talking in the staff room.'

'That's what you say.'

Then, stupidly, because he was preoccupied and also irritated, he said, 'A little girl, Helen, was talking to me.'

'In the staff room?'

'No. I was walking down road, coming home. She's supposed to be ESN but you should see her – she's as bright as a button. Sometimes she walks part of the way home with me.'

'How nice.'

'Cora, I'm worried. You see, she doesn't realise I'll be leaving soon. She's what they call a clinger.' He regretted his words at once, but a perverse imp inside him wanted to say more.

'I see. She's got a crush on you.'

'Don't be foolish – she's eleven.'

'How very sweet. If you could only just for once be honest with me.'

'Can't you understand what I'm saying? She's attached herself, that's all. I'm a sort of stand-in father. She'd try the same with anyone. One day soon I'll be back at college, I won't be there any more. What d'you think – should I tell her or not?'

Cora pushed past him, on her way down to the kitchen to join her mother. A mirthless smile formed on her lips. Over her shoulder she said, 'You make me sick.'

9

It was another day. 'How did you meet your wife?' Ruby asked.

Daniel looked into her broad pallid face. Her brown eyes were perfectly neutral; she was simply addicted to confidences, as he well knew. All the same, he thought, surely she feels some emotional involvement – any woman would. That is, if she had begun to attach herself to him, as he suspected. Cora could never forgive him his few relationships with women, though he had told her truthfully they were unhappy, and before he and Cora had even met. He didn't like to think of jealousy in connection with Ruby, or of sex either. She had already told him naively, after only a few exchanges, that someone had once given her a booklet on how to do it if you were disabled.

'Do what?' he asked, trying to joke.

She laughed at his expression. 'Get satisfaction,' she said.

He nodded sagely, secretly in conflict within himself. Why shouldn't she seek what she called satisfaction? But that was the point – he saw it as the opposite of satisfying, as a cruel illusion. But how would he know? He prided himself on being a realist, not a hypocritical romantic. Always waging a private war with the puritan under his own skin, he was the last person to view dispassionately the question of sex and disability.

They were in a small room, no more than a lean-to,

called the Social Club, next door to the industrial-therapy unit. Daniel hardly ever went there, and only after dark, so he was never sure of his bearings. Around them, towering to the skyline, was the wild moor, erupting in jagged tors, with its dangerous bogs and sudden engulfing mists. Yet in daylight, when the sun broke through, it looked a masterpiece, a vision of heaven on earth.

There were individual tables sat back against unplastered stone walls. Lamps with pink tasselled shades on wrought-iron brackets provided the subdued lighting. He asked how it was possible for inmates to come in here and consume alcohol when they were heavily sedated. He knew Ruby would enjoy telling him.

'These are the short-stay people only. You're the privileged ones.'

'Don't my drugs matter?'

'It depends what you're on.'

'Something called Parstelin.'

'Don't you carry a card?'

'Yes, it's here. It says nothing with yeast in.'

'Then avoid the beer.'

'I've already had one!'

'Calm down, Daniel – you're so excitable! When did they issue you with that card?'

'Yesterday.'

'That's fine,' Ruby said, smiling. She gripped his forearm with her big puffy hand. 'Now stop worrying. That's far worse than half a pint of beer. Don't have any more. I'll take care of you, my plum.'

Suddenly, as his wave of panic subsided, he felt safe and foolish.

Ruby swung back greedily to the subject of his wife. He should have known how it would fascinate her. Although he wasn't averse to discussing Cora, she had turned into a shadow. So was he a shadow.

'What would you like to know?'

'Anything you feel like telling me.'

'Am I in therapy here?'

Her face fell. 'No, of course not. How can you say such a thing?'

'I'm sorry. Joke. Right, I'll cut it short.'

'Not too short, eh?'

Cora had a husband when he first met her. Alan was a shoe-shop manager, a conventional, decent fellow, utterly bewildered by his wife's animal-like outbursts of frustration. She would leap up without warning and snatch his paper as he settled down for a quiet read in the evening. 'Talk to me, say something interesting!' By interesting she meant cultural, literary, artistic, and the poor devil was an ignoramus in such matters. It was that kind of situation. He was kind, sweet, his feelings dammed up, and in her terms limited. Daniel encountered him for the first time after Cora and he ran off together. Alan tracked them down, rushed to their country guest house and dragged his sobbing wife back home. The actual scene was both ludicrous and horrible. Daniel made no attempt to defend himself against this enraged bull of a husband. Sick to the stomach, dodging a fist, he stumbled backwards and tipped into an empty bathtub like a clown, wearing only his pyjamas. His legs waved in the air.

This Alan had a handsome head of tight curly black hair, a fine physique and a ninny's voice which grated on Daniel's nerves. Still, he was devoted to Cora in a way Daniel could never be. Utterly reliable, patient, trustworthy, he worshipped Cora dumbly. She overawed, frightened and subjugated him, whether intentionally or not Daniel could never decide. He felt inadequate before her cultural tastes, not to mention her appetites. All the same, whatever had drawn them together in the first place remained alive for another seven years at least – as longing in him, remorse in her. It could be that she was intent on punishing him for being so dominated by his mother, who took him back again after Cora's desertion. Alan's widowed mother was by all accounts a devourer of the old school.

Every year Cora would receive a sumptuous birthday card smothered in red roses. Alan never forgot. After Daniel's daughter was born he even paid them a visit. Daniel was now working at a job every bit as dull as Alan's and twice as menial. The cuckolded ex-husband took Cora and her child up the lane for a walk while his usurper sat clerking in a city office miles away. No doubt when they reached the steep part, Alan pushed the pram. He hadn't changed: when it came to expressing emotion he was as tongue-tied as ever. Gazing at Cora like a loon – so her account went – he pleaded lifelessly to be allowed another chance. He would be a loving father to the little girl too. He said doggedly and repeatedly that this was his great mistake – he should have given her a child. Cora shook her head. 'You still can't understand, can you? I was dying, dying with you, I wanted a different life.' He thought by this she meant art, and said he would enroll in an evening class and learn about it. 'These conditions aren't for you, Cora. You weren't brought up to live like this. When your mother saw what it was like here, no inside toilet, no bath, no hot water even, she was horrified – and no wonder.' Coming home from his daily treadmill, Daniel found Alan seated at the round table where they ate and on which he dumped his old office typewriter, hammering away at manuscripts most evenings and weekends. He said, 'Hello.'

Alan nodded bleakly, treating him to the stony stare Daniel expected and felt he deserved, sitting bolt upright in his grey lounge suit, polished brown shoes tucked under his chair, elbows pinned to his sides as his mother had taught him to behave when dining out. Then he averted his pale Jewish-looking face. In fact he wasn't a Jew, though in the business world he would sometimes be taken for one. Clare, in a high baby chair, was being fed mush with a spoon, letting it ooze out again blithely from the filled pouches of her cheeks. It was perhaps Clare's resemblance to Daniel, Cora subsequently maintained –

'she's got your eyes, your bone structure' – which caused Alan to abandon hope at last. Whatever it was, he didn't visit them again.

Ruby's absorption in Daniel's life story ceased abruptly when she became concerned for Phil Hucker, a tall beefy fellow who always wore a white polo-neck sweater of thick wool – knitted, so he told Daniel, by his wife. Now he was silent, except for sudden inexplicable fits of rage, when he became irrationally quarrelsome over mere trifles. Daniel had been a witness to one of these tantrums, standing behind him one lunch-time in the meal queue. In a flash Daniel felt more alive, excited, although alarmed for Hucker and what the consequences might be. Two days later the man electrified the entire dining room by hurling his new issue of multicoloured pills across the floor.

'What's likely to happen to him?' Daniel asked Ruby.

Ruby's eye movements were unusually rapid. She kept pulling at her fingers and moving her head restlessly, as though in a corner. He could never decide where her curiosity ended and her compassion began. 'He was making such good progress,' she said worriedly, 'and now he's started having these relapses. You'll see, they won't let it go on for long – it disturbs the others too much.'

Daniel was in two minds about this. Everyone seemed to liven up and become expectant, more alert, at the least hint of any drama. 'Will they put him somewhere else?'

Ruby answered him like a professional, 'Not yet. They'll warn him first, to see if he responds, and then they'll change his medication, give him another kind of cocktail. That's probably happened already. Well, I hope not.'

'So it's not working – is that what you're saying?'

She nodded gravely, and fell silent for a moment. 'Poor Phil – he was all set to go out at the end of this month. I was talking only the other day to his wife. She seemed really happy.'

71

'If they do transfer him, where to? Where's this other place?'

Ruby became so guarded, he wondered at first if she was about to deny all knowledge of it. They were near one of the large windows overlooking the long slope. The wet glistening roof of another low building, set apart like theirs, showed below them. Ruby pointed to it. 'There,' she said. 'The Scott Clinic.'

'I've heard the name, yes. So that's it. Is it grim in there?'

She frowned, then said carefully, 'More restricted than here.'

'She means a locked ward,' he thought at once, and by the way she spoke he gathered that she was unwilling, or maybe too superstitious, to say more. As though reading his thoughts she added, 'You mustn't believe the rumours flying around up here about the Scott. It's just a myth.' Then she dropped her official-sounding tone and looked candidly at him. 'But nobody wants to slip backwards, do they?'

He shook his head, thinking that poor Hucker was about to slide downhill in more ways than one.

'That's why I feel so bad about Phil,' she said. 'How do you feel?'

'The same.'

It was true; he meant it. On the morning of his admission, it was Phil Hucker who came up before anyone else to ask if there was anything he could do for him. I'm on my way to the village shop,' he said. 'Do you need anything?' Daniel lay there feeling utterly ashamed, officially ill for the first time in his life, confined to bed while everyone else came and went freely. The fair-haired serious man in soft white wool hung over him, looking big and friendly as he stood by the bed. 'Any razor blades?' he asked gently.

Daniel said no, thanking him feebly with his ghost of a voice. He stared at the white sweater. Rising on the chest was a great eagle with outstretched wings. The man clothed in this bird nodded and moved off. Something about him, his appearance, or it may have been his simple kindness, brought Daniel close to tears.

Hucker's wife would come on visits, a shy woman in her thirties with a trim figure, wearing glasses. She looked like a teacher. They seemed fond of each other. In the Day Room one afternoon she was telling him news of their children, while Hucker nodded away and gave her small smiles of amusement. He was an engineer. Once or twice Daniel saw him examining his hands intently as he sat alone. He turned them over in slow motion, first one and then the other, as if puzzled by their idleness. He seemed to be expecting them to provide him with answers if he waited patiently enough.

10

Daniel was going home now on weekend leaves. The charge nurse signed his pass, handed over sufficient medication in a tiny buff envelope bearing his name, and he walked out down the gravel drive which curved and sank in a long snake past the main block.

The picking-up point was outside the library. A magnolia tree in the middle of a circular plot was well advanced, about to begin opening all its great creamy flowers together. The thought of this act of triumph put a faint smile on his lips, as did the sound of the gravel crunching under his feet. 'I'm not beaten, I am up and about, in motion,' he told himself jubilantly. And detected yet again the tremor of astonishment darting along his veins. There and then he made a vow to paint a picture, no matter how crude, inspired by the magnolia, with its leafless upraised arms carrying its buds in cold air, burning.

In the dark blue hospital bus which was provided free of charge he sat nursing a grubby duffle bag between his knees. Nothing in future weeks would equal this wonderful experience. He sat trembling with anticipation like a returning sailor. As they raced down the new dual carriageway he didn't miss a thing, his eyes busy at the endless task of joining every morsel he saw to the intricate bits inside him which corresponded so perfectly.

He approached the front door, unable to believe that nothing had changed. The house looked exactly as when he had last lived here – and why shouldn't it, after an

74

absence of only a few weeks – except that now it had nothing whatsoever to do with him. He stood there like a visitor from abroad, or from outer space. Cora was out, he knew, visiting a friend. She would be back later.

He was expected, but evidently his transfigured state was a complete surprise to Cora's mother. Nellie opened the door, its bits of broken stained glass rattling just as he remembered, and tottered back as if pushed, her mouth open. He noticed as if for the first time how unsteady she had become on her wasted legs.

Her manners recovered first. Finding her voice, she managed to say to this apparition, 'Come in.'

Her last sight of him had been with filthy hair, uncut for six months, his chin nicked and bloody from his attempts at shaving. Now the hospital barber had given him a short back and sides, not too brutally. Each morning he shaved carefully and with pleasure, and he was wearing a newly washed and ironed shirt. Even his shoes were shining.

He followed the old woman dreamily into the sitting room, loving every moment. He saw again her own bulky, worn-out suite, and the ancient lined curtains and threadbare carpet, all of which belonged to her, pathetic relics of her past life in another town and age. Originally it was intended that she should have this room entirely to herself when she moved in with them, but somehow the separation into two households never happened.

'Sit down,' she said meekly. 'I won't be a moment. I imagine you'd like a cup of tea.'

'Yes I would, thank you.'

She took small steps, the way girls were taught to walk in another time. Coming back in with her oak tea tray, she sat on the edge of the lumpy armchair by the window, a chair no one else sat in. She poured the tea, then took a cup and saucer for herself after serving her son-in-law. Her stick-like legs were pressed tightly together. She waited politely for him to speak first. Much as she disliked him, he was nevertheless some kind of man and therefore deserving of respect. These ingrained attitudes didn't affect the veiled irony – and sometimes the contempt – in her sharp grey eyes.

Now, though, she was staring at him as if seeing a ghost. He felt like one. It was strange, not in the least unpleasant. Either he was risen from the dead or he was already dead and this was the afterlife, he thought happily, and sipped at the tea instead of gulping too hastily at it, in an attempt to please the old lady.

It was like meeting her afresh. He noticed things he had forgotten about completely, or had failed to notice, such as the sharp purplish ridge of her hawk nose. 'Nana, why is your nose bumpy?' Clare would ask as a child. 'And Cora is mad about falcons,' he recalled. Looking at Nellie's nose had reminded him.

The doorbell rang. Nellie jumped violently. 'Oh dear,' she cried out, flustered, 'it's Saturday, that'll be the milkman. Oh what a nuisance, I should have had his money ready.' She was already struggling to her feet.

Daniel leapt up at once. 'I'll see to it, don't worry – have another cup of tea.'

Making for the door he glanced back and smiled, keen to show her how capable he now was. Everything had pleasure in it for him – the tingling pleasure of accomplishment. The bell rang again, more insistently this time.

'Stupid man!' Suddenly Nellie was glaring mad. 'Ask him where the fire is.'

Daniel settled the week's bill, took the milk down to the kitchen and glanced round automatically for the refrigerator, accustomed to the one in the hospital kitchen. He had forgotten that they had never owned one. Moving into this neglected old house, faced with bills for rewiring, plastering, burst pipes, roof repairs, replacement windows, he bought a new cooker and then had to stop. After two years at college living on meagre grants their savings were virtually wiped out. He signed on for benefit but couldn't face applying for a teaching post. As if inviting disaster, he

76

began an affair. Soon he was ill – he believed from a failure of nerve in the face of life – and of no use to his lover or anyone, bursting into tears for no reason, feeling ruined by women and yet lost without them, his mind revolving madly like a windmill.

Nellie had taken him at his word, and sat sipping a fresh cup of tea. She liked what she called her little pleasures. She still sat bolt upright, knees pressed together as if glued, but she was smoking a cigarette. When she spoke, her voice was almost coquettish. 'I've poured you a fresh cup,' she said.

They sat in a peaceful silence, which for her must have been a trifle embarrassing. She wasn't accustomed to sitting alone with him like this. With Cora present, she became a silent ally, stiffly opposed to his presence. Well, that was how it had been. He saw himself as responsible for Nellie's predicament, her misery and Cora's, everything. Persuading Nellie to join them had been his idea.

Now the atmosphere was almost friendly. He saw again how frail and desperately old she was, older than her years, with her withered neck, fleshless cheeks, her claw-like fingers as she raised the cigarette to her mouth negligently and smoked, a veteran whist player who was every inch a lady.

'I can't get over it,' Nellie was saying. 'You look so well. It's a miracle.' Her shyness made the business of conversing with a stranger – for that's what he was – quite an ordeal. But to remain silent would have been bad manners. She tried again, this time not so awestruck. 'How do you feel?' she asked doubtfully, as if suggesting that it might be some kind of trick. Her northern caution hadn't deserted her. She spoke primly, but with a distinct accent.

'I'm fine.'

Too polite to stare, she lowered her eyes demurely. Daniel's sunken cheeks had filled out and he was now a stone heavier than his normal weight. He wondered, not for the first time, if he was high on drugs without knowing it. Whatever the reason, he kept feeling an urge to rush out and buy things, presents, surprises, which for him was certainly abnormal. If medical science alone had achieved this, why wasn't the hospital itself happier? What about Phil Hucker? Certainly he was exceptionally happy, and because the tender feelings he had were impersonal, running out of him in a steady stream towards people and things indiscriminately, there was no fear of loss. If he owned nothing, how could anything be taken from him? That shadow over his life had vanished, he thought for ever.

Nellie sighed, and began to fidget. 'This is very nice, but I ought to stir my stumps. I've got a shopping list this long' – she measured in the air with her hands and pulled a face.

He had always detested shopping. He jumped up. 'Let me go, will you? Just give me the list.'

'Oh, are you sure?'

'Definitely, I'll enjoy it.' Which was the simple truth. He knew how the steep incline coming back made her gasp and clutch her side. Once she had clung to the garden railings of a house for half an hour before daring to move again.

Nellie provided him with a capacious shopping bag and he set off. She came to the front door and opened it, peering cautiously into the street. She even smiled sweetly at him like a girl. He went down the street feeling childishly pleased with himself for doing Nellie a favour. God knows it was little enough. What else could he do? Hearing her climb the stairs to her room at night when he was ill, knowing by her dragging steps that it was her, lying in his fetid room in dirty bed linen, he would have given anything to be her, often in pain and near the end of her days but honourable, upright, pious, not a cheat and a liar like him. He wanted to call out and beg her forgiveness for bringing her into this disintegrating house, crumbling around them like his marriage.

Passing the glittering display in a wine shop window, he stopped. Obeying an impulse he went in. That's right, Nellie liked a drink. Her husband in his heyday was a partner in an upholstery firm. Their massive sideboard would be crowded with bottles, a box of cigars, a tantalus, glasses of all shapes and sizes. Daniel remembered that she enjoyed a drop of whisky. Eager to buy the biggest bottle available, it struck him that this might seem too crude a gesture. He settled for a half bottle of Teacher's.

Nellie was a pensioner, more or less penniless, but he felt bound to take her proud nature into account. She had invested the last of her savings as her share in this foundering house of theirs, making it a condition of her coming at all. After the stroke which had killed her husband she lived on for a while in the Bradford terraced house which had belonged to his mother before him. Now the district was run down, virtually an immigrant quarter. For all her race prejudice, Nellie was in fact more afraid of break-ins by whites.

A Pakistani who worked for British Rail came knocking on her door. He was most polite, his beard pitch-black with streaks of grey. Was it possible that she intended to sell her house? Frightened, she shook her head, closed and double-bolted the door. How could he have known? What was he, a mind-reader? Her letters to Cora were full of this possibility, together with her loneliness and fear. Although Cora replied that she shouldn't be living alone, and too far away to be visited regularly, she made no concrete suggestions. It was Daniel, the sentimentalist, who kept saying she ought to move in with them. Eventually his mother-in-law consented.

The Pakistani – who was in fact a Sikh – returned. This time Nellie said yes. The house was leasehold and there was a loan owing. All she received on completion of the sale was six hundred pounds. Daniel went up on her final day to escort her back on the train.

Her house was half empty, the large pieces of furniture,

Sheraton and so forth, already in store or on the road to them. Daniel rolled up carpets and tied hairy string around the long cylinders. Nellie's entire life had been spent in this city – she knew no other. Since the age of eighteen, after her marriage to a seemingly prosperous businessman in his forties, her days and nights had been consumed by this house. Nellie took a last look round. 'I've got nothing now,' she said, and seemed to be speaking to the walls. 'This was my one and only home. I'll never have another.' Seeing her choke, turning away and beginning to wring her hands, he went out hastily and waited by the front gate. He stared blankly at its peeling paint. There was a taxi coming. Their train was in forty minutes.

The half bottle felt like a big stone at the bottom of the shopping bag. Daniel swung on down the long hill and on to the Plain. As always the main thoroughfare was loud, seething, congested. Cars and vans crawled along bumper to bumper. Only a few months ago he would have loathed these crowds and their ant-like activity. Now he glanced eagerly into faces to his left and right as if they were shop windows, set out to tempt and sparkle. Old and young, ugly and pretty, they were all significant, important, part of the scene. Men and women alike seemed to be smiling pleasantly. Clouds broke, the sun came out.

How simple life was when you gave up the struggle and simply went along with everything! 'So that's the secret!' he told himself, exuberant as a child with his discovery. His sexual desires were still dormant, maybe lost for good, or possibly having a game with him, perhaps lurking in the big toe of his right foot. What did it matter? At the greengrocer's, where everyone had to queue in a space no wider than a passage, he waited contentedly behind a tall girl with thick chestnut hair dropping to her shoulders in deep somnolent waves. Every so often she would claw absently at it with her fingers. Sometimes she would

80

plunge in her hand and leave it there, as though her hand was her hair's lover. She had small sloping shoulders, then her body swelled heavily at the hips. Standing with no name or identity close behind this succulent goddess he felt curiously at peace, sniffing at her like a ripe pear and imagining he could smell her moisture.

The shopping done, he went on a personal spending spree. At the hospital, wandering on jaunts down to the cafeteria or over the field path to the village, he had kept wanting to make a visual record of his journeys and what he encountered. Yes, he needed a camera. He imagined himself taking shots of gateways, paths, trees, inmates in the distance, even the grass and common plants known disparagingly as weeds. He would be trigger-happy in no time, capturing moments of wonder struck by light. In a chemist's he bought a cheap automatic, then marched from there straight to a music shop and picked out a cassette recorder. At the back of his mind too was the idea he had long considered of preserving on tape some of the voices he heard daily in his carefree new life. This lost its point as soon as he got back there again. He remembered a nice story that he hoped was true: a painter shows one of his pictures to his young son and asks for his comment. The still life, pears and apples in a bowl on a red table-cloth, was so representational that you were tempted to touch them. 'It's all right,' the boy said, 'but why do you want two of the same thing?'

Now what he needed was a present for Cora. He had this ridiculous feeling of innocence bubbling in his veins day and night, jostling to be let out, to be given expression. Surely Cora, who knew him better than his own mother – and wishes she didn't – would accept his gift and see him as the basically good fellow he really was? The terrible winter, *their* terrible winter, was over, he reasoned. Why prolong it? He passed in front of a florist's. Flowers affected Cora strongly, he knew. How about taking her back an armful? Yet even in his state of permanent euphoria he could anticipate difficulties. Being nice to Cora could be tricky. Into his mind floated a memory of one of her simple desires – rum-flavoured ice cream with raisins. He wanted very much to have something good happen to her for once. A surprise – but what? He decided to act with circumspection; she would have said deviously. Not that it mattered what she said or thought, he was in love with whatever kept reminding him that he was in possession of a new, guiltless and pure heart, pumping away invincibly in his chest like a baby's. He had been given a clean slate, he could do anything, he thought. Babies, after all, could do no wrong. Unlike a baby, however, he could also act.

He walked into a showroom full of hard white light from the many fluorescents burning overhead. There was an excess of heat. Brilliant white box-like appliances stood about the glossy floor and on stands, with only a small area left clear for the salesman's table and chair.

A ginger-haired youth hopped from behind a screen. He wore brown, and had the twitchy bulging eyes of a rabbit. Daniel pointed to a refrigerator which looked suitable, not too enormous for their high boxy kitchen. 'I'd like to order that.'

'Certainly, of course sir.' Suddenly a solemn old man, the young assistant rubbed his hands together. 'Would you like to see inside?'

'Inside?'

'To see the various features of this model?'

'No, no, it doesn't matter.'

The young man led him to the table. 'Please take a seat.'

'Thank you.'

'Now – hire purchase, sir?'

'No.'

'Credit sale?'

Daniel nodded. As an ex-clerk of the Electricity Board he was familiar with this term. The brown-suited youth gripped his pen and set to work. He flicked importantly at the carbon copies.

'How soon can you deliver it?'

'Monday's the earliest, I'm afraid.'

'Monday's fine.'

Outside, the crowd surged as thickly as ever. He was in no hurry. People in a rush shoved past him. The full bag of shopping tugged at his arm and shoulder. On the hill climbing to his street, the hill Nellie dreaded, he took it easy, pausing for a breather now and then.

At the door he searched for his key and couldn't find it. He rang the bell. Nellie let him in, looking strained and cold. She hobbled ahead down the partly decorated hall, not speaking. From behind she looked horribly emaciated. He thought she might be suffering again from an internal malady which came and went, though she never complained. But her coldness was obvious. Then he heard Cora's voice call, 'Mother?'

'Yes, coming, dear,' Nellie said. She even put on a burst of speed on her way down to the kitchen on its lower level. Daniel followed her in with his load of shopping. The two women stood by the cooker, staring wide-eyed at him.

'Well, this is a surprise, I must say,' Cora said, in an unnaturally neutral tone. Her flushed face and shining eyes told him that she was anything but cool. Looking at her, he was at a loss. The clear skin of her cheeks bloomed as freshly as ever. He was glad to see her looking so well, in spite of all he'd inflicted on her.

'Did you forget I was coming?' he asked mildly.

Cora glanced at her mother and laughed. 'Oh, we didn't forget, did we, Mother?'

'You said it's a surprise.'

'It is, it is!'

'Why, what's surprising?'

'Your recovery. It's unbelievable, isn't it, Mother?'

For some reason Nellie was avoiding his eye. She looked distinctly uncomfortable, he thought. Not for the first time, he felt pity for her. Basically, for all her snobbery and disapproval, she was a kind person, with no vindictiveness in her. He always saw her as going about half petrified by a fear of scenes, of emotional turmoil, the warfare of their marriage, always about to break out. She was beyond violent passion herself but seemed to sense it in the air, as the old often do. If she heard raised voices, or her daughter weeping and raging, she would start passing out with severe palpitations. He wondered if her fears stemmed from a lifetime spent with her husband, a squat, fiery, unpredictable little man, all barrel chest and bald skull, who had had a breakdown in the Depression when his business ran on to the rocks. From then on he was subject to terrifying outbreaks of black rage, followed by silences full of ugly menace lasting for days. At least half a dozen times Daniel had heard Nellie – prompted by Cora – go over the story of one incident. Creditors had come banging on the front door. Nellie was expected to answer. For once she refused. Arnold would never face them. They stood glaring at each other. Suddenly he grabbed his wife by the wrists in a fury and squeezed. Nellie cried out and fell to her knees. Arnold hadn't uttered a word, and he didn't then. He just went back to his armchair and picked up his paper. 'Oh, he was a terribly strong man, your father.' At this point Cora seemed to exult and grow powerful herself, smiling secretly at some thought of her own.

'Let me take that,' Nellie said, carrying off the bag of shopping. Her voice had taken on a cold edge and a touch of sarcasm. 'Aren't you an angel,' she murmured slyly.

'That'll be the day,' Cora said, but without bite. Daniel, still under a compulsion to do nice things, felt no remorse, none of the old tendency to grovel. Pain and suffering, lies and debasement had been replaced by a kind of thrilling happiness which he wanted to share with others. There was something Biblical in all this.

'I've ordered a fridge, a new one,' he told her. 'It ought to fit all right over there, next to the cooker. They'll deliver it on Monday.'

'Which Monday?'

'The day after tomorrow.'

'Wonders will never cease, my God,' Cora muttered. Then she turned quite brightly to her mother. 'Did you hear that? After all these years, a fridge!'

'I heard,' Nellie said grimly.

'Will somebody be in?' he asked.

'On Monday? Oh, I expect so. We're always in on Mondays, aren't we, Mother?'

'Yes, we are.'

'We have such an exciting life here, just the two of us,' Cora went on wildly, then stopped. Abruptly, she added, 'God, I'm old before my time.' She managed to scowl and laugh at once. Daniel was staring in surprise, expecting a long bitter monologue which didn't develop.

'Don't you like the idea?' he asked.

'What of?' She gazed blankly at him.

'A fridge.'

'Oh, that,' Cora said dreamily, as if miles away. 'Yes, very nice, a great help. Thoughtful of you.' She had a wistful expression. Then her eyes sharpened, as though recognising someone she had once, years ago, known intimately. 'Daniel,' she said, in a changed voice, full of sad yearning.

'Yes?'

'Nothing. You can use your old room. It's all clean up there.'

'All right.'

'I can't get used to it.'

'What's that?'

'How you look.'

Their old relationship was suspended, as it were by common consent, and yet they were here together, in this house of hatred and woe. Could she have forgotten? Cora's eyes watched him warily, her animosity in abeyance.

That evening they settled down in the shabby sitting room on Nellie's worn-out furniture. Daniel hadn't managed to decorate this room. The original porridgy wallpaper was still in place, lifting off with damp around the mouldy window frame. The TV laughed and chattered but he made no effort to make sense of it. Instead, he examined the interesting stains at the corners of the ceiling above the fireplace, the signs of ruination and neglect which would once have filled him with gloom.

Nellie got up two or three times and pottered around. Finally she left the room, moving with a crippled step like a woman of old China whose feet had been bound in girlhood. Probably she was unnerved by the tranquil atmosphere, he decided. She came in again with a ball of dark green wool and a brown paper bag. She lowered herself down timidly on the sofa next to her daughter.

'Socks!' Cora said scornfully.

Nellie didn't seem to hear. She was getting deaf, but he preferred to think of her silence as diplomatic. She was knitting a sock on four needles, a present for someone's husband. Everything she did was for someone else. Daniel stopped studying the ceiling and became absorbed in the action of Nellie's arthritic fingers as she looped and recovered the wool with deft graceful movements.

'I can feel a draught round my ankles,' Cora said. 'Did you close the door properly?'

'Were you speaking to me, dear?'

'The door, the door!'

Daniel jumped up. 'I'll do it.' The door didn't fasten until you pressed on one of the panels with the flat of your hand. He went over, pressed hard, the catch clicked. Something else he would probably never fix now.

'Thank you,' Cora said.

'Oh, the door,' her mother said. Cora gave a snort of laughter. An overgrown bored child getting her own back, she darted a knowing look at him.

Like old times, he thought; except that now he was quite detached, like a spectator. He sat receptively, craning here and there like a plant that receives the light, listening like

86

a cat, but weirdly desireless, and with no opinions about anything, thinking that if everyone stopped expressing opinions the entire world might change, perhaps unrecognisably. 'We'd see what a blessing life is,' he thought, feeling as he did so the sensation he had known as a boy when ducking his head and drinking from the sink tap, sighing with pleasure as the water slopped over his chin.

The mantel clock struck ten doleful notes. Nellie let the knitting fall into her lap, groaned, coughed, struggled to her feet and said she was going to bed. 'Goodnight,' she said politely to them both, suddenly shy and unable to look, embarrassed by them as a couple. She shuffled quickly to the door.

Daniel soon followed her up. It had been an exciting day for him, and at the hospital everyone was encouraged to turn in early after swallowing their sedatives. There, he would go into the kitchen and get down the huge jar of Horlicks from its shelf, spoon in a generous helping, mix in the cold water to a gritty paste and pour on the hot milk, then head for the charge nurse and his pills, a nightly ritual which for some obscure reason gave him immense satisfaction. Was it because he had become responsible for the well-being of his body again? Cora had always been a night creature, rising late in a deep depression and then gradually coming alive as the day wore on and darkness fell. By midnight she would be another person, smoking, listening to music, prowling about restlessly. Looking across at her, he saw she had no intention of moving.

Upstairs, he filled a glass with water, swallowing his ration of two pills from the tiny envelope in his pocket. That night he lay perfectly content for at least an hour. He couldn't – didn't want to – get over the fact that he was back in this small dank room which had held such terror for him only in January, and which had always seemed airborne, hung in space over the city as though over a chasm, liable to topple and crash – so his madness kept saying – in the next violent blast of the gale.

There was a clean pillowcase, snowy sheets, and some-one – surely it was Nellie – had taken down and washed and mended the curtains. The rip in the left-hand one had been repaired, he noted with a little thrill of recognition. The light bulb was still bare, no shade; something else he hadn't got around to fixing. Over the built-in cupboard a long strip of ceiling was badly cracked. He lay with his legs pleasantly aching and stared at this broken plaster, tracing a path from one zigzagging crack to another. It was a maze to explore with interest, idly, as a child might. Just two months ago he had worried endlessly about it, about whether the next raging storm would fetch it down, and with it the whole house, crashing round their ears. What a joke!

His abandoned desk still stood in the window bay. The bottom drawer on the right needed attention – it jammed when you closed it in a hurry. 'So this is the room where I tortured myself for months,' he marvelled, moved almost to tears. He let his gaze roam over every inch of it. And he had half expected to hate it. Of course it was only a room, he told himself. But the walls were soaked with meaning, and so was the bed, the floor, the ceiling with its cracks, the curtains. If he listened hard he could hear again his own hopeless cries. Every detail was precious to him. All he wanted was to go on wallowing in it, and then after-wards fold it up with its contents very carefully inside himself and carry it off.

The next day, that was what he did. He had brought a duffle bag containing a pair of blue pyjamas and a few toilet articles – comb, toothbrush, a plastic dispenser for blades, and the weighty metal safety razor in its chrome case which Nellie had passed on to him after her husband died. He went down the stairs with these items, together with the wordless message from the once-hated room.

Naive as it seemed, he had begun to allow himself to feel forgiven, lulled by the evening before into imagining they could perhaps make a fresh start. Cora quickly shattered this illusion. Besides, the day was dark, rainy, one of those filthy mornings she detested since it depressed her spirits even further in these dangerous early hours. He was surprised to find her up.

They were on the doorstep. He turned to go. 'Heard from Margaret?' she asked innocently.

'Who?'

Cora held something behind her back. She thrust out her hand. There was a book in it.

'What's this?'

'It came the other week. It's for you, isn't it? Read the inscription, I should. Have you lost your memory?'

The book was *Confessions of a Disloyal European*, by Jan Myrdal. Inside, the nervy jagged handwriting said, 'For Daniel – love, Margaret.'

He gaped in bewilderment. What had possessed her to sent it to him? Who was Jan Myrdal? Over a year ago he and Margaret had said farewell, sorrowfully on her part, thankfully and with shame on his. Disenchantment had set in: it was all they would ever share. 'Why me?' he asked, without knowing whom or what he was addressing.

'Put it in your bag. Otherwise there's no telling what might happen to it.'

'Yes,' he said in confusion. He was still fumbling with the cords of his duffle bag when Cora said, 'Goodbye,' and shut the door with a bang. The loose bits of stained glass rattled dryly. One day they'll fall out, he thought, turning up his coat collar against the cold spring rain.

11

It was another sunless Monday. Phil Hucker failed to appear for breakfast, but that wasn't unusual. Daniel came out of the dining-room to find Ruby waiting, her chair slewed at an angle. Her face was set.

'You did go home for the weekend?' she asked anxiously, without any preamble.

'I did, yes.'

'Was it a success?'

'Very nice.'

'Oh, good.'

'Any drama here?'

Ruby lowered her voice. 'Yes. Phil's gone.'

'Gone?'

'They've transferred him to the Scott.'

'That's bad news. Why, did he do anything spectacular?'

'I don't think so.' He was behind Ruby's chair. 'Push me to the end.' When they were out of earshot she said, 'He was throwing his pills back at them. He's done that before.'

'Yes.'

'Daniel, I feel upset.'

'I know.'

'I can't stop thinking of him.'

'No, it's too bad.'

'Will you push me down as far as the library?'

'Of course.'

'Are you upset?'

'Yes, very much.'

'He's not dead, far from it,' she said suddenly, vehemently, as if warding off demons, or contradicting some thought process of his own. Twisting round her head, she asked, 'Won't you need a top coat?'

'No, nurse.'

She laughed in spite of herself. 'Do they say that to you?'

'Now and then.'

'I'm not them, you know that.'

'They mean well. This is a thick sweater.'

A sharp wind was blowing, whirling down from the moor in sudden brutal gusts. The light was harsh, the bushes of evergreen glittering, full of knives, the gravel dry and glittery underfoot. Daniel stared at the bright roofs, straight walls. Slates and bricks interlocked freshly, as though fitted into place that instant.

'So, was your wife glad to see you?'

He laughed. 'Yes and no.'

'You were glad to see her, though?'

'What a question. Yes, I was.'

'You must have been pleased. Don't tell me you weren't pleased to be home?'

'Ruby, everything pleases me.'

This kind of answer seemed to make her impatient. 'Well, what did you do? Tell me.'

'Very little. Sat about, ate food, drank tea, coffee, failed to understand TV, lay down in my room. Did shopping. Oh, I bought a camera.'

'Did you? How nice, a camera! Are you going to take my picture?'

'If you like.' Not sure that she would approve, he kept quiet about his real motive, and the mania he had for making a record of the place, each stick and stone, and maybe even writing a book one day, a documentary but with a personal slant. (Years later he still had the rough notes, in shaky old man's handwriting.)

'Daniel, listen. Can I ask you something private?'

91

'You will, anyway.'

'Please don't say that!'

'Go on, ask.'

'It's this. Does your wife want you back?'

'I couldn't say. The subject didn't come up.'

'No, but surely you've got a clue. You must have. Can't men sense things like that?'

He laughed again. 'Why not ask instead what the husband wants? You've got him here, ask him. Why don't you?'

Ruby said very firmly, without hesitation, 'Because you don't know what you want, that's why.'

'Is it that obvious?'

'It is to me.'

'That's very interesting.'

'Tell me, right now, what you want.'

'Is this a challenge?'

'Yes.'

He turned the chair round and they began to go back up the steep slope. 'I can't. That's because there's nothing I want. Absolutely nothing. No needs. It's a funny feeling, like floating.'

Ruby wasn't impressed. 'Take my picture now,' she said. 'By the magnolia. Look, the sun's coming out! Go and get your camera.'

'Why do women always end up by ordering me around?'

'Same reason. You can't decide what it is you want, so somebody has to tell you. You prefer to let things happen to you.'

'And land up here.'

They had reached level ground. 'If you're going, will you hurry up? I shall get chilly sitting here in this wind.'

'I'll be quick.' To let her see how positive he could be, he broke into a run. As he sprinted away up the gravel he was thinking, 'What does it matter, see if I care!' But he did. Like it or not, he was regaining his normal solitary self; ambivalent, observing, difficult.

* * *

The outside world drew closer. He both wanted and resented it. In his mail on Tuesday morning was a large book of watercolours by Emile Nolde, a gift from an American he had met briefly in London. Next, he opened an invitation to read poetry at a residential centre in Devon for aspiring writers. Finally he tore free a letter from Bridget, expressing anxiety and remorse and taking the blame for his breakdown. Bridget was a madly active, searching young woman whose final act with Daniel had been to drive him to Taunton and leave him there, after making sure he had a single ticket for home in his pocket. While they had walked distractedly up and down, up and down, she had devoured a whole bagful of chocolate raisins without even noticing. She saw only that he was incapable of handling his affairs or making a single clear decision, and to avoid further contagion with this walking disaster and at least save herself she had driven off weeping in her ugly old car, their accomplice for the past fortnight. It was the first sensible thing she did.

Leonard Rowe, his oldest friend, called in on Wednesday afternoon to see him. This was his second visit.

Leonard approached him looking strained. On his previous visit, Daniel had sat inertly on a hard chair as if being interviewed, in the bare cubicle used by Alcoholics Anonymous. They had gone in there for some privacy. Having been admitted only ten days before, Daniel was in no condition to see or be seen by anyone. He simply endured it, waiting lifelessly for the meeting to end. At one point he mumbled, 'No way out.'

And now look at me, he was saying to himself, inwardly rejoicing but not uttering a word. Surely his smile was eloquent enough? Leonard stuck out his hand cautiously, eyeing his stricken friend. What a shy pair they were. Even after twenty years they would still be awkward with each other for the first few minutes.

Seeing Leonard gave him a warm, glad feeling, and yet his friend's deadly seriousness seemed misplaced. It made no sense to him now. Obviously Leonard had come dutifully but in trepidation, prepared to undergo a second harrowing experience. Daniel's first impulse was to cheer him up, as if he were the visitor. Somehow their roles were reversed. And he did truly feel in possession of some amazing and precious secret, which was in fact an open secret, to do with man's primordial need to be happy. 'Man is born for happiness,' he had read long ago when he was an idealist, 'as a bird is born for flight.' It was Maxim Gorki, perhaps from his diaries. Nowadays he preferred Isaiah's 'And man is bowed down and man is humbled.' Looking at his friend reminded him. Leonard seemed to be hunched over troubles of his own – his marriage was in difficulties, it transpired later – whereas Daniel no longer understood problems or the necessity for them. To think that in the old days they had laughed their heads off at the sheer preposterousness of everything!

Taking charge, Daniel said, 'Come out here and sit down – it's a real sun-trap.' Beneath the glass canopy at the rear of his room was a discarded armchair, parked on the cracked flagstones for collection later by the waste disposal men. 'There, try that. Watch out for any busted springs.'

Leonard smiled a wan smile. He was handling the convalescent gingerly and Daniel wanted to laugh. At the same time he longed to pronounce a magic word, one which released his friend from his burden of duties. He did too much teaching, and anyway he hated it. He was pinched and resentful, a bundle of responsibilities, twisting in a trap of his own devising, writing copiously in his spare time as a way of justifying his existence and getting nowhere with indifferent publishers.

Daniel went off to make coffee, one for Leonard and one for himself. He came back accompanied by Ruby, who wheeled herself up to be introduced. Daniel observed Leonard chatting more freely to Ruby than to him. He sat back and enjoyed listening to them both. Ruby, however, refused to stay more than a few minutes for fear of intruding. Afterwards she told him, 'I did like your friend.'

As she went off, Leonard watched her. He had perked up considerably. Daniel guessed that he would have liked to jump up and push her chair – he was strangely drawn to handicapped people. Daniel wasn't so good with them. If they were robust, like Ruby, that was fine, but more than once a victim of severe disability had somehow undermined his will to live.

Instead of asking a direct question – they knew each other too well – Leonard said gratefully, 'What a change in you since the last time I was here.'

Daniel waited curiously, like an onlooker, eager to hear about this lost soul who bore his name, whom he remembered perfectly but without strong emotion, just a kind of wistful tenderness. How odd; he was even happy to have fallen into a crisis – and how odd to have forgotten all about his guilt. But he could never have explained this. He made no attempt to try. The sun came out. His friend blinked, shielding his eyes.

Leonard waited till his coffee was nearly cold, then drank it down like a task, in two hasty gulps. He shifted his legs unhappily. For years now it had been difficult to persuade him to stay long. Then Daniel had an idea – or rather his mania took over. 'Stay where you are, don't move – I need to take your picture.' And he added truthfully, 'For the record.'

Leonard managed to laugh, assuming the remark to be a joke, but he sat obediently where he was, his body too low and his knees too high, like someone wedged in a hole. Daniel went in through the open french window to his room and snatched up the Instamatic from his bed.

The photograph, when developed, was both comical and sad, showing a man who had got stuck in mid-life, his face wrinkled in a grimace. Daniel stood outside the village post office chuckling at what he saw. Then he stopped. He shook his head over what could have been a depiction of their stalled friendship.

12

Later that week, stepping out of his room, he saw a young woman wandering towards him like someone lost. It was Friday afternoon. The newcomer wore dark glasses, so that her face and the movements of her head seemed blind. She came groping up the corridor. Her straight fair hair was cut short. She was tall, rather ungainly, with an anxious stoop to her round shoulders. The dark glasses and the newly cut shining hair, curiously neat, made her look unfamiliar, but there was no mistaking her mud-stained baseball shoes. He said hello to Bridget.

'Hallo,' she said, very tentatively, and ventured a smile. 'I nearly didn't recognise you. Why should that be?'

He was about to say exactly the same. 'You found the place, then, no trouble?'

'Of course.'

'Why of course?'

'Don't you remember what a good map-reader I am?'

'Yes, I do.' She was referring obliquely to their exploits. My God, he thought, it was less than nine months ago.

'You were hopeless.' She was making a big effort to sound light-hearted, her face tense. In her eyes, if he could have seen them, he would have read her perplexed nature, the terrible eagerness and the appeal coming and going.

Defending himself smilingly, he said, 'I wasn't fast enough sometimes, I'll admit that. I've always been fascinated by maps.'

'You can't use them, all you do is admire them.' Bridget

96

twisted up one side of her mouth in the lopsided, rueful smile he remembered only too well.

'So you say. No, the trouble was, you were always in such a tearing hurry. I didn't get enough warning.'

'Rubbish.'

'Come and inspect my private room,' he said, and opened the door proudly for his visitor.

'Oh yeah.' Bridget advanced a few uncertain steps and then stood nervously on his blaringly new carpet. Strange surroundings always gave her the jitters. So did anyone who stared fixedly at her, as he was doing. Once, Daniel took her to meet an acquaintance of his who lived in a spacious St John's Wood flat. He was trying to impress her. What a mistake. She refused to take off her winter coat and chose a seat in a corner of the room. Oh well, he thought; his room was too small for any kind of retreat, if that was now her problem.

'Nice?' he asked.

'Very nice,' she said emphatically. 'Yes, I see,' and she began to nod in the vigorous way he had always admired.

'They give you this for good behaviour,' he joked.

'You always were a jammy sod.'

Daniel sat on the bed watching her. 'Why don't you sit down?' He pointed to the one and only chair.

'I've been sitting down for hours, driving here,' she said, with her characteristic obstinacy.

'Take your sunglasses off – I can't see who I'm talking to.'

'Shades. They're called shades.'

'Right,' he said.

'Daniel, I can't stay.'

'It was good of you to come.'

'Oh shit, this is stupid!'

He gazed mildly at her. 'What is?'

She removed her glasses. What an anxious frown, he thought. Nothing has changed for her, only for me.

She said, 'This. Us,' and waved her glasses in the air.

'What's wrong?'

'This isn't at all what I expected.'

'No?'

She screwed up her face, became a pug, tossed her head. The search for the right word always exasperated her. 'It's so – formal.'

'Would you like a cup of tea?'

Bridget burst out laughing, her face flushed. 'So's that!' she cried, in her old style. 'Oh Christ, why not? In a minute, not yet,' she went on hastily. 'Let me say my piece first, I've been rehearsing it all the way here. No, it's no good, it makes no sense any more. You see – well, when I heard the news about you I was horrified, truly. It was all me, I thought, I'm to blame, I did it to him.'

'Did what?'

He was genuinely puzzled. She was staring at him wild-eyed, the picture of remorse. Yet something didn't add up. For one thing, he looked too well – maybe that was it? She gave up, shrugged, waved her arms. 'Ah, forget it. What the hell. Listen, I tell you what – fancy something to eat? I could murder some fish and chips. Is there anywhere round here?'

'There is, yes, about three miles down the road. Have you come in your car?'

'What a question. You haven't changed. I didn't drop out of the sky. How else could I have got to this godfor-saken place? Didn't I say I'd been driving for hours?'

'I forgot. The same car?'

'No. That one died.'

'The one you were so fond of?'

Bridget shrugged dismissively. Her emotions fluctuated like the weather, and what was dead no longer existed. In this respect she was truly modern. He caught her examin-ing his face closely, and thought, so that's her mission – to make sure I am in one piece, alive and kicking.

As if tuning into his thoughts, she said, 'Are you all right, really?' But when Daniel tried to describe his sensations, his elation and so forth, she became at once the sceptical university graduate of last year. 'You're on cloud nine. That means you'll come down,' she predicted, with an unaffectedly warm smile. She suspected him of experiencing manic-depressive swoops similar to her own. Maybe she was right, he thought. He didn't think so. He stood before her calmly, a placid smile on his face, totally convinced of his uniqueness.

They spent a few hours together. In the fish restaurant she ate ravenously, perhaps to console herself. Whenever his attention wandered – or she thought it did – she darted sharp looks at him. Saying goodbye, she assumed a mournful expression and he wanted to laugh. I'm immune, he told himself, safe from her helpless caprices. She clambered in behind the wheel of her car and suddenly cheered up, her hands strong and stubby with purpose, the road waiting for her with its bends, junctions, flying houses, magic carpet fields, all that distance to be covered, hills climbed, valleys to be ploughed through. Though she denied liking it, he had always had the impression that her whole being was focused by the act of driving. It sewed things together beautifully and she felt in charge of her chaos for once.

As for him, waving goodbye to that purposeful forehead and the demon will it concealed, he felt the finality of a dark chapter that had closed for good.

13

The following weekend he went home again. Again he sat quietly over meals, and even did the washing-up when he could beat Nellie to the sink. In the kitchen the new refrigerator was in position, plugged in, humming busily and cutting off.

'Do you like it?' he asked Cora. 'Is there an instruction book?'

'I *am* capable of using one,' she said tartly. 'I *have* seen one before.'

'How do you get rid of the ice?'

'Open the door and switch off.'

'Nothing else?'

'No.'

He hung up the teacloth. It was Sunday, late afternoon. In about an hour he would be walking down to Waterloo Road to pick up the free bus. He enjoyed coming home, and the return journey was equally pleasant. Which was home? Really he had no idea. The faint tingling in his veins as they swept along the roads simply meant that he was in touch with his myriad active feelers, a survivor who found himself miraculously alive – and like a child about to have his first glimpse of the sea. He had a house but it wasn't the same any more; it no longer belonged to him. He came and went, leaving no impression. This wasn't in the least disturbing; on the contrary it was delightful. He sat inside the house as though savouring a dim memory. Its doors were open, he was free to stay or to go. Leaving was just a matter of walking away. A few miles in the bus and it was erased from his thoughts: he looked forward to returning to the faces of men and women he knew, in a transit camp of casualties, doctors, nurses, caterers, gardeners and cleaners. The whole spectacle, complete with its buildings, set down on a hillside in the midst of fields, would arise in his mind's eye and fill him with an inexplicable fondness. He sat in the bus and experienced what he hadn't known since early childhood, the apprehension of life as a miracle. Paradise was here on earth.

On Monday there was talk of terminating his stay. He sat in the office before the charge nurse. Connor's sour rumpled countenance and his bulky shoulders in the snowy coat had become familiar, reassuring even. He would miss them. Not that he liked the man particularly.

'So what's your reaction?' Connor said, surly, the creases deepening around his mouth. He played his old game of not bothering to glance in the patient's direction.

'About going?'

Connor sat impassively, his face averted. Maybe he's applying some sort of severance technique, Daniel thought, and sat observing the man closely. Connor nodded – or at least inclined his head. At last he said, 'Say next week.'

'I'm getting to like it here,' Daniel said lightly, smiling.

'That's a sure sign,' the man grumbled.

'What of?'

'Time to go.'

All at once Connor seemed satisfied, and actually swung round to confront his patient, then nodded almost cheerily to indicate the end of the interview.

Cora had sent a message to say she was coming to see Daniel. This was a surprise. As far as he knew he was going home again at the weekend. Still, he looked forward to seeing her. He imagined a pleasant stroll through the grounds. Maybe, if the weather held, they would venture up a rough track he'd noticed but not yet explored, leading past a clump of firs and on towards the edge of the moor, high up. It would depend on her mood of course.

She stepped down from the bus. Men he knew by sight were assembled there to meet wives and relatives. In the midst of these embraces, warm cries and affectionate reunions, Cora's face looked sadly forlorn.

She had news for him. The hospital authorities had asked her to call that afternoon at three. Daniel faltered. His hand fell to his side. 'Why?'

'God only knows.'

He found himself staring at a big fellow in a thick white sweater who stood with his back to them. Yes, it was Phil Hucker. So he was back in circulation! His thin earnest wife stepped off the bus and greeted him fondly with a peck on the cheek. Hucker bent over her dutifully like a son. Daniel decided against speaking to him. If his recovery was an illusion then he preferred to hang on to it. While he dithered, the Huckers moved off in a different direction.

Cora had spotted them too. 'They seem fond of each other, that couple.' Daniel told her of Hucker's recent relapse. She wasn't listening. 'Not like us,' she said bleakly, following her own train of thought.

She dabbed her eyes, sunk in a misery which excluded him. At least in a mutual hell you were still bound together. He understood, without a word spoken, that he had long ago forfeited the right to console his wife. They walked senselessly along the paths. Cora broke her sullen silence by asking, 'What time is it?'

'Nearly three.'

'Hadn't you better show me where to go?'

He led her to the consultant's door. 'I'll wait for you in my room.' Cora made no answer. She was white and tense. She glared angrily at the consultant's blank door, thumped on it with her fist and went in.

In his room he wandered up and down on his few yards of carpet, sat on the bed and swung his legs, got up and

102

peered out of the window. Ten minutes went by. Cora poked her head into the room, hot-faced, eyes jumping with anger. 'I'm off, then,' she said. 'Oh, by the way, his nibs want to see you now.'

'What for?'

'How the hell would I know?'

She left in a flurry. Daniel sat down again for a minute or two, then walked down the deserted corridor. What on earth could they have said to upset her? He seemed to have lost the capacity for tormenting himself – all he felt was a mild astonishment. Yet it was sad to see her so agitated and unhappy, after all she had endured because of him. She deserved better: anyone did. Now she would rush home and unload her fury on Nellie, and the poor woman would suffer grief. Though he could picture the scene and be affected by it, nevertheless it seemed to exist on another plane, remote from him.

He knocked on the consultant's door.

'Come in, come in,' the doctor called. His name was Sanderson.

This was the man who had admitted him. He appeared younger than ever, his black hair meticulously parted. He wore glasses with sturdy black frames and sat up straight, very slim and sharp in his grey suit. His narrow face was shrewd and twinkling.

He waved Daniel to a chair, at the same time giving an impartial little smile. 'Now, your discharge is really dependent on one factor only, and that is a decision you have to make,' he said rapidly. 'Where do you intend to go from here?' He glanced down at his papers. 'This is essentially a question of your marriage. It's your own business, naturally, whether you rejoin your wife or not, but I think you need to decide one way or the other. I put this to your wife also. She was rather cross, I'm afraid. She sees it as entirely a matter for you.'

'She's right.'

'Oh, you agree?'

Daniel nodded. 'I'll go and stay with my mother. She's a widow.'

'Good. Leave whenever you wish. I'll issue the necessary instructions.'

A surge of love for this efficient, sleek person, whose succour was so constant and whose demeanour was so self-effacing, rose up in his breast. He felt an urge to take hold of his hand and thank him, but it wasn't possible. Wasn't the professional life of such a man a continual warfare against the turmoil and squalor of misdirected emotions? Daniel mumbled something ineptly and took his dumb feelings of gratitude away.

Clare, his newly married daughter – no longer a child but a young woman of eighteen – arrived at the hospital with her husband to give Daniel a lift as far as Taunton. They were en route to their first home in Newcastle, where Brian had taken a job.

Brian was a newly qualified engineer. Despite the fact that he was a mere youngster of twenty-two, just to look at him inspired confidence in Daniel. He grasped luggage, door handles and the controls of his car without doubt, as if born for responsibilities. Now he was responsible for Clare, who sat beside him docilely, her small eager face peering from a mass of dense brown hair. Clare had chosen someone as unlike her father as it was possible to be. Brian was a logician. He dealt with problems coolly, one at a time in order of importance. He excelled in sports. Daniel imagined he could actually see the energy packed into his deep chest and shoulders, rippling through him with irresistible force. He was growing a thick moustache.

To Daniel, their marriage of eleven months ago belonged to another age – to the worst time of his life. Shown photographs of the wedding, he stared at pictures of himself in a grey woollen off-the-peg suit, a white nylon shirt bought for the occasion, cheap suede shoes. Already he was losing weight and in the photographs looked famished, tense with cold and stress. A bitter March wind blew fiercely. The photographer acted out his fantasy of the artist – his composition on the church steps wouldn't come right. Clare flowered, exquisite in her white glory, a goddess who had dropped out of the sky and was holding on to his crooked arm. His thoughts as he guided her down the aisle were as split as his inner life, between his wife and daughter and Bridget, between Bridget and his mother. He took one look at himself caught by the camera and saw all his lies exposed.

Now he was clean and well, a ghost with full cheeks, saved as if by an act of Providence. 'Are you ready, Dadda?' his daughter called. It was like being collected from a hotel at the end of a pleasant holiday. Neither Clare nor her young husband gave the hospital a second glance. Daniel stowed a few items in the car boot: a hand-woven waste-paper basket made in therapy (not by him), a square low coffee table, its top covered in black vinyl, a good print of van Gogh's 'Sunflowers' which he had had framed as a present for Clare. The basket might make a gift for his mother, he thought. The coffee table represented his one and only possession, apart from shirts and underwear and the clothes he stood up in. Cora had the rest. It was wonderful not to be impeded, relieved of the shackles of ownership.

They set off, rolling down the hill towards the main road, the open countryside unfolding maternally. It was a day in early spring. Everything spoke tenderly of beauty on earth, the sunlight pulsating with growth, with hope, overhead a sky rinsed clean of murk, as if specially prepared for them. He felt no desire to look back. He hadn't said goodbye to anyone. Nobody there did.

Clare seemed to have the knack of picking up the mood of the person she was with – or maybe they were two of a kind. As they emerged from the lane and joined the flow of fast traffic she jerked round her head to ask pertly, 'Is it a funny feeling?'

'No,' he had to say. 'That's what's so strange. I can't feel a thing.'

'You will, later,' she said confidently.

How were women so sure about these things? They offered to make a detour for his sake but he said no. What was his hurry? At Taunton he could pick up a bus heading in the direction he wanted. He had roped the basket and table together, so as to leave his other hand free for his weekend bag. It would be good to wander about and make his own arrangements, a free agent. His mother had no idea when to expect him. True, he could make a phone call at some point, but he knew this would alarm and confuse her. Phone calls were to her like telegrams, the bringers of bad news.

Since his father's death his poor mother had become increasingly muddled about time. Her disorientation came from a lifelong fear of the outside, of society, and now her main bulwark was gone. In any case she'd come to accept over the years her son's haphazard comings and goings. Often Daniel felt she was like Clare, and could divine what he was thinking. If so, she rarely questioned him, presumably because she was too fearful of the answers. Although born afraid, like many timid persons she possessed an iron will. Once she had set her sights on an objective her tenacity was unrelenting. Gradually he had come to realise that his mother was sustained – until it rose against her like a black treacherous floodwater – by a secret inner life.

Though her first name was Beatrice she was called by her second name, Mary. Quite early on he grasped that she had made herself into a Mary as a way of embracing a fate. Whenever she spoke of the past it was in terms of hardship, injustice, sacrifice, suffering. She had grown up in a street court embedded in a web of slums, where lavatories and washhouses stood outdoors in squalid clumps, infested with insects and sometimes rats. Her tales of bygone days were nearly always horrific. Her own father, a short-legged deaf man when Daniel knew him as a child, had been a day labourer all his life. As a young worker he would stagger home on Saturday nights drunk and unrecognisable, ready to beat up the whole family in his rage. It was the terrible anger of the submerged man, the senseless fury of a beast caged up in his ignorance, cursing fate and maddened by the poverty of his curses, a little roaring bull with only his females to trample. But when Daniel was a boy his grandad was benign, deaf, diabetic, a diminutive Santa Claus who happened to be living with them, beaming hopefully at remarks he hadn't managed to understand.

His mother's dream of a country cottage took root after a visit to a friend and became reality after the war, when many found to their surprise that they were better off. Daniel's father, abandoning a lifetime of clerking, sold their mortgaged bomb-damaged house and then bought an insurance book with which he hoped to support them both. By then Daniel had left home, his brother years before. His nervous parents travelled south to bid for a Somerset cottage at an auction. It went for seven hundred pounds, the sum total of their savings. His father too had a dream, of moving from slavery to redemption by means of self-employment. It soon faded – he couldn't earn a decent income as a rural insurance salesman no matter how hard he worked. Farmers were too stingy, and he was over-scrupulous, never a natural seller of anything. Defeated, he found a job in a helicopter factory and was again back behind a desk. Their tiny hovel was renovated in slow stages and connected to the mains drains, and they installed a bathroom in the repaired outhouse and covered the backyard in crazy paving. The cottage glowed with new gold thatch; white roses straggled over the stone porch. Then he retired.

This seemed to be the signal for Daniel's mother to write down her childhood memoirs. Winter and summer for the next two years she disappeared upstairs to scribble compulsively at a card table in their bedroom, filling school exercise books with her rapid scrawl and then pounding away at final drafts on a mail-order typewriter. A vivid, terrifyingly raw and brutal past began to emerge. Her education was rudimentary: sentences read like the spilling speech of someone caught up in a tale of pity, love and terror, the testament of a witness which had to be recorded at top speed, otherwise it would vanish. This lost world ran out on the page, scalding hot, bubbling like a cauldron, and took shape as *Hurdy Gurdy Days*, the book of her spirit.

Down below her husband sat ignored, mutely putting up with it or turning it into a wry joke for visitors. 'I'm a widower. She's up there at her book again.' Slowly, as the months passed, he was sucked in by the force of his wife's curious passion. Then he started to take pride in her achievement, urging her on to finish the latest version. He became a voluntary reader and adviser, correcting her wild spelling and smoothing out her rough grammar. Daniel was asked to recommend manuals on writing and on how to prepare material in a form suitable for publishers.

Eventually Daniel's father took over from her the task of submitting the manuscript. It was now his baby as well as hers. With each rejection he set about parcelling it up again carefully and composing a fresh covering letter. By now he seemed fanatically identified with her ambition. Whereas she was now more or less resigned to her book's fate, the desire to see it in print never left him. The parcel went back for the fifth time, after a letter expressing mild interest in kindly phrases had caused him to smell victory. This, he convinced himself, was going to be it.

Daniel's mother told him how the story ended. The village postman banged on the door, in his hand a sickeningly familiar package. 'Thank you,' Daniel's father said. He closed the door. His face grey, he broke down and wept. His wife begged him in a shocked voice not to be so silly. 'It doesn't matter that much, not any more,' she told him.

'Let our grandchildren read it.' Nothing she said made the slightest difference – he refused to be consoled. His whole life had become centred on the fate of a book.

Clare and Brian dropped him in the middle of Taunton in the rush hour, only a couple of streets from the railway station where he had finally parted from Bridget. As he stood on the pavement with his luggage figuring out his next move, they drove off – just as Bridget had done. Recollections of past misfortunes were all secret pleasures now, fed by the tremors and tricklings of his wellbeing. He was happy to be left alone. When Bridget had waved goodbye and then driven off, hadn't he been at the mercy of his fears, befuddled, emaciated, growing weaker by the minute? Look at him now: by a great stroke of luck he had regained his strength. More than that, he was at peace with his mind. Although he owned next to nothing he was free of guilt, with a destination and a warm welcome waiting. Millions the world over faced starvation and death, their bellies empty and their hopes extinguished. He began to walk awkwardly in no particular direction, encumbered by his bits and pieces. As though urged upwards by his euphoria, the sun made an effort and broke clear, bathing the crown of his head. He took it for a benediction, smiling to himself at this nonsense in which he half believed. The walls around here were of a warm, honey-coloured stone. An aroma of freshly ground coffee wafted out of an open doorway. He turned and retraced his steps, blundered into a woman shopper, apologised, reached the coffee shop and saw how full it was. Reversing again, he collided with customers who were about to enter.

Near the graveyard of a church he spotted a bench with a brass plate screwed to it. The inscription said: DONATED FOR THE USE OF THE ELDERLY AND INFIRM. He sat there anyway, telling himself that at least his greying hair was appropriate. Compared to his virile son-in-law he supposed that he was definitely old, yet he felt young, healthy as a flea. An old man came by, bluish at the lips, his eyes like dead stones. All appetite for life seemed to have left his body, Daniel mused, yet he lived on. After all, what choice did he have? Daniel made ready to make a space for him on the bench but the old fellow kept going, concentrating on his painful shuffle.

PART TWO

MIDNIGHTS AND DAYS

Which of us has overcome his past?
JAMES BALDWIN

14

His mother's cottage, one of a row of thatched dwellings, slumbered in the mid-afternoon silence, sunk down low as if grown from the earth. Such a picture of serenity! Daniel knew of course what an illusion that was. Massively thick damp walls and blackened wormy beams ticked with beetles. Spiders hatched out by the hundred each season in the underside of the straw roof. It was a cave, a refuge, or had been, until his mother's fears multiplied in her darkened mind and sealed her off in it. He had thought of it once as a womb. Alas, she was never going to get reborn from its low door. Through the lattice window she gazed out despairingly on a landscape of open fields, a stone trough like a bath, munching cows, distant bluish hills, the reddish bristles of a fir plantation, vehicles with glinting roofs buzzing faintly in a straight line along the main road, their movements no more intrusive than the rustle of insects. In order to peer from this window he had to stoop, his head only a few inches from the ceiling joists.

His mother was now severely deaf, in a cave within a cave. The unchanged idyllic view only seemed to mock her. Since his father's death she often spoke as if her own days were numbered. Terrified of what might await her, she still longed to join him in death. Daniel opened the black studded door cautiously, so as not to frighten her out of her wits.

'Anybody in?' Hearing nothing, he called loudly, 'Mum, are you there?'

She wore, as he knew, a hearing aid, a gadget of little use, wired to a little box containing a battery which was fastened to the inside of her cardigan. The cruel handicap of deafness put a double strain on her. When strangers spoke to her and she couldn't catch what was said, that was humiliating, and before acquaintances she would be ashamed of her failure, since they were making a special effort for her benefit. More than anything she hated to be in anyone's debt.

Daniel put down his things and stood looking round. He was familiar with every detail: the old plank doors, iron latches painted black, the uneven surfaces of rough plaster. Coming home had always been a joy, awakening a love for his ageing parents in which was mingled the sense of a long-lost childhood restored to him.

First to appear was the fat marmalade-coloured cat, sauntering in so complacently from the back regions that it didn't even raise its head. His mother appeared, a small dumpy woman with loose unhappy cheeks, her hair less grey than his own. Alarmed, she cried out, then did her best to smile welcomingly. Pained by her obvious woe, he urged kindness towards her. From her expression he understood how pleased and yet confused she was to see him. She said, 'Oh dear, I must look a mess – I must have dozed off in the chair. I only sat down in the kitchen because my legs hurt. What time is it?'

Her sad fretful voice begged to be forgiven, and between sentences she tutted at her dishevelled state, glancing at him with anxious brown eyes while she pulled at the twists in her thick woollen skirt. She stared blankly at him for a moment. 'Have you been here long? Are you tired? All the things you've brought, good lord! I didn't expect you till this evening, but I wasn't sure. It doesn't matter really. I'll be all right in a minute – oh dear, I hope I've got enough for you to eat –'

'I've just come through the door,' he said, shaking his head and laughing, 'and already you're worrying about everything.'

She put her head to one side like a bird. 'What? Say that again.'

Her eyes were blurred with sleep – or so he thought – and she swayed unsteadily where she stood. Immediately she made a lunge for his bag. With his head close to the ceiling, Daniel felt as he always did, a bringer of chaos to her tiny sitting-room. 'This can go upstairs out of the way,' she was saying, 'and then I'll get you something to eat. My, you must be hungry, have you been travelling long? Did you come on the bus or the train? What a journey!'

He allowed her questions to break over him without attempting to answer. In order to read his lips she needed him to face her, as he well knew, and even then that cheap gadget of hers might not be switched on. 'No, I'll take that up,' he shouted. 'Leave it to me.'

'Are you sure you're well enough?' she cried after him. He ignored her, hauling himself up the steep narrow stairs which wound round in a spiral. Then he clattered down again to mouth loudly into her face, 'I'm well! I'm very well! I never felt better. Look at me!'

'Do you have any pills to take?'

He took in the alarm on his mother's face and decided to tell the truth, reasoning that she'd be better off with something tangible to worry about. Confronting her, he wagged his head up and down reassuringly and said, 'Yes, but they're tailing them off. That's what they have to do. It's normal procedure.'

Her disbelief was obvious. In her experience, 'nerve trouble' persisted for months or years, if not for ever. Her own sister had broken down so catastrophically in middle age that she'd been given a lobotomy. Mary herself was a prey to black moods which transformed her normally meek disposition. Once, a year before his death, Daniel's father took him aside and, his face haunted, related an incident in strict confidence. 'One night I came home from work and there was no sign of your mother. I tried next door but they hadn't set eyes on her for a fortnight. That

114

woman, that old gasbag, she said she thought she'd heard funny noises through the wall some mornings. "You mean crying?" I said. She didn't know, or she wouldn't say. "It sounded, well, like screams to me," she said, and asked Tom, her husband, who nodded agreement. He's as deaf as a post, how would he know? I came in and searched upstairs, even in the wardrobe. It was getting dark, a cold night. I went out the back way and wandered round in the fields, calling, and then over towards my allotment. Where d'you think she was? All the time she was hiding behind a tree out there, watching. She let me look high and low for an hour, then sneaked in and sat waiting for me. I'll never forget the look she had on her face.'

'What kind of look?'

'Hate. Malice. I don't know what else to call it.'

After his father died he asked his mother if the story was true. Her version was substantially the same. He expected her to be reluctant, but she blurted it out willingly. She said she wanted to explain, but couldn't, how malignant she'd felt, how she'd exulted at the sight of her husband running to and fro in a torment. Yet she loved him. 'Wasn't it horrible?' she kept asking. 'I just squatted there and let him suffer. Wasn't that awful?'

Daniel stood before her, gazing round at the little room as if he couldn't look at it enough. He was full of quiet joy and amazement. He wanted to tell her how desperately he had longed to be here when he was lying ill in his mockery of a home. If he could have crawled here, he told himself, he would have done. If he could have found the strength. If, if. And if he had, what would his mother have done with him?

'What's wrong?' his mother asked, fear in her voice.

He tried to laugh. 'Why should anything be wrong?'

Two high-backed wing chairs – to ward off the draughts – faced one another on either side of the hearth. One was used by his mother, and the other, now sadly vacant, waited for him. His mother perched rather than sat. Her puffy wrinkled hands seemed lost with nothing to do, waiting helplessly for their next task. The room seemed even smaller than he remembered. So did she, though she wasn't stooped.

'You must be ready for a meal,' she implored. 'Would you like scrambled eggs?'

'Yes, all right.'

'And beans?'

'Yes.'

'Pardon?' She fumbled angrily with the hidden box. 'This blasted thing, it's gone wonky – I shall have to get it mended again. Daniel, what did you say?' She watched his mouth, frowning with concentration. Hot flushes mottled her sagging throat.

'Yes.'

'What?'

'Yes, anything!'

Left alone, he bent his head to admire the view, once such a source of pride to both his parents. Unless he craned his neck and squinted sideways, the grassy vista stretched out to the skyline and a long hill like a bank with not a building in sight.

He must have day-dreamed, or dozed off on his feet. 'It's ready!' his mother was calling, her voice agitated. 'Don't let it get cold.'

He entered the dark narrow kitchen, a thick-walled den smelling faintly of damp earth. Like the sitting-room, it exuded memories. He was conscious of permanence, of being safe. At one end was a dining alcove. He sat down. As always it was difficult to arrange his long legs under the gate-leg table. His mother noticed at once. 'What's the matter?' she asked.

'Nothing.'

'Sit further round. There – sit there. It's not very good, is it?'

'This is fine.'

116

She carried over the plate of eggs and beans and tinned tomatoes, clutching the rim with a cloth. In her clumsiness she nearly spilled everything into his lap. 'Oh, what's wrong with me,' she moaned, on the verge of tears.

'You're in too much of a hurry, that's all it is,' he told her. She didn't hear, scurrying back to the cooker. 'Aren't you having some?' he shouted.

'What's that?' Her face was scarlet from the heat, her hair coming unpinned.

'Where's yours?'

'I'm doing it, don't rush me. I'll cut some bread in a minute.' A spoon dropped to the floor with a clatter. She let out another half-suppressed moan. 'You get on with yours while it's warm, never mind about me. Please!'

Daniel gave up. Nothing changed. They had all day, all the weeks to come, yet everything had to be done at the double in a mad race against time. His food looked unappetising, the eggs rubbery, slopped on hastily, a heap of beans mounting to the edge of his plate. If not quite this bad, it had been pretty much the same as this for as long as he could remember. He recalled his mother's comic phrase, 'a bag of nerves', at which no one had ever laughed, since she was such a perfect example. On visits home, Daniel would begin by feeling stricken, then would soon be gritting his teeth in exasperation. But not this time, he assured himself, none of it mattered any more, and he sat dreamily, prepared to accept the situation as he did now with everything, wherever he happened to be.

His mother sat down at last with her own plate. He wanted to shake his head, wanted to laugh. It was both sad and hilarious. Even sitting down she was twisted sideways, her feet pointed towards the cooker, ready to jump up at a moment's notice. What if he wanted the salt, the sauce, something she might have forgotten? She was as tense as a sprinter.

She began to gobble hastily at her meal. Attacking the last of her beans, she chased them round with the blade of

117

her knife. Sometimes, attempting this balancing act, her aim wasn't good and she smeared her mouth. Daniel felt a pang of shame. Now his father was dead she ate only to stay alive. She had given up on her appearance and her speech had deteriorated, become slovenly, to such an extent that it was like a regression to her childhood in the slums. On the table was a scrawled shopping list, written, so he suspected, at breakneck speed. Noticing it, his mother fumbled with a plastic case and put on her spectacles. He couldn't help noticing how grubby and speckled the lenses were. His knife and fork weren't too clean either. A thought struck him – was she on some medication or other? Though unwilling to ask, his concern for her forced the question from him.

She looked tearful at once. 'I keep going back to the doctor. He's hopeless, I can't talk to him. He doesn't bother to look at you, and his finger's always on the bell – that button he presses under his desk, to call in the next patient. Nobody listens. He gives me anti-depressants, huge orange things, gob-stoppers . . . it's as much as I can do to swallow the things. And I've got sleeping tablets, blood-pressure pills, I get mixed up, I forget which is which. In the morning my mouth is so dried up, it's horrible, my tongue sticks to my palate. Nothing makes any difference . . . they can't bring your father back with a pill. I stay up later and later because I hate to go to bed so much, hate it . . .' She was weeping silently. She took off her dirty glasses and wiped her eyes. 'I only think of one thing, just one, and that's being with him again.'

Daniel's throat was thick when he tried to speak. 'Let me make you a cup of tea.'

Instantly she was scrambling to her feet. 'No, you sit still, I'll do it. What about you, shouldn't you be taking your medicine? You mustn't forget, Daniel. You'll be ill again.'

To ease her mind, he took a tumbler of water and swallowed the pills down in front of her: one Librium, two

Parstelin. She looked visibly relieved. It's the same old story, he told himself. Medicine is for children, whereas mothers are beyond help. He opened his mouth to explain that he must avoid yeast, then closed it again. Later – one worry at a time. He guessed, knowing her as he did, that she was about to launch an anxious enquiry into his non-existent future, what he intended to do, where he would go and so on. He could almost see the questions brewing behind her eyes, clouding her sad forehead. They ate some cheese and biscuits and drank tea, then she was off, unable to delay a moment longer. Typically, her approach had to be indirect, and via the subject of nourishment. 'Are you sure you've had enough to eat?' she asked.

'Yes, plenty.'

'It wasn't very much.'

'For me it was. I've got a small stomach.'

She gulped, staring down at the table. 'That's what your father used to say.'

'It's true. I hate to feel bloated.'

'I made some jam tarts specially for you – as soon as your letter came. Have one, they're only small.'

'Perhaps a bit later.'

'They're raspberry, the ones you like best. I brought some to the hospital that time I came to see you, remember?'

He nodded. How could he forget? He recalled it again, all of it, with the pleasure of a masochist who has full control of his actions and could choose one misery rather than another, just as he could now actually choose what or what not to eat. When his mother arrived he had been in hospital for less than a week and was still confined to his bed in an open ward. Suddenly – it was three in the afternoon – there she was, coming through the swing doors with Cora.

He sat on the edge of his bed, at bay, still skin and bone, and with the expression, he was told later, of a hunted animal. His mother turned in bewilderment to her daughter-in-law, who had forced a ghastly smile on her lips.

119

They found hard chairs and drew them up, sitting there mutely to confront him. Cora at one point put out a hand. Ever the sentimentalist, she was moved to touch the man she had once known, now a pitiable object. Daniel jerked back as if stung. With the frightened voice of a small girl, his mother pleaded with Cora, 'Why not come back in a minute, when I've spoken to him?' Even though incapable of speech, Daniel felt with anguish that to be referred to in the third person by one's mother meant that his helpless passivity had rendered him virtually invisible. To be lost from sight in this way was to experience the total despair of someone who was no longer a man.

His mother must have been devastated to realise that now she had no one to turn to for help. What use was this lost son to her, or to anyone? Although he was still unable to dwell on this moment of mutual loss, he could see with great vividness the squashed cardboard box she tugged free from her bottle-green zipped bag and handed over, before hurrying away without a word to rejoin his wife. The ward was empty. He sat on the bed in his dressing gown. The moment the doors closed behind his mother he tore open the damaged carton. It held six clumsily made jam tarts. Two had been smashed in transit. The pastry was the grey, leaden sort she always produced. He stood facing the wall, up against his locker, cramming the sweet mush into his mouth wolfishly before anyone could see him. He polished them off with incredible speed, crumbs and all. He even licked out the box like a dog. Since then he had often wondered at the brutal fury of his greed. Was his metabolism still awry, his chronic hunger as acute as ever, in spite of three meals a day and vitamin shots, or had he been trying to literally stuff his mother inside himself, in the gaping hole left by her withdrawal?

Daniel's mother hovered before him, present in the flesh but with her spirit elsewhere, longing to depart. She was gazing at him so imploringly that he said, 'All right then, I will have one.'

'Daniel, what are you going to do now?' she asked.

He stared at her. Did his chaotic affairs have to be sorted out immediately, this very minute, on his first day home, before life could continue? He burst out laughing. 'I'll tell you what I'm going to do – I'm going to eat a jam tart and then digest it!'

She looked startled, then perplexed, and finally anxious, all in the space of a second, as if the illness he had suffered was permanent – he *was* mad. 'No, I mean about Cora,' she said. 'What's going to happen to her?'

He thought at first she meant money. He said, 'Well, she's all right for the moment. There's still a bit left in the joint account.' But she meant more, much more. In her world a woman needed a man to protect her, keep her from harm, dispel her fears, deal with the thousand bristling dangers outside, beyond the door. And how could she survive without love? Daniel could see his mother identifying transparently, though the real situation, as he well knew, was very different. She and Cora had never taken to each other.

'You can't abandon her, Daniel.'

'It's not like that.'

'What is it like?'

'I don't know,' he admitted. Which was the truth.

His mother watched his face closely, intent on not missing a word. Suddenly she changed tack. 'You know you can stay here as long as you like,' she said meekly. He thought he detected a hint of slyness in her expression as she added, 'But you can't leave her in the lurch, can you?'

'No.'

'And how about you? It's your house, after all.'

'I don't want it.'

'What did you say? Who doesn't?'

He raised his voice to a near shout. 'It's complicated – it's not easy to explain.' Really he was asking to be let off.

Deaf as she was, she still responded as sensitively as ever to his changes of mood. 'I don't know, I really don't,' she murmured sadly, and seemed more or less resigned for the moment.

'There's no need for you to worry about it all,' he said. 'It's my mess.'

'Somebody's got to.'

'I suppose so.'

'If she has the house, where does that leave you? Where will you live?' She had worked round at last to what, after all, was her chief concern. But she was having trouble hearing him again. She leaned closer. As she concentrated she screwed her face into a monkeyish expression.

Aware that he sounded ridiculous, he said loudly, 'I'll probably look for a cheap place, a cottage say, something off the beaten track. One up, one down – that's all I need.'

She heard this perfectly. 'You want money for that.'

'Yes, well, I've got about two hundred left in the building society. The rest I can borrow from a bank.'

She said after a moment, shrewdly, 'Do you have that in a joint account as well?'

'What, the building society?' He was startled to find she had jumped ahead of him. 'I think so, yes.'

'She might not let you touch it. Have you thought of that?'

'Why shouldn't she? Hell, I've got to live somewhere.'

'She might not let you,' she repeated gloomily.

The truth was, he was becoming bored with all this fuss. He went over to his dead father's chair, sat down and stretched out his legs. His mother followed, perching like a wan owl in the chair opposite. What a surprise when she settled and came to rest for a few minutes! Yet he could see her mind endlessly at work, tussling with the next problem and the one after that. He kept smiling at her because it was also funny. His mother believed in punishment, while he was a convert to the idea of rewards. He no longer knew who was the most ignorant. He felt an urge to preach the gospel of living in the present, but the concept was too new; he was feeling his way. If by waving a wand he could have changed his mother back into a young girl, would she still be a lost cause? He thought so. Even out in the open, waiting at the bus stop on their rare shopping trips into town, she cowered as though in a cave. She was his crazy mother, frightened out of her wits by everything since the day she was born. All the same, her own ill fortune took second place in her thoughts to his. She loved him and it was unconditional, in the terrifying way of mothers who admit nothing and accept everything about their sons.

'If she's angry, she might not let you touch any of it,' she repeated fearfully. 'Then what will you do?'

'We'll have to see.'

Then her face changed and she became vigilant, sharp, as befitted a mother faced with a hopelessly unworldly – and possibly loony – son. 'Where do you expect to find this cheap little cottage?'

'In Devon, probably.' Not until these words were out did he grasp that he was truly free of burdens. Only then did he realise with astonishment the strength of his dream to live isolated and alone, in a wilderness if possible. 'I was glancing through a local paper I picked up in the hospital. On the edge of Dartmoor there are tiny villages, right off the beaten track. Some real bargains for sale.'

'What sort of bargains?' His mother's mouth turned down in a grimace of suspicion. 'Daniel, listen, you might be letting yourself in for a pile of trouble.' She gazed at him with reproach.

He laughed at her fears. 'No, I won't – stop worrying.'

'Be sure to get it surveyed, won't you?'

Again he had to laugh. 'Get what surveyed? I haven't found anything – I haven't even started looking yet!'

'No, well. When you do.'

She sat pouting, looking darkly at him. He had the strange feeling that these reproofs of hers were more self-ishly motivated than he'd thought. As for him, was he in fact serious, already planning his escape without even admitting it to himself? He was amazed to find that he could actually contemplate burying himself in some god-forsaken spot in the middle of nowhere like a hermit. Yet he believed he knew why he was being pulled back to a region which had meant absolutely nothing to him before his collapse. It was magic ground. That was where he had broken the mould. His eyes were opened and he woke up and saw things. Merely to think of it made him feel rejuvenated. Was it just nostalgia for the hospital, the only community he had ever known? Could it be the terrain? Certainly he loved the country around there, but he was no countryman – he scarcely knew one tree from another. Yet at the mere thought of those moors, the magnolia, that restless sky, he wanted to make for it there and then as a place infinitely alluring. He longed to go there now, this instant, and fall down on his knees and kiss the rough turf he had so rapturously photographed. It was altogether beyond his understanding why this should be so.

15

The weather grew steadily milder, warm shouldering
westerlies and sprinkles of rain, with bright flower-like
skies between the showers. Daniel was in a mood for
tramping around out of doors. The intermittent sun invited him. Outside, in contrast to the gelid atmosphere of
the winter-bound cottage, the air was surprisingly kind.

For the first few days it had been easy enough to fit into
his mother's routine. About nine she would wake up with
a jolt, exclaiming to herself in a voice of dismay at how late
it was. Daniel could hear every sound she made through
the thin partition. He heard her struggle out of bed and
immediately make for the shamefully drawn curtains, to
wrench them open. No one was out there, only cows in the
field across the road, but there was just a chance someone
might be walking by at that hour and think she was a slut.
Then he would hear her fumbling and whispering in the
kitchen below him, full of unrestrained self-pity because
she imagined he was asleep. She filled and switched on the
kettle, and made her way out through two doors to the
meagre bathroom to empty her chamber pot, grumbling at
the cat to come in and eat its breakfast. The docile creature
was too fat to do more than waddle.

When his mother came up with a cup of tea, she always
cried out in a shocked voice, 'It's ever so late!'

It always was. After breakfast she did some perfunctory
cleaning. Then, while he was still dozy, he would sit listening to potatoes being scraped, cabbage being washed

and torn. He sat there blearily with the remains of his toast and tea.

Nowadays his mother had a box of groceries delivered from the village shop weekly, ringing through her order on the unpredictable phone, her voice humble, making a change or two and then apologising profusely. Paraffin would be delivered from the local garage. Twice a week she bought chops or liver or the occasional chicken from the travelling butcher who pulled up in his white van on Tuesdays and Thursdays. Wednesday and Friday the bread man came. That left the sudden uproar of the refuse collection on Monday, for which the dustbin had to be lugged through the rooms from the back yard into the road.

Several of these tradespeople she knew personally, and wished she didn't. Their wives would try to coax her to the Sunshine Hour at the chapel or to the Women's Institute hut for a talk or for amateur dramatics, and if she couldn't fend them off she dolled herself up, dabbed powder on her flustered cheeks, stuck pins savagely through her felt plant-pot hat and hurried off down the road in a torment of shyness. 'I won't be very long,' she assured him, like abandoning a lover. 'Oh, they're such pests, I wish they'd leave me alone!' But, like him, she was a coward when it came to saying no. At the door she would call back in, 'Will you be all right? Are you sure?' She felt obliged to watch over him in his convalescence. He supposed that in her eyes he had, in a sense, always been recovering from something. She saw him as basically weak and vulnerable, like her: not robust. She often made him feel it was a miracle he had survived this long.

He had never been able to ramble pointlessly. Now it was no problem. 'Who wants a destination?' he would tell himself airily. Stepping out into the fresh air, sniffing the wind, he would walk off slow as a policeman, in whatever direction his feet took him. A favourite route was down past the pines on the corner and over the main trunk road, then descending further on a lane which sank below a garage and a large sluttish cottage called *Underhill*, its thatched roof like a heap of decaying rubbish. Behind it rose a hill of scrap metal accumulated by the garage above, the car corpses and tyres threatening to overwhelm the rotten fence. He came to a bridge, the ancient stone parapet damaged by a lorry and roped off, not yet repaired. This was where Bridget had once picked him up by arrangement in her car and carried him off to their final illicit excursion. A stream full of rocks trickled underneath. On from there the landscape was rather featureless, in the distance a solitary farm and the next scattered village.

Daniel smiled as he walked along, pleased by the monotony of the silent fields. A melancholy which had always been part of him felt expressed, and seemed at home here. If the sky stayed overcast and grey, that pleased him too, as did this countryside, which had nothing to do with him, imposed no burdens, giving him the feeling that he was now free of people and their endless complications. And because he was such an ignoramus about country matters, his thoughts could wander like smoke. Scuffles in the depths of hedges meant a surprised bird – he didn't know what kind, even when it broke cover. One flashed across his vision, curved beautifully and was gone; black with startling white markings.

Soon his aimless activity became another source of worry to his mother. 'Shouldn't you be doing your writing?' she asked one day, after he had come in with muddy shoes from one of his jaunts.

'I'm thinking.'

'Don't you *want* to do anything?'

'Not just yet.'

'You will, though?'

'I suppose so. Soon.'

He thought she hadn't heard him, but she countered accusingly, 'How can you? You haven't got your typewriter with you.'

'That's true.' And he gave her a smile.

'Can't you write with a pen?'

He tried to explain his peculiar aversion to writing by hand, brought about, he theorised, by his years as a clerk. Bad memories would sabotage him. He objected to desks for the same reason. 'Sounds stupid, but there it is.' He omitted to mention that he sometimes felt nauseated by words, or that when he was falling ill he had been unable to open a book, so great was his disgust for print.

'Well, you won't need to avoid a desk here.' The sudden jab of sarcasm startled him, but he appreciated it. In some unaccountable way it brought them closer. His mother's eyes had brightened. For a brief moment they were in perfect accord, he felt, like twins.

'Good,' he said.

She began to outline a plan, so swiftly that he suspected her of hatching it out beforehand. 'Use my machine – the one your father bought for me to type out my book. You'll need a table, so we could put the Vono up in your bedroom.' The Vono was a card table, covered in green felt, with folding legs. 'If it's cold up there you can plug in the fan heater. It went wrong again, and Alfie – you remember, the odd-job man whose sister runs the post office – he fixed it for me. That was ages ago. I still can't get him to give me a bill, silly man.' This unnatural trait clearly bewildered her. 'He's just not interested in money – he's ever such a funny chap.'

Funny chap! This was a phrase he'd often heard his father use. Hearing it again gave him a start. A voice inside him asked, Why do I still think of him as a stranger? What had made him tick? Was I a disappointment to him? On a visit here one autumn, Daniel had volunteered to help his father dig over the rough ground of his allotment, a field away to the rear of the cottage. It was like old times. As a boy of fifteen he had done the same – only not in this place. As they came in together for their Sunday dinner his mother cocked her head quizzically to ask, 'How did you get on today with your assistant?' His father answered gruffly, 'He's been a good chap.'

He agreed to the use of the Vono and the typewriter. Before he could change his mind his mother was clambering upstairs, eager to get things settled. 'Don't come up yet!' she beseeched, directly over his head. She set to work arranging the room. Thumps, crashes and the odd whimpering sound came down to him through the low ceiling. Convinced that his lack of purpose signified dejection, the one cure for this as far as his mother was concerned had to be work. The noise over his head became more frantic, then it abated.

'Come and see if this'll do,' she called, almost sobbing as she caught her breath.

Daniel went up and pretended to survey her handiwork. 'That's fine.'

'No, wait a minute. Let me stand out on the landing. Now you go in.'

There was no space in the tiny room for both of them, now that the table and chair were in position between the two single beds. He went in obediently. 'Good,' he assented.

'Go on, sit down properly.'

Feeling foolish, he sat there at the wobbly card table. 'Yes, fine.'

His mother was frowning. 'I'm worried about this heater. Is it too close to the bed there, Daniel?'

'No.'

'You say no but are you sure? You're so impractical. This is a thatched cottage, remember.'

'And this is a fan heater. You can't set fire to anything with one of these. Anyway, I'll be here.'

She wasn't listening. 'Will you promise to keep an eye on it?'

'I'll watch it, yes.'

'What about when you're miles away?'

He tried to joke, not easy with his voice raised to a yell. He told her, 'One eye's miles away, the other's watching.'

She eyed him sceptically. 'Which is which?'

'I'm not sure.' He shook his head and smiled. She knew him too well.

'Oh,' she said suddenly, and pulled a face, pressing her fist into her side.

'What's the matter? What is it?'

'A pain.'

'Go and sit down, have a rest,' he urged; a useless suggestion. She would need to feel she was dying first.

She turned away and began to descend the stairs, grumbling as she went. 'It's the best I can do, so you'll have to manage.'

'Thank you.'

At the bottom she called up, 'Are you going to do anything this morning?'

'I might, yes. I'm not sure.'

'I'll make you a coffee soon.'

'Right.'

'Would you prefer tea?'

'No thanks.'

'Pardon?'

'I said no!'

Though he had no desire to do anything he sat down, wound in a sheet of paper and tried out the machine. The action was stiff, unpleasant, the typeface crabby. He reminded himself that once he began to spin out a world from his insides, afterwards lodging in it like a bedbug, he would forget the typewriter, the room, everything. But the urge to try was missing.

He got up and peered out of the back window. To do this it was necessary to bend nearly double; the ceiling sloped down and the window was near the floor. There was a small council estate out there, deserted at this hour. He could see rooftops and vegetable patches, and could hear a child bawling, then its mother screaming empty threats. This violent outburst set off the frenzied barking of two or three dogs. Then the rural silence returned. He sat submerged in it.

130

His mother knew everything and yet next to nothing about him, he reflected. She sensed, for instance, that he was at a loose end, floating, feeling his way obscurely to a new beginning. If there was one state more than any other which she couldn't bear it was uncertainty. Though this was her problem, not his, and there seemed nothing he could do to ease it, living in close proximity with her meant that he was entangled in her fears, her darknesses. If he stayed here very long they would become his too.

He always longed to confide in her, yet he held back, warned by an instinct even deeper than filial devotion. More than once, when she pressed him to say what he intended to do about Cora, he felt like shouting, 'You don't know her! What about the time when she ran off with the Irishman?'

He had kept his mother in ignorance about that. There was no reason why she should know. Since then nearly ten years had rushed by. If he poured out the story of this upheaval now, so long after the event, would it do anything to lessen her concern for his wife? He doubted it. He wanted to explain that though he may have been at least partly to blame for that betrayal, neglecting Cora, ploughing away obsessively at his own concerns, nevertheless her action proved one thing beyond any doubt – she could act for herself when she was driven to it. He wanted to cry, 'She's not helpless, she's not a child!'

The Irishman was his punishment, he could see that now. It was as if he had perversely begged for him to arrive, irritable as he was to the point of madness with everything, desperate for change at any price.

16

His fingers punched at the arthritic keys, a machine-gun rattle now and then to please his mother, who would he knew be downstairs in the kitchen with her ears cocked. There was in fact a daunting task waiting for him – he had some notes to prepare for an agent who believed he could obtain a commission for a study of D. H. Lawrence, a project he'd been avoiding for years, even though he had dreamt it up in the first place. At times the very subject seemed preposterous: a crazy, marvellous man, a hectoring little bully, totally dependent on women and – for that very reason – resenting them bitterly, managing to resurrect himself by the skin of his teeth each spring, dying in the flesh and refusing to admit it, and so on and so forth. And after all, he was dead, wasn't he? Daniel was alive, with cold feet. He shivered, plugged in the fan heater, switched it on and it whirred out some warm air and a smell of burning dust.

Outside it was spring – and it was in him, too. The very season was an incitement, impelling him to draw closer to the little scarecrow called Lawrence, who had told anyone who would listen to him that the whole world was going to hell. Daniel agreed. Even when Lawrence was absurd and wrong he was somehow paradoxically also right. That was why he maddened everyone, why it was ridiculous of him to feel let down by others. What did he expect? How could a man so implacably right fail to be insufferable?

Daniel heard his mother climbing the stairs. She entered

the room with a cup of tea and two digestive biscuits, backing out again respectfully because she thought he was busy. There was a sliding door to the room which she kept open for some air. 'Thanks,' he said absently, as her head sank out of sight.

The typewriter burst into angry life once or twice, before stuttering weakly and falling silent. He pounded on it again, in an effort to overcome its resistance. He gave up. Sitting there, he fell to day-dreaming, remembering the Irishman. Lawrence meant a great deal, and always would, but Stephen Gonne was, he assumed, in the land of the living. Daniel wondered where he was now, at this moment. Had it really happened, that episode he saw now as ludicrous, which had seemed so calamitous at the time? What did it mean? And how did it come to happen in the way it did?

When Stephen first entered the picture, Daniel's situation couldn't have been more wretched. Recalling it now, he saw it as all his doing. Working long hours as a clerk to support himself and his wife he had ceased to love, travelling miles to an office and back and having to use buses and ferries, struggling fanatically each evening and at weekends to write a novel, he never relaxed. He became a proud but distracted father, too impatient to give himself up to such simple joys. Some months before, he had found a terraced cottage by the side of a tidal creek, wedged up against a hillside, just inside Cornwall. It was incredibly small, with no hot water, no bathroom, no back door. The outdoor lavatory was in a yard five yards away down the village street. Only two young romantics would have looked twice at such a slum. He owed money to a solicitor's client who had invested in his private mortgage. The cottage's previous owner, a retired Cornish farmer who was going blind, kept lowering the price whenever Daniel told him there was no hope of raising the cash. Finally the man came down to eight hundred pounds. Even then it was a disastrous purchase.

133

'There must be more to living than this,' Daniel used to mutter under his breath, unaware of his nearness to despair. Life in its true sweetness was embodied in a tiny daughter sitting in the sink in her birthday suit. Awareness of her beauty only served to madden him. He ladled the water over her little shoulders with a saucepan and she quivered, she crowed, her peach skin mantled to a flush of rose. When he picked her up from her cot all stuck with sleep he was embracing life and it was sweet, whereas the world he saw as a cruel and sick place. Something had split him in two and he had no idea how dangerous this condition was. He went round disgusted by the stupidity of everything, yet absolved from blame. He washed his hands of it. All this sickness, this error, he remembered telling himself, had been set in motion before he was born.

Stephen Gonne was a friend of another Irishman, Robert Cronin, a novelist, and of Cronin's German wife, Hermine. One day Cora brought home a library book. She had been fond of Cronin's books for some time. This was one of his post-war novels. Picking it up idly, Daniel read it at one gulp as though famished and afterwards sent the author a fan letter. At that time Cronin lived in London. He was a much-travelled, wandering Irishman from Dublin who had been educated at Rugby. Daniel struck up an acquaintance by correspondence with this neglected writer who for some unknown reason was taking an interest in him. One winter Daniel was sent two tickets for a play of Cronin's, *The Dominique Affair*, about to be produced at a theatre club in Hampstead. Overcome by the desire for an outing he travelled up to London with Cora and Clare. He had no idea where they would spend the night.

The four adults and one child met in a nearby pub. Daniel took to the older man at once. Robert Cronin was tall, square-shouldered, deeply quiet, the lips of his long mouth pressed tightly shut. He sat in silence while his wife and Cora chattered away vivaciously.

No one in the pub objected to the child. Clare was now nine years old. In company she would appear to be waiting, her face tranquil, for something extraordinary to happen. Outside, the December air was bitterly cold. As they had left the station, flakes of snow fluttered down. In the warm noisy pub Clare sat very still, like an insect on a leaf. Hermine seemed captivated by her, to such an extent that Daniel wondered if she perhaps yearned for a child of her own. 'So, pretty one, you have come to London?' she crooned, and she touched Clare's cheek. 'How cold you are, darling!'

Afterwards Daniel couldn't recall how they had got on to Stephen. Cora was excited: she loved to talk and talk. Daniel took pleasure in her pleasure, observing her pale skin flushed with excitement. To her this was real living, these cosmopolitan, fascinating people.

Cora's rapidly gyrating monologue, and her alarming habit of spilling herself out to strangers with total abandon, must have appealed to Hermine. All at once she and Cora were discussing someone called Stephen with an intimacy which astonished Daniel, their heads close together. It was if they had both known him, as well as each other, for years. When he glanced over at Cronin it was to find him smiling remotely like a Buddha. He looked wise and detached, brimming with experience, yet with the dreamy aspect of a genuine mystic. He had lived in Berlin, Paris, Geneva. Hermine had once been a student of his. She was maternal, but with green tigerish eyes. Her hair, scraped back and wound up in a knot, with inserted curved combs, put Daniel in mind of a teacher. At her throat, contradicting the apparent severity, was a coquettish piece of mauve and orange chiffon. Her accented English, the warm gush of her speech and her Continental gestures set her apart from the pub's clientele, but not from Cora, who was lapping at her avidly with her eyes.

Hermine said, 'Stephen loves dressing up, doesn't he, Robert?' and received a grave nod from her husband.

'Oh, so do I,' Cora cried. 'When I get the chance, that is.'

'No, no.' Hermine lowered her voice. 'As a woman, you understand.'

'Really?' Cora's eyes popped open wide. 'How fascinating.' At once another story began to pour from her lips. 'I knew a boy once, he was the same. Such a beautiful dancer. We used to dance together in contests. Fabulous. The poor boy, he lived with ignorant parents who kept trying to knock what they called sense into him. It was tragic. Can you imagine, in a mining village?'

Hermine smiled, shaking her head as she flashed Robert a knowing look. 'No, no,' she laughed. 'Stephen is hardly in that sort of situation. His mother keeps him, you might say. He lives alone, but on funds from her. When he was small she dressed him as a girl, not wanting a boy, you know?'

'How old is he?'

'In his forties. Well, maybe. You see, he's slim and looks younger. But his hair, yes, is grey. We are so fond of him!'

'He lives in Ireland?'

'A few miles from Dublin, on the coast. A little resort.'

Before another minute had passed, Daniel heard Cora say, 'Could I write to him, do you think?'

'Oh, I imagine so. Yes, I'm sure he'd like that. Don't you agree, Robert?'

Yes, Robert thought so too. Or did he? A silent nod was his only response. Daniel noticed a hint of weariness in those sad sunken eyes.

'Let me write you down his address. He lives in a bungalow by the sea, a quite ugly building as a matter of fact.'

It was time for the play. Daniel went off with Cora and Clare to locate their seats. When the performance, which was in the round, began, his mind kept drifting from the players – who seemed ridiculous to him at close range with their unnaturally loud voices – to thoughts of the tall man he had just left. He was sitting impassively next to Hermine in a front row directly facing them.

The play over, Daniel went out with Cora into the freezing streets. They were immediately lost in the dark. Clare wailed. Daniel counted his money, found a taxi and they rode as far as Euston. He remembered that in Gower Street there were hotels no larger than houses, one every few yards. They tramped along, wincing at the cold. Cora stopped. 'Does it matter which one?' she asked, her teeth chattering. Clare jumped up and down. 'It doesn't matter, Dadda!' They entered one nearest to where they stood, opposite the blinded windows of some institution. In this period of his life, though he was often stimulated by the thought of London, its pace and glamour, he would be swamped by its vastness after a few hours.

Their room was on the second floor. It had a high ceiling and a window that rattled. It was icy. Cora rushed downstairs to see if she could beg a hot water bottle. She came back with a grimy red bladder, worn dangerously thin. 'Look at this,' she said disgustedly. When she went to fill it at the wash basin there was no hot water.

Daniel heard himself say, 'Let's get into bed.' The cold seemed to have half-frozen his brain.

There was a cot for a child, but they ignored it, opening the cold sheets of a wide saggy bed and huddling together in one heap in an attempt to generate warmth. Clare was frightened at first by the continuous rumbling of heavy traffic. It pounded by so hard and fast that the floor shuddered.

'I don't like it here,' Clare whispered.

Home was a long way off. The double bed sank in the middle like a hammock. Daniel could feel a broken spring under him. Soon he was the only one left awake. He watched the lights move over the ceiling, his wife on one side, this shrimp of a girl aged nine on the other. He told himself he was their protector, and yet fear clutched at him. He was their provider, that was all. Somewhere he had read that London was built entirely on mud. Lying there at the dead centre of the huge metropolis, more scared than his daughter if she had only realised, he imagined them sinking down through the floor together, then through the mud, layer after stinking layer. His dreams sucked and bubbled. He dozed off, waking in a panic, unable to make out where he was. Turning to clutch his wife, he embraced his child.

17

Back home, the routine went on as before. Daniel was now in his late thirties. Ten years of marriage had flashed by like a day. Yet each day seemed immense. The travelling he had to do meant that he would be away from home for twelve hours, even longer if he was forced to do overtime. Cora would be left stranded in a dormitory village where the men poured themselves at six-thirty each morning into a vast dockyard across the Tamar. Their wives, most of them born in the place, kept on cleaning and cooking and pushing their babies to and fro. Cora had to get Clare off to school, then she retreated to her bed and fantasies. On afternoon walks she would venture as far as the abandoned quarry within sight of the dock cranes. She gathered sloe blossom, spindleberries, whatever happened to be in season, finding solace in her trophies.

Otherwise it was a life of incessant reading, usually novels, and of waiting for Clare and then for Daniel. It was clear that fantasy didn't banish loneliness. Her dreams were of the kind that had to be indulged, shared with someone. She had dreamt of building a life upon Daniel, but he was absent in mind even more than in body. Often she spoke of ending it all, and once took an overdose, not sufficient to kill but to 'blot myself out' as she said later. Not knowing this, he thought she was dying when her legs gave way under her. He ran out in the night to gabble down a phone and raise her doctor from his bed. The doctor drove three miles, then in his village surgery went searching through records to estimate the number of pills she might have swallowed, 'stupid woman'. Even after this night of ugly surprises Daniel was soon complacent again, since she often spoke out of bleak moods which changed with bewildering rapidity to outbursts of childish enthusiasm. Stephen Gonne was her latest enthusiasm. She seized on him as a dream come true, as if this was her last chance on earth to taste the joy of living she saw as her right.

Another drama began for her. She posted off long rambling confessionals, and was wildly happy as the replies came shooting back. Not the least like her stuff, his were short cryptic messages in an elegant hand, full of puns, witticisms, teasings. Cora wouldn't have cared if they had been in Chinese; they were addressed to her, proof that she really existed and had a future. She was being taken seriously, perhaps even wooed by means of these skittish verbal pranks. This Stephen, whoever he was, seemed intrigued by her. And why shouldn't he be?

She made no attempt to disguise her triumph, and although now and then she acted secretively, often she wanted to include Daniel in this fantasy being conducted with such ardour on her part by post. He was touched. Watching her face, looking into her eyes, he fancied he saw regained hope, gleams of mad hope that something permanent could come out of it all. His bad conscience about her flew out of the window.

Sometimes Stephen would write a single sentence on a postcard, exclamatory and mock-urgent. These were coded messages, meant for her eyes only. Cora showed one to Daniel. It meant nothing, but she was smiling blissfully. He asked her when it had come.

'Oh, I don't know. What does it matter? The day before yesterday.'

'He's asking for a quick reply.'

'Is he?'

'Haven't you read it?'

140

'Of course I've read it!'

'He sounds desperate. Is he, d'you think?'

'Probably. I'll write when I'm ready.'

She was beginning to feel her power, he thought, and he said, 'Don't let the poor devil wait around too long,' suddenly afraid that the correspondence might fizzle out. That would be awful. It had begun to dawn on him that he had a stake in it too. Just to think of a resumption of their old strain and misery was enough to make him nervous. This was such a pleasant respite. His hopes as well as Cora's were now pinned on Stephen. He would have the curious sensation that this faceless person, dancing brightly in the far distance, was his freed self, a kind of secret brother who would recognise him instantly if he ever did turn up.

Cora grew steadily happier. There seemed no end to the possibilities: either she could go over there on a visit – several hints had been dropped – or Stephen could join them for a holiday. Daniel pointed out that their cottage, only three tiny rooms piled one over the other, contained two adults, one child, a cat, a small dog, and the results of Cora's hoarding instincts, such as several hundred back numbers of National Geographical Magazine, mustard yellow stacks of them, ever increasing. No matter, they would fit in a visitor somehow. It had become vital. And he was keen to meet this man whom the Cronins held in such high esteem. Would Daniel and he hit it off? Admittedly their tastes in literature didn't appear to have much in common. Cora exclaimed in delight each time a name familiar to her cropped up. 'Daniel, he adores Anaîs Nin!' 'Guess what – he collects first editions!'

'What of?'

'Mainly modern novels. French, he loves anything French. Genet, Camus, Mauriac. And would you believe it – Gide's *Journals*! He owns them! You know how I've been searching for those for absolutely ages.'

'I do.'

'He's got them all!'

'So you said.'

'Isn't it incredible?'

'Wonderful.'

He meant it. After such a build-up he had become identified with her hopes and dreams. As well as this, a voice whispered to him that anything which so clearly banished her depression was bound to be good for him too. He so much wanted it to succeed now that he was beginning to anticipate a possible hitch. If this bibliomaniac suddenly and mysteriously dried up, or went cold on her, what then?

One night he came in soaked to the skin after being caught in a rainstorm. One look at Cora's face told him, without a word being uttered, that she had won. She waved it under his nose triumphantly, the letter with its firm invitation. So when should she go?

'Oh, any time,' he said wearily. 'God, look at this. My socks are soaked. It's even gone down my neck. Can I have a towel?'

'No, you don't understand!' Cora cried. 'Daniel, I'm not asking you – it's him, he's asking me. He wants to know when. Isn't that fantastic?'

'It is, it is. Let me get a towel.'

'I thought next week.'

'Can't you make it sooner? He might change his mind.'

'Don't be silly, of course he won't. I've got to write and accept, and let him know my time of arrival. Daniel, you're not listening to me!'

He was peeling off his trousers, underpants, socks. 'I'm listening.' The cheerfully blazing coal fire in the little grate put fresh heart into him, and so, the more he thought of it, did her news. He dropped on another lump of coal. The cottage was so damp, they had fires throughout the year.

'Now, don't moan at what I'm going to say next. Don't say what you always say, that we can't afford it. Good God, it's only once in a lifetime.'

'What is?'

142

She drew a deep breath. 'I thought of flying. From Exeter.'

Without waiting for his reply she went through to the kitchen on the other side of the fireplace. This was a primitive lean-to affair, squashed against the mountain of damp earth pressing up behind the cottage. There was a cooker, a deal table for working on and nothing else. Everything was stored on shelves he had fixed up on the end wall. Soon after they first moved in, a period of heavy rain lasting for days caused the stone wall backing the earth to stream with moisture. He came down on the third morning to find a fat slug making its way upwards towards the light. The only daylight came from a skylight which leaked. Since then the back wall of rocks had been cemented over. What a thin skin it was! Thoughts of what lay behind it still haunted his mind, the heaped tons of darkness crawling with slimy life, and with the power to crush them all.

Cora came out again with his steaming dinner. She was smiling. 'Are you ready for this, love?'

'In one minute.' Daniel scrambled up the narrow stairs for a change of clothes. What a foul day it had been, and here was Cora in an excellent mood. A wild urge to laugh rose through his body.

Sitting opposite Cora, tucking into the hot food, he asked, 'Have you ever flown before?'

'No, never.'

He raised his head, gazed at her and smiled. 'Then you should do it.' The words just popped out of his mouth and he heard them as if someone else inside him had spoken. Cora's reckless spirit was certainly contagious, he thought. They were hard up, living from week to week, but that no longer seemed to matter. Things were moving swiftly at last. And he saw suddenly how everything had begun expanding for her, walls collapsing, air rushing in, the clear light of a succession of thrilling days shining down. He was sick of always being prudent – all at once he felt wild

143

and generous like her. Sitting at the table with his elbows tucked in – she had asked him often enough not to be uncouth – he took a great leap into space with her, leaving his mean upbringing far behind.

Clare asked, 'What's flying, Mamma?'

'In a plane, sweet.'

'What's a plane?'

Cora stopped acting nice. 'Stop talking and eat your food. Use your fork properly. Look, you're dropping it! Watch that orange squash, for heaven's sake. If you knock it over once more this week I'll scream.'

That trip of hers, Daniel reflected later, must have been an astonishing adventure. And such an escape from everything that oppressed her, winging out over the sea towards a perfect stranger who stood waiting at the airport full of anticipation (so his words said), a tall slender man, cultivated, travelled, with beautiful manners. First, though, she had to pack her bag, catch a rackety bus down to the ferry – the one Daniel boarded daily on his journey into work – and then at the other side she would need another bus to reach the station. From there she would travel to Exeter. How did she propose to get out to the airport?

'Oh, there's bound to be some arrangement laid on,' she said blithely.

'If there isn't,' he told her grandly, 'jump into a taxi.'

'Am I hearing right?'

'Of course.'

Off she went, one Tuesday morning as he paced around restlessly in his cage of an office, glancing out from time to time at the sky and wondering if she was already up there, in flight. In flight! His boss, Mr Hughes, pretended not to notice his air of distraction, his nose well down as usual over his papers. Daniel could tell though by the grasshopper twitching of the man's fingers that he was struggling to control his irritation. He and Daniel knew each other like an old married couple. Finally Mr Hughes asked pointedly if there was a shortage of work by any chance. Daniel shook his head. The three other clerks grinned and exchanged glances, hoping for a diversion. Moving to the steel cabinets near the window, Daniel made a big business of tidying up the filing system. That way he could stay in touch with the sky.

Cora didn't know how long she might be away; she would have to see how it worked out. Maybe a week, she thought. On the other hand, they might not see eye to eye. He told her, 'Stay as long as you like,' and meant it, still behaving generously from mixed motives.

Coming home nightly to the empty cottage, letting himself in, he missed her. Without her there was no core to the house. The silence was deathly. Clare was away too, staying at the house of a school friend. Cora's pug dog bulged its eyes at him. The cat ate up its food and then leapt out of the small rear window at the top of the first flight of stairs. Daniel felt deserted.

He wandered about aimlessly, neglecting his typewriter, picking up Cora's books, staring blankly at nothing. He even touched a dress she had apparently considered for the journey and then rejected. There it was, lying across the bed as if it had just that second landed there. He draped it carefully over a chair. In the morning he woke up and it was the first thing he saw. He stared at it as if seeing a ghost.

On the third night he was unable to sleep for a long time, seized by feelings of insecurity, and by a burning jealousy he didn't know he possessed, which seemed to stimulate him sexually. Returning home one evening, he came up the cobbled alley from the bus garage and saw the ground floor window of the cottage alight. He pushed open the door. Cora was there inside: the meagre room was a home again.

Clare was back too, sprawled over the carpet and tickling the dog's pinkish belly, its nipples like tiny studs.

Everything was in order, as it should be, gloriously normal.

'Hello,' Cora called, not even showing herself. 'This is about ready, if you are.'

The matter-of-fact sound of her voice unnerved him. Immediately he assumed that the visit had been an utter flop. He dived straight into the kitchen to hear the worst and to come to terms with it. Seeing the triumphant glint in Cora's eye he realised his mistake at once. Her neutral voice was assumed, her indifference an act. Whatever news she had, it was good, stored away inside her for an appropriate moment. Vastly relieved, he decided to play-act himself. Anticipation could be pleasurable, if one had the patience for it.

He went up and kissed her, and then asked, 'Was everything all right?'

Cora gazed coolly at him. 'Why shouldn't it have been?'

Knowing her as he did, he translated this to mean: So you didn't have faith in me! 'Well,' he said lamely, 'it was a blind date after all. You didn't know the first thing about each other.'

'On the contrary, I knew exactly what I'd find.'

'How?'

'Intuition perhaps.'

'And were you right?'

'More or less, yes, I was.'

She seemed to be teasing, hinting at things he couldn't possibly know, shared secrets, affinities. She said, 'This is your plate, here – the one with the most potatoes. Is that enough carrots?'

'Yes, plenty.'

'Are you hungry?'

'Starving.'

'That's good.'

He received another flashing look, a radiant smile. In the space of a week she had changed into a happy person. Daniel beamed gratefully at her. He wasn't concerned, if

146

he told the truth, with what news she had. He had shed his cares and was prepared to splash about as happily as her in this lovely new atmosphere.

Sitting around the table with his reclaimed family was another new joy. He ate the delicious hot stew, helped himself to fresh crusty bread and feasted his eyes on them both. How glad he felt, how fortunate he was! With each mouthful of dinner he swallowed down as well half a dozen questions he was having to save until later. The boring routine of everyday living he now found amazingly pleasurable – even the washing up, coaxing Clare off to bed, promising to come up and tuck her in later, and then having a shave to freshen up.

This evening, though, he had no intention of lugging down his cumbersome old typewriter and setting to work. Hearing what Cora had to say would be a hundred times more interesting. It was bubbling madly in her, he could see, the kind of drama she loved. And if she didn't tell him soon she would burst. Yet he had to admit that her preoccupation, or whatever it was, gave her a self-sufficiency and a restraint which he found strange. Where was the Cora who spilled things out compulsively, like someone without a second to lose?

He climbed the stairs to Clare's top room. Maybe she would insist on a favourite story, not just a goodnight kiss? It wouldn't matter, he had lost his tiredness. The room was in chaos, looking as if a dustbin had been up-ended in the middle of the floor. For once he kept calm. There was a bad smell. He decided to ignore it. He waded through the rubbish of broken toys, torn paper, woollies, and opened the window a little.

Clare could be very stubborn. Evidently she was set on mending an old doll, getting angry with it. The arms had come unhooked from their sockets. She wouldn't let him help her, either. Her feet were bare, but she had put on her pyjamas. 'Get into bed, Clare,' he urged. 'It's warmer. You can do that in there.'

She sat on the floor, not answering, saying 'Oh,' each time her attempt to hook an arm into the empty hole failed. He left her to it and descended the steep stairs. As he reached the bottom he heard a maddened scream and something hitting the wall with a thud: the beloved doll, presumably.

Cora had prepared coffee. She sat back on the small red settee. Beside her was a pack of Sobranie cigarettes. If she smoked at all she preferred foreign brands. She favoured the exotic in all things whenever possible – Stephen was a good example – as a way of countering the mundane, and as a result was endlessly frustrated.

Clearly this was going to be an occasion. He sat opposite, admiring Cora's new confidence, her air of gleaming satisfaction. The sweet smell of her cigarette seemed to be in his nostrils, even though she hadn't yet begun to smoke. She told him about the plane, what a fantastic feeling it was, and about her first sight of the Irish coast, the sea laid out below them. Hanging up there in defiance of nature had been for her a magical sensation. Her eyes lighted, she smiled seraphically. Not for the first time, he felt that something peculiar was happening and that it excluded him.

'How about him?' he broke in impatiently. 'He was there to meet you, I take it?'

'Yes, of course, what do you think? Daniel, I had the shock of my life! Can you imagine, I had no idea what to expect, how he would look physically, and there coming towards me was this weird character, very thin, rather haggard, and yes, tall, in well-cut tweeds, the most beautiful hand-made shoes, and a stringy frizz of salt-and-pepper hair down over his shoulders. Yes! I was so shocked. And it was such a shame, all wrong, it made him look simply comic. Yet when you did look into his face, when you managed to find it, well, he's really quite handsome. A narrow, sensitive face. Always laughing, creased up. God knows, he hasn't much to laugh about. As you know he loves to dress up, it's his mania. He has this wardrobe "blazing with secrets" – that's how he refers to it – and it's crammed to the doors with dresses, fur coats, hats, scarves, underwear, the lot. At night he goes out alone, parades up and down. Now and then the police pick him up and have a brutal little game with him, cross-examining him and so forth. Isn't that vile? It's not as though they don't know all about him – of course they do. Stephen is well off, kept by a generous mother, who maintains his bungalow and gives him an adequate allowance. And so she should provide for him – she did it!'

'Pardon?'

'Never mind, I'll explain later. Oh, and he loves Paris, frequents all the famous transvestite clubs. I tell you, it was quite an experience. On the very first night he asked me to accompany him, parade with him out in the open. Two women taking a stroll. Naturally I said yes. First, though, I told him, I'm going to cut your hair. Believe me, he looked dreadful.'

'Did he submit to that?'

'He sat like a lamb. You see, he adores attention. To him that's the essence of being female. When I think of it now – such a nerve I had. And at our first meeting. He ran into his squalid bathroom for a towel and then sat on a chair without a murmur while I made him presentable. I just tidied him up.'

'How does he look now?'

'Very handsome.'

'So where did you walk at night when you went out, you and your lady friend?'

She threw back her head and laughed at the extraordinary memory. Or was she laughing, he wondered, in sheer delight at being chosen as his accomplice? Yes, this was surely her real pleasure, the contemplation of what she had achieved. She had passed the test, she had been essential to someone. To think of it now made her so gleeful. If he had been sitting next to her at this moment she would

149

have dug her elbow into his ribs exuberantly. Yet in a sense none of this was so exceptional, not in his experience. Cora was capable of feeling perfectly at home with the oddest people. Only supposedly normal behaviour baffled her. Conventional types bored her, made her uneasy, even frightened her with their intolerance. 'I don't know where you find your friends,' her mother used to say to her. 'It seems to me they're not quite the ticket, any of them.' Cora would always answer, 'Mother, you don't understand anything. It's their peculiarities I'm *interested* in. Would you like me to explain what I mean?' Her mother would shake her head, lips pursed. 'It's nothing to do with me, none of my business what they get up to.' 'But aren't you even the tiniest bit curious?' 'No, thank you very much.'

'We walked along the promenade like two old friends,' Cora was saying. 'Two women friends! We promenaded. Under the full moon. At midnight.'

'Anybody about?'

'No, worse luck. Stephen was so disappointed. For him that's part of the thrill, deceiving the respectable, risking discovery, inviting disaster.'

She talked on, giving him further illustrations of Stephen's style. For instance, he'd once sat in a restaurant with a woman who was stark naked under her mac. The waiter asked if he could hang up her raincoat and she declined graciously. 'Well,' Cora said, 'do you get the picture? We walked along, a perfectly acceptable couple. Never mind, it was a glorious night. Stars, moon, the sea coming in.'

It was a small seaside resort, down the coast from Dublin. At this time of year, end of September, it must have been deadly quiet. Daniel asked her if that was so.

'Yes, oh yes. Shutters going up everywhere. Rather forlorn really. But you know me, it's the kind of melancholy I like. Autumn's always been my favourite season.'

150

He looked at her. What had happened to his usual scepticism? He was affected by her triumph, and by the dreamy nostalgia which had a touch of regret in it. It was wonderful, her experience, but over. The entire visit must have flashed by with the speed of a dream. He wished for her sake it could resume, continue. She ought to have more of the same, and so should he. Had she begun to see herself as Stephen's permanent helpmate? If so, he, Daniel, was beginning to see him as theirs, as a mutual friend, necessary to them both in some peculiar way.

He said, 'So what happens now?'

Cora was silent for a moment. Then she looked candidly at him. 'It depends.'

'On what?' He was reminded of a child, dreaming up more daring exploits and about to defy its parents.

'Well, on whether you mind him coming here.'

'For a holiday?'

'Yes.'

'Mind? Why should I mind? Did I object to you going there?' He had begun to bluster like someone uncertain.

Her large eyes watched him. 'You might not take to him. There's no reason why you should.'

'Is there any reason why I shouldn't?'

'No. Except that he's not in the least like you.'

'We're all different. Would he care for me, d'you think?'

'Oh, I'm sure he would.'

'Then it's settled.' A thought struck him. 'Only one problem that I can see.'

'What is it?' she demanded, her voice hard, not like her own.

'Where the devil would we put him?'

Cora smiled. She said slyly, 'I've thought of that.'

Now it was his turn to smile. He could only say, 'All right, tell me the arrangemet. When did you work out the details? Don't tell me, let me guess.'

She was nodding. 'On the plane crossing over. No, listen, Daniel, what I thought was, if we moved up with Clare, then he could use our bedroom.'

'Fine. Do we lie down anywhere?'

'Of course, don't be silly. We'll unfold the portable bed. Have we still got it?'

'Yes, somewhere – at the bottom of our junk heap. I'll have to excavate for it. It's only a three-quarter, if you remember.'

'Oh, we can manage, surely. I don't suppose he'll stay more than a few days. He'll soon be bored with us.'

18

Stephen Gonne stayed for three weeks. Eager now for the disruption of his routine, Daniel waited as impatiently as Cora for him to arrive. The prospect of even a temporary change in their situation enlivened him. Could something unpredictable really be about to happen? He fished for extra tidbits. Cora was maintaining a certain reserve, he felt. This uncharacteristic secretiveness of hers puzzled and obsessed him. Was he jealous after all? How ridiculous, he thought, when he had encouraged her from the start to cultivate the friendship. From what he knew of this Stephen he could rule out sex. Yet it was odd – each morsel of information he managed to coax from her seemed to have a sexual flavour. But then she did have a mischievous tongue. She was indulging in a kind of happy spite, perhaps that was it. He didn't know or care. Why should he? Let her have her fun.

He reasoned that if he waited for her to fall into a reminiscent mood, then she might tell him things. He even wondered whether Stephen actually existed somewhere or if she had invented him, conjured him up out of one of her fantasies. The next evening he probed again.

'He likes attention, you say.'

'Yes, definitely.'

'Anything else he likes?'

'Let me think. Females with long hair, the longer the better. Mermaids.'

'That's a water thing.'

'What is?'

'His hair fixation. Psychologists have a name for it – I can't remember it. A famous poet had it – was it Shelley?'

'I've no idea.'

Cora's hair was shoulder-length, abundantly luxuriant and bushy when she unfastened it. Usually she piled it on top of her head in a dense glossy edifice, dark as night. At home her mother had a framed studio portrait of Cora, looking like a movie goddess.

'What else?'

She began to answer, and stopped short. Her expression changed and became wary, her eyes tinged with slyness. Evidently she distrusted his motives. Daniel noticed, but was too far gone to stop now. Cora said irritably, 'Oh, I don't know. He likes to have his face slapped.'

'He likes what?'

'You heard me.'

'Why does he?'

'How should I know? From what he's told me I imagine his mother used to do it. Now it seems he's developed a taste for it.'

'That's sad.'

'Don't be naive. It's more complicated than that.'

Daniel fell silent. Cora's whole posture was taut, distrustful. He could almost see her temper simmering, and each time she spoke she sounded as if she were addressing a simpleton. Goaded, he asked. 'Did you oblige him, then?'

Cora's anger broke over him. 'For God's sake, what's this interrogation about? It's got nothing, absolutely nothing to do with you. He's my friend, do you understand? This friendship belongs to me. Keep out of it.'

'I'm sorry. What have I said?'

'He's a person, he's not a case history.'

'Of course not. I agree with you.'

'Just drop the subject please, if you don't mind.'

'It's dropped.'

She sat there fuming, her face angry. She burst out again, 'Look, we might as well get one thing straight. If he comes, I'm not sharing him with you or Clare or anybody. It's my business, what we say or don't say. We have certain interests in common. That's a private matter between us. Now, is that agreed or not? Now you know what's at stake, do you want to back down?'

'No.'

'I'm perfectly serious about this.'

'I can see you are.'

'I've told you the truth. I'm trying to be honest.'

'Thanks.'

'Can he still come over?'

'I'm looking forward to it.'

Cora's eyes flared. Daniel sat very still, doing his best to calm her down but also himself, while a storm of consternation swept through him. Not trusting himself to speak, he nodded mutely.

'It's up to you,' she said flatly.

'I know.'

Then, more contrite, she said, 'Daniel, I'm sorry. I didn't mean to put it like that. It's just terribly important to me, don't you see?'

'I do now.'

'Are you sure?'

'Yes. I don't need telling how unhappy you've been lately.'

Her face was shadowy, half-frightened. She seemed about to glance back naively over her shoulder. 'God, don't remind me. And not just lately. I haven't dared to tell you. What's the use? For years now I've woken up every morning feeling suicidal. Years of hopeless mornings.'

'Has that stopped?'

'I'm afraid to say yes.'

'Cora, I'm glad.'

'So now I'm seizing this chance,' she said fiercely. 'Don't

155

spoil it.' On an impulse she held out her arm. 'Come and kiss me.'

He went to her to be comforted, and became the comforter. She broke into a clamour of tears like a small child. Was he being told something by this – something about her entanglement? Like any man faced with the inexplicable, he looked round for an errand or a duty. 'Let me get you the tissues,' he said.

Stephen Gonne arrived suddenly one day in early October. They had issued an invitation, but for a few days later. For some reason he had had to change his plans. When he got home from 'business' – Cora's name for his job – that evening and opened the living-room door, there the guest was. Daniel stepped into an expectant hush.

He would always come home feeling drained and bloodless, like the white paper he sorted and shuffled all day long. But their visitor disarmed him at once. He had a soft smile and an even softer voice. Daniel had half-anticipated this, yet the reality astonished and beguiled him. How could anyone in their right mind entertain an unkind thought about such a person? The lean man said, 'Daniel, how are you?' as he jumped up to greet his host, and it sounded more of a caress than a question.

Daniel's fatigue slipped from him. He was mumbling something or other. He felt totally inept, a clumsy ungracious oaf. Then within minutes he had begun to respond in kind. An early fear of the world had planted in him a need to please others. From this came his ability to ingratiate himself.

Cora returned to the kitchen, then came out again. She looked pleased, if a little keyed-up and watchful. Daniel wondered whether Clare was irritating her, racing upstairs and dragging down armfuls of toys and books for inspection, hogging the limelight, something she did on the rare occasions when they had guests.

Glancing at Stephen surreptitiously, he saw that sideways on he looked frail, with a slight stoop. His expensive oatmeal tweeds lent the man a little extra bulk. His hands were elegantly bony and so were his wrists. What he hadn't bargained for was the Irishman's wit. Though he didn't talk a great deal or say anything hilarious, his face exuded wit and a kind of wanton intelligence that Daniel found irresistibly charming. As well as this, he could act the child to perfection. Clare was drawn to him like a needle to a magnet: she wouldn't leave his side for a second. 'Now darling, stop being such a pest,' Cora said. She glanced sourly at Daniel. Stephen smiled, dropping back on the settee. He crossed his thin legs.

Later, the subject of a play of Daniel's came up. He had written it in the space of a fortnight, eighteen months ago, just to see if he could pull it off. Though it was meant for the stage, he had no interest in the theatre. Indeed, he hadn't seen more than two productions in his life, both of them amateur. What did captivate him – he had no idea why – was the writing of dialogue for its own sake.

An agent showed interest, then promptly sold his play to a TV company. Daniel didn't even possess a TV set. He signed a contract for five hundred pounds, was sent a sample script and told to copy that when he rewrote. Eventually the entire second act was thrown out. Nevertheless, the words remaining were all his. His writing had earned real money at last. His parents were impressed.

With the lump sum he brought a wooden bungalow up on the cliff, no more than two miles from where they lived. It was an attempt to realise a dream he had, which was for them to live up there one day in complete freedom, overlooking the sea. From the weekend bungalow he now owned he gazed down intoxicated over swaying bracken to an enormous spotless beach and out at a wall of sea, telling himself that there was nothing between them and the coast of France. True, at weekends he scarcely glanced in that direction. Instead he worked fanatically to replace damp-stained ceiling boards, plug holes in the tin roof, yank up rotten fence posts, install a sink in the kitchen. As he sweated, he cursed his dream for gobbling up his precious writing time. It was at this point that Stephen arrived. Now his leather bag stood on the rug in their little bedroom in the cottage.

The evening passed swiftly and pleasantly. Stephen had brought along wine to go with the meal. After they had eaten, they finished off the wine and followed it with coffee. At midnight they went off to bed. The atmosphere was relaxed, even jolly, a rare pleasure for Daniel.

In all the excitement he had forgotten how whacked he was. Climbing the steep stairs reminded him. He trudged past their relinquished bedroom and went on up to Clare's room. Cora was still below, making sure that her guest had everything he wanted.

Clare sat up in bed, wide awake. 'Dadda, isn't he nice – I like him!'

'Lie down, go to sleep.'

'Do you like him?'

'Never mind that. What are you doing awake at this time of night?' He went over and tucked her in. Down below the voices sounded conspiratorial. Now and then he heard Cora's hooting laugh.

'Say yes, Dadda!'

'Yes, yes. Now shut up, it's very late.'

Thank God, the portable bed was already made up. He crawled between the sheets, groaning under his breath. In six hours he would be out again, preparing to go off to work. He was virtually on the floor, which was where the unpleasant odour in Clare's room seemed strongest. He crept out, got up and opened the window at the top. Cora came in. She whispered, 'What are you doing?'

'Trying to get rid of the smell in here,' he croaked, lying down again.

She undressed rapidly. He couldn't remember ever see-

ing her so happy. She knelt down. 'I can't smell anything.'
She was sniffing. 'What kind of smell?'

'A bad one.'

'Nonsense.'

'You're not concentrating. Your mind's somewhere else.'

'You're imagining it,' she hissed.

Exasperated, he opened his mouth to appeal to Clare,
who lay watching them with avid eyes. What was the use?
A sweet child, she was a little savage at heart, like all small
children.

Cora plunged the tiny cupboard of a room into darkness
and came to bed. Without walls or ceiling the room
seemed to enlarge, to encompass the night. Cora lay on her
back beside him, sighing contentedly. Daniel thought,
Thanks to Stephen, we're closer than we have been for
years. Cora clutched his hand. He began to drift off.

At the weekend they went for a walk, the four of them,
through the twisty lanes and then up a steep track leading
to the top of the cliff. They were on their way to the bungalow. Sometimes Daniel saw it as no more than a shack.
Cora had fancy names for it – 'studio', 'retreat' – but in a
black part of himself he had already christened it 'The
Workhouse'.

The view from up there was staggering. Whether in the
mood for it or not, you were lifted up into a different region, one glittering with light, a vast space inhabited by
gulls. It still took his breath away, and he forgot his worries. This was what had seduced him in the first place. A
tremendous sweep of bay curved grandly for at least ten
miles. Stephen merely glanced politely at it, though the
trip was supposed to be for his benefit. Clearly he was
unimpressed. Daniel concluded that nature and its mar-
vels bored him.

It was the same with the shack. Cora drew attention to
the brick chimney piece, told the story of the dockyard
family who had lived there throughout the war to escape

the Plymouth blitz, took him inside and pointed out the fireplace, various improvements, the ultramarine curtains she had made up herself. He listened courteously, nodding, yet seemed far away. 'He must think it all rather droll,' Daniel decided. Or maybe he just didn't notice things. Half an hour later he heard Stephen telling Cora of his preference for artificiality, mirrors, night-time – and games. Returning down the steep track again, Stephen skipped gaily from side to side as he chased after Clare. He had the agility of a goat. They were playing tick. He leapt at her nimbly and shot out his long arm. She uttered a piercing shriek. 'Clare, that's enough,' Cora cried. 'You're getting too excited, stop it.'

This was the moment, Daniel would tell himself later, when he came to his senses and understood what he had done. Stephen flicked a look at Cora which was full of devilment. That's it, Daniel thought – he was using Clare to make Cora jealous. They had invited the devil to stay with them; a charming devil, to be sure, with a faint brogue and a gargoyle cast to his eye.

Soon, the evenings – especially on weekdays – began to irritate him. After a sterile day juggling figures under the eye of a crabby boss, the non-stop gaiety at home now seemed a bad joke. A growing perversity made him more and more unwilling to smile or act pleasant. He was only too aware of the sour set of his mouth, his dull resentful eyes. The visage staring back at him each morning from the mirror told him what he most feared to know, that he was indistinguishable from his fellow clerks, a wage slave who had ceased to hope for anything better.

Cora had always been a night bird. Now she had a companion. At eleven each night, collapsing with fatigue, Daniel would mumble goodnight and leave them to it. They sat cosily on the settee, close together, sometimes with a single book open between them. They pored over Anaïs Nin novels in unison, their heads almost touching. Certain passages would intrigue and delight them. They whispered together, arch collaborators in a parallel creation of their own. What were they discovering, if not that their solitary passions had made them partners? If Stephen jabbed a long bony finger at a spot on the page, this would cause Cora to hoot uncontrollably and then clap a hand over her mouth. Stephen hissed or giggled, or simply raised his eyebrows mock-quizzically. Daniel saw them, with puritanical distaste, as a school of hedonism for two.

19

On Saturday he caught a train to London, supposedly to visit an agent, but the truth was that he found it impossible to stay in the house for the whole weekend. As it happened it was also his birthday. On the train he composed endless drafts in his head of a speech to Stephen, making it clear that it was time he left. He had begun to seriously doubt that he would ever be rid of the man. Cora, he could see, was unaware of the problem. She would speak to Daniel politely, never lose her temper, and she no longer noticed his irritating habits. It was so unnatural: he missed her complaints. Catching her eye now was difficult. When he did manage it, he wished he hadn't. She gazed at him, he thought, without any intimacy, as if she had changed places with Stephen and was now a guest in the house. Thinking this, he felt sick. His innards knotted, then froze. On the train he stared out blindly at the rushing landscape. The windows of the carriage streamed with rain.

At Paddington he changed to an underground train. In the West End, the heavy shower became a continuous deluge. By force of habit he had packed sandwiches. How was he going to eat them? Where was he? What was he doing here? The rain drove through his clothes, softened his shoes. He looked down at his feet. The shoe leather was piebald, blackened by water where it had soaked in, the rest in weird yellowish patches.

He found an empty phone box and stood there, wondering if he should ring the agent's office for directions.

Would they even see him without an appointment? What kind of impression would he make in this sorry state? The trip had lost whatever flimsy purpose it once had. London was turning into a vast gurgling sink-hole. When he got bored with staring at it through the glass of the call box he unwrapped his sandwiches and ate them where he stood.

The rain eased off. Outside, in the Charing Cross Road area, he tramped around, splashing through puddles and walking hastily like everyone else. He tried to interest himself in the contents of secondhand bookshops, fighting down a growing nausea for print. Finally he gave up and turned for home.

Another pounding train carried him westward again. He sat in an open carriage, and kept noticing newspaper headlines. At Taunton the passengers around his table disappeared. Someone had left their *Evening Standard* behind. Daniel read the front page, below its banner headline screaming CUBAN CRISIS. Apparently the world was about to blow itself up. He felt damp, cold. His shoulders shivered of their own accord. Miserable or not, he still wanted to live.

By the time he reached home he was beyond caring one way or the other. Long journeys always tended to lower his appetite for experience. He would be disorientated, saddened. Glimpses from the train of lighted rooms, seated figures, a woman in a kitchen, left him feeling blank, aware of the curious pathos of living things. Numb and dazed, he tried to relocate himself. He imagined he had left something or himself behind at each station the train had rushed through.

The cottage had shrunk incredibly. How did they manage to lever themselves into it and exist? Getting into the living-room from the narrow street was like trying to edge sideways into a corridor. There was a fire burning in the grate. The atmosphere was jollier than ever. Clare jumped up and down, running to him for a kiss. 'Happy returns, Dadda! Have you brought me anything?'

'No, not this time.'

'Why not?'

'How was London?' Stephen asked, smiling.

'Dirty,' he said.

Cora came up. 'Happy birthday, dear.' She pecked at his cheek. 'Look at what Stephen's bought to celebrate the occasion – isn't it nice of him?'

She pointed at a large coffee cake, layered with a sort of pale fudge. They waited for him to wash, then sat around the table with cups of tea. Cora sliced the cake ceremoniously. Clare clapped her hands and wriggled. 'Oh, is that mine, can I have that?'

'You can wait,' Cora said. 'And remember your manners.'

Cora and Stephen were using forks, so Daniel did the same. He dug into the fat sticky wedge, grimly determined not to enjoy it. The cake was beautifully moist and light, oozing with sweetness.

'Delicious, isn't it?' Cora said, eating delicately. Daniel mumbled something with his mouth full.

Afterwards they sat close to the fire, and there was an attempt at conversation. It kept foundering because Daniel wouldn't respond. A stone was lodged in his chest. He was intent on sabotaging the evening, yet without admitting it to himself. He could feel the anger bulging up, forcing through the pores of his skin into the room. The word 'crisis' ran through his head as though printed on a loop.

Stephen sat smiling, immune it seemed to Daniel's boorishness. This baffled and enraged him. 'It's all a sham, a lie,' he thought. Cora suddenly stood up and took Clare off to bed.

Daniel sat on in silence with this enemy who continued to elude him. He stalked him, but to no effect. This was ridiculous. He felt like his own father, immovable and stupid as a rock.

Forcing himself, he asked, 'Have you heard the news?'

'What news?'

'About the crisis. Haven't you heard?'

Stephen laughed, clownishly raising his eyebrows. 'News is an invention, it seems to me. But then, journalists have to live.'

'Invention? We're going to be obliterated. This time it looks certain, unless a miracle saves us. Doesn't it bother you at all?'

'No, not really. Naturally I'd prefer it not to happen. Anyway, I'm hardly likely to influence the outcome with my little wishes. Certainly not with my opinion, since I don't have one.'

'And you don't even think about it?'

The man was doing his best not to smile. 'I'd rather think of coffee cake,' he said.

Daniel felt his face burn. 'How about Clare?'

'I'm afraid I don't follow you.'

'If you don't give a damn about yourself, can't you think of her?'

He didn't answer immediately. Daniel was sitting facing him now with clenched fists like an adversary. Stephen said coldly, 'That's rather a devious question, I would have thought.'

He got up and wandered to the table as if bored, put a hand to his mouth to cover a yawn, picked up a book and sat by the window. Cora came in, her face stiff. The hostile silence made her stare at Stephen with a hurt look in her eyes. Daniel felt in contact again. By inflicting this strain on her he was at least somebody, not excluded. The moment of bitter triumph came and went in a flash. He went past Cora to the door, his hands trembling. 'By the way,' he said to Stephen, 'when are you leaving?' He paused, half in and half out of the room.

'Possibly next week,' Stephen said. He glanced over at Cora fleetingly and shrugged.

Daniel tried to express his fury by slamming the door. He should have known better – the carpet underneath was too tight a fit. The matchboard door shuddered, flimsy as

a stage prop. He dragged it shut and climbed the stairs,
banging on the partition with his fist a time or two. He felt
misshapen beyond recognition. A horror of his own ugli-
ness rose up in him. He imagined himself cut off from
everyone, the hatred in his heart reversed, levelled against
him, and he understood the words 'lonely as hell'.

'Who was that banging?' Clare said. She sat up.

'Me.'

'Are you coming to bed?'

'I am.'

'Why now?'

'Because I'm tired. Look the other way, I want to get
undressed.'

She always peeped, he knew that. Only the other week
she had asked Cora, 'Why has Dadda got a middle leg?'

In bed, he turned to face the window. Clare, behind him
now, was unusually quiet. She must have decided that
adults are incomprehensible creatures, his mind mumbled.
Then he heard her singing softly to herself. After another
long silence, she said loudly, 'Now you settle down and
go to sleep, do you hear me?' He lay there, startled, his
eyes wide open. 'Do you want a good slap?' she said loudly. She was reprimanding one of her dolls in an astonish-
ingly exact replica of Cora's tone.

Hours passed. Finally Cora came up. She groped about
in the blackness, undressing. Stumbling over his shoes, she
swore under her breath. She lay down beside him, motion-
less, terribly distant and cold. He had been waiting all this
time with his rage and jealousy and wounded pride, tick-
ing like a bomb. Before he could speak she aimed the first
blow, hissing savagely in his ear, 'I hope you're satisfied!'

Instead of anger, it was self-pity which overwhelmed
him. 'So it's my fault. I'm the one.'

'Yes, yes. You're disgusting.'

'I feel it.'

'How I hate you.'

He ground out in a choked voice, half swallowing his

words, 'I want him to leave. That's all. I don't want to find him here when I get home on Monday.'

'What makes you think he wants to stay? Would you?'

'Tell him.'

'Daniel, I shan't forgive you for this, ever.'

'Just do it.'

Monday was a day of fierce gales and hard slanting rain. Leaving the office, Daniel missed his town bus to the ferry, then missed his usual ferry by a couple of minutes. The next one, due in half an hour, arrived late. He reached home at last and was fumbling for his key when the front door swung open. It was Clare. There was an odd silence behind her. Fear clutched him. He imagined disasters in rapid succession – accidents, illness, suicide, sudden death. He said, 'Where's Momma?'

'Gone away.'

He entered the living room. A note propped up on the tiles of the mantelpiece said, 'With Stephen. Don't try to follow me. Take Clare to her grandmother's. I'll be in touch with her. Cora.'

With the paper in his hand he sat down on the settee. Stunned, he covered his face. Clare came and sat beside him. When he'd composed himself and was able to look, he saw by her apparent unconcern that she was waiting patiently for the situation to resolve itself. 'Shall I make you some tea?' she asked.

He nodded dumbly, and she went into the kitchen. His mind racing with crazy ideas, how to set off in pursuit, in which direction, what to do first, he sat with his life in chaos. Jumping up, he called, 'Wait a minute, that's awkward. I'll put the kettle on for you.'

'I can do that.'

'You can?'

'Momma lets me. I'm allowed to.'

'I didn't know.'

'You sit down,' she said firmly. 'You'll feel better in a minute.'

In his mind he snatched at a name, Robert Cronin. He might be able to help. Daniel saw his rocky, sympathetic face; the face of a kind man.

Over tea, he told Clare he would be taking her to her grandmother in Bradford for a holiday.

'What about school?' she asked interestedly.

'I'll write them a note.'

Then he must have dozed off, or fallen into a stupor where he sat. Clare was shaking his shoulder. 'Dadda, Dadda.'

'Oh – what is it?'

'You should go to bed,' she said, his solemn-faced little nurse.

'Yes, come on, then,' he agreed, and stood up, feeling as he did so deplorably weak.

They went upstairs together. The sight of the dismal, sad bedroom with Cora's belongings strewn around would have made him whimper if Clare hadn't been ahead of him, marching in sturdily. His utter bone-weariness frightened him. It was as if he had aged prematurely. He stood staring at the two divans.

'Can I sleep with you, Dadda? Can I, in your bed?'

'It's too narrow, I think.'

'I'm only small,' she said cunningly.

'I suppose so.'

They lay for a long time with the light on. Daniel feared the dark. Clare's eyes were bright and seemed enlarged, her skin incredibly soft. She wriggled a lot at first, then was still.

Daniel closed his eyes. Clare whispered, 'Are you asleep?'

'No.'

'Nor me.'

'Try, then.'

She was silent for a moment. 'I spied them through the letterbox,' she remarked.

'Who?'

'Momma and Stephen.'

'When?'

'Dinnertime.'

'Why did you do that?'

'The door was locked.'

'Where were they?'

'At the bottom of the stairs.'

'What doing?'

'Kissing.'

He waited, wanting more and yet afraid to ask. After a few minutes he got out to switch off the light. Clare lay mutely without stirring, a model of good behaviour.

In the night he woke up abruptly from a merciful oblivion and the dreadful truth rushed back. Where was Cora at this moment? What was she doing? Jealousy has little to do with love: he became loathsome and maggoty, squirming about inside himself. Clare was lying with her back to him. The extraordinary peacefulness of her slumber calmed him to some extent. He snaked an arm around her waist. She didn't stir. In the dark she seemed no bigger than one of her dolls, a mere bundle of bones. He thought of a bird, as he pressed up gingerly against her spine.

Falling sleep, his dreams were more tumultuous than ever. Mostly they had running through them a speechless rage against some injustice or other. In one, there was a knock at the bedroom door and a sandy-haired Australian – he actually lived next door – came in, followed by a dwarfish bald man. Against the wall was a bath, although in fact he didn't possess one. A pasty young clerk, known to him by sight, sat in the filled bathtub fully clothed, his face covered in flour. His black raincoat floated about his waist. Dennis, the Australian, asked how Daniel had paid off his mortgage. Where did he get hold of the money? When Daniel demanded to know what business it was of his, he retreated. The dwarf companion followed him out.

169

Clare shook him by the shoulder. 'I think it's late.' She was already up and curious.

'What time is it?'

'Half-past eight. Do I have to go to school today?'

'Yes.'

'Not tomorrow.'

'I don't think so.'

He scrambled out, weak as a winter fly. The unaltered daylight world threatened to crush him, and yet something in his mind was frantically demanding action. He longed to close his eyes on it all, but stood and swayed about, scratching his head. His pallid ankles and skinny feet stuck out from faded blue cotton trousers which had shrunk in the wash. Clare was yanking her long nightgown over her head. Suddenly she had grown up and become skinny, elongated like him. When did it happen – in the night? She had arms like peeled sticks.

Downstairs he splashed cold water on his face, gave Clare a kiss and ran out without breakfast. Already he'd missed buses and ferries.

In the office, he was so obviously distraught that his boss asked him what was wrong.

'It's my mother-in-law,' he said. 'I think she's dying.' His own lie bewildered him. Why mother-in-law, why not mother?

'You'd better fill in a leave form.'

'Thanks.'

'She lives up the line, is that right?'

'Yes, Bradford.'

That afternoon he sat imagining the details of a reunion with Cora. His speech was all prepared, he knew every word by heart. Mr Hughes, assuming Daniel to be consumed by mother-in-law worries, said, 'Have you got anything urgent on your desk?'

'Not really.'

'Then you'd better go.'

Daniel put on his coat rapidly, desperate to escape and be alone with his thoughts. 'Thanks.'

'I hope the news isn't as bad as you fear.'

'Me too.'

'It couldn't be worse,' he groaned to himself. He bolted through the door. In the glass pane he caught a glimpse of his gaunt staring features.

At Bradford station he queued for a taxi, and got into one with Clare. Soon they were standing on the doorstep of his in-laws' house. Cora's mother Nellie and her husband would, he knew, welcome them because up here it was the courteous thing to do. Also, since he was bringing Clare to them unexpectedly, they would be more than pleased with him. They both doted on her. They wouldn't ask questions either, though he had to tell them something. 'Cora's gone for a short holiday in Ireland,' he would say. 'She's gone to a friend. I'm on my way to join her.' November was a peculiar time for holidays, but that couldn't be helped. They weren't fools – no doubt they would guess he was lying.

The door swung open. Nellie stood there, a suspicious look on her face. Spotting Clare, she crowed with delight and opened her arms wide. Daniel followed them in, thankful to be plucked out of the cold night, even though his own night accompanied him everywhere now with its washing fears and great empty holes into which he kept falling. Nellie fussed lovingly over Clare. Daniel longed to step into his daughter's place and receive unconditional love. What a paradise childhood was, if he had only realised.

In the gloomy high sitting room he shook hands with the stocky old man who was Cora's father. The master of the house – he was still indisputably that – sat down again with his Sexton Blake. A massive fire of coal slabs blazed. The old man lifted his head now and again to glare fiercely in his son-in-law's direction, not uttering a word but rubbing a dry palm over his shiny bald skull. A slight tremor ran through his hands. When the coal scuttle was nearly empty Daniel took it down into the cellar to fill it, and for an excuse to stand there alone with his thoughts.

Pain, rage and despair surged through him, sometimes all three at once, horribly entangled. He felt bitterly ashamed of the mess he had created. He was close to some kind of outburst, either laughter or tears, he wasn't sure. He stood registering the shapes of strings of onions, old newspapers tied in bundles, jagged black coal rearing beneath a manhole, a hillock of firewood. The weight of the house above seemed to rest on his head and shoulders and crush him deeper. To fill the scuttle, he began dragging at flat boulders of gleaming coal with his bare hands. Clutching a hatchet he smashed away, shielding his eyes with his free arm as best he could.

Later, he went out in search of a phone. There was a call box a hundred yards or so from the house but he had forgotten in which direction. It was near a blackened church. When he rang Dublin, someone, a man, answered at once. 'Who's that?' Daniel cried, hearing his own anxiety and fear.

Robert Cronin identified himself. Daniel stumbled over his words as he tried to explain Cora's desertion. 'I can't find Stephen's address.'

'We have that here. Hold on a moment.'

Daniel heard the man call to his wife in his soft, slow voice. The sound put hope into him. When he had the address, he wanted to hang on, to prolong the moment of contact, but could think of nothing further to say. Cronin said, 'Goodbye now,' and hung up. He stepped out of the phone box. He was alone again.

20

At last he was on his way. He travelled to Leeds on the
Interchange, then at nightfall caught the Liverpool train. It
was Bonfire Night: from the squeaking, slow-moving train
he watched dozens of fires in backyards, gardens, on
waste ground, and saw the first rockets race upwards,
bursting prettily on the night sky. He could hear nothing,
but in his mind they hissed like jealousy. Each time the
rushing snakes of light went out the sick emptiness in his
stomach came back. Yellow street lamps illuminated the
neat new estates. He felt a compulsion to stare at everything. He noticed how badly lit the old streets of terraced
houses were, with mean damaged pavements. If they ran
at right angles to the train he took imaginary walks up
them, back through the intricate grooves and channels of
his childhood. Some of these streets were uglier than any
he could remember.

At Liverpool he was lost. He bought a ticket for the
crossing, asking the way like a blind man until he found
the night boat. He had no confidence, now he was at the
mercy of his anxieties. On board the ferry he discovered
that the cabin allocated to him was similar to a train
sleeper, only shabbier. A man sat on the lower bunk, nursing his head in his hands. As he opened the cabin door
and stepped in, the man exploded in a violent sneeze and
fell back on the bed, a fellow in his thirties with red
streaming eyes. 'Oh my Christ,' he moaned. Dragging out
an enormous white handkerchief he went on spluttering

and sneezing into it. 'At least I won't have to attempt a conversation,' Daniel thought. Relieved, he climbed up the stepladder and crawled on to the top bunk.

An hour passed. The walls and floors of the cabin creaked suddenly. He heard violent cracking sounds, as if everything was coming apart at the seams. He peered out of the porthole but saw only a sea of blackness. He lay down, feeling a strange sensation. Chains rattled, he heard shouts.

'Thank God for that,' his companion muttered below him, then said something inaudible through his blocked nose. He started sneezing and groaning again, blowing into his handkerchief like a trumpet.

'Are we moving?' Daniel said, for something to say.

There was no answer. He hadn't expected one. Lying on his bunk, he experienced the anguish a man feels when he has lost all faith in himself.

At Dun Laoghaire he disembarked, shivering in the cold of a sunless November morning. He boarded a bus and travelled down the coast a few miles. The roads were wet. After about a mile he saw a signpost and understood that Dublin was in the other direction. The bus passed through bedraggled flat country and pulled up at last on the sea-front of a deserted resort. This was Bray, the town where Stephen was supposed to live.

He got out. Gusts of panic were making him shiver. Neither Robert Cronin nor his wife seemed to know whether Stephen was at home or away somewhere. He was often away, they'd said. There was no phone apparently. What if he was still in England, or some other country? He muttered aloud, 'No, no.' Taking one look at the dirty grey sea, the boarded-up ice-cream kiosks, deserted benches, torn posters, he half-walked, half-ran into the streets. In the corner shop selling stamps, vegetables and groceries a woman gave him directions. He was to make for the big grassy hill – she called it a mountain – which dominated the town. There it was on the skyline, no matter where you stood.

As he reached the higher streets he lost the sense of being on a hill. He found the avenue he wanted, then the number, nine. Stephen's bungalow backed on to the crest of the so-called mountain, now no more than a hump of bare ground. The bungalow, grey, poky, just a featureless box made of cement blocks, wasn't at all what he had expected. How could Cora and Stephen be spinning fantasies inside this place? It had a derelict air. Curtains were drawn, one sagging in the middle. He walked up the concrete strip between a tangle of weeds. From this spot he had a bird's-eye view of the town below. The wind whistled and blew steadily, with nothing to stop it. He glanced over his shoulder for a sign of life, a child, a dog, anything. Nothing stirred.

Banging on the door seemed like committing an outrage. The dead bungalows on either side remained dead. He banged harder, and at the same time seemed to observe himself – as one does in dreams. He pictured himself, a dishevelled bony figure, floating in space high up at the edge of the sea and hammering to be let in, to be included, the unwanted guest who always turns up, the despised foreigner nobody understands.

A curtain at the smaller window moved, to the left of the door. He thought he heard sounds. Nothing happened. He was about to raise his fist again when Cora opened the door. She had a white face, and dark marks under her eyes. In a low, unsurprised voice she said, 'You damn fool. I told you not to come after me.'

He felt such an idiot, unable to utter a word of his endlessly rehearsed speech. He was simply overjoyed to be recognised, and by his wife. Cora stood in the doorway staring and looking irritable. She could have been anywhere but she was here. In a flash another life, full of sun and of hope, began to rise mysteriously through him. This woman had betrayed his trust, but why? What had he done to her?

'You'd better come in,' she said, her voice bored and

spiritless. As if reading his thoughts, she added, 'You're lucky. We nearly went on to Paris from London.'

Daniel followed her in, nearly sagging at the knees with weariness and relief. He still felt himself to be, inexplicably, the luckiest man alive. A voice inside him, a malicious, exultant one, was saying, 'She doesn't look too happy. Has the magic between them flown out of the window?' Thoughts racing, he began to weigh up his chances of restoring the status quo. Did Stephen belong in her life as he did? He doubted it. On the other hand, he admitted Stephen's charm. The man was attentive, full of clever and interesting tricks. Where was he now, by the way?

Cora led him into a shabby lounge. It smelled sour and airless. The first thing he noticed was a large white refrigerator, smeared with fingerprints. It was pushed against a wall next to a cluttered sideboard. In one corner were tottering stacks of old newspapers and periodicals, in another some dirty washing in a plastic basket. The whole room was a shambles.

He noticed that Cora moved stiffly, and when she sat down she lowered herself into the armchair gingerly. She winced with pain.

'What's the matter?' he asked.

'Why?'

'You're in pain.'

'So would you be.'

'Why, what have you done?'

'Only cracked some ribs.'

He gaped at her. Forgetting that they were estranged he said, with old familiarity, 'How the devil did you do that?'

'I fell down in a public lavatory. In Piccadilly. They'd just washed the floor, I think. I slipped on the tiles and crashed down on my back. Now I'm all strapped up with elastic bandage. Tomorrow I've got to see the doctor. What fun!'

She sat there glaring furiously at him.

'How many ribs?'

'Oh God, I don't know. Five. Six!'

Daniel shook his head. 'The things that happen to you,' he intoned mournfully.

'Don't they! Don't they!'

He said, after a moment. 'I thought when you opened the door, how glum you looked. Well, no wonder.'

She flashed him an angry look, and said grimly, 'It's not only the ribs.'

He sat waiting, listening to his inner self. Cora refused to say more. 'What is it, then?' he coaxed hopefully.

Still she wouldn't speak. Whatever it was, she clearly held him responsible in some way. Changing tack, he asked where Stephen was.

'He's in the bedroom.'

'Asleep, you mean?'

Cora laughed harshly. 'No, not asleep.' In a bleak mocking voice she went on, 'He spends a lot of time in the bedroom.'

Conscious of the thin walls in modern homes, he lowered his voice. 'Doing what?' he asked, not expecting an answer.

'It's got a mirror, a large one,' Cora said sarcastically.

He managed a weak grin. 'Will he be surprised to see me?'

She shook her head. 'I doubt it. But he'll be curious. Oh yes, he'll definitely be curious!'

Hearing sounds, her eyes came alive and gave a malicious sideways flick. Stephen came in. He eyed Daniel brightly, without visible fear. He drooped a little and his chest caved in, the kind of posture adopted by men of poor physique who are unsure of their reception. Daniel recognised himself. Cora would tell him, 'You ought to stand up straight, your posture's terrible, you look pregnant.'

'Hallo,' Stephen said. 'How was the journey? Not too nasty, I hope?' He wore the pale blue sweater Daniel remembered. His trousers of fine black and white check were in sharp new creases.

177

Daniel felt light-headed from sleeplessness and worry. I always have to please everybody, he thought. Now it's the seducer of my wife, the stealer of my child's mother. The blind fury he had felt surging through him at the cottage seemed to belong to another, quite different situation. He had the odd feeling that the word 'adultery' could never be made to fit this person, and not only on account of his sexual ambivalence. As if genuinely glad to see him, Stephen said, 'Won't you sit down?'

He sat wearily, feeling his anxiety ebbing away. What happened now? It was as though his will, which had driven him here tirelessly, had suddenly stopped functioning. He decided it was best to wait and do nothing: one false move could ruin everything. Cora kept eyeing him suspiciously – she was familiar with his bouts of ill-temper. He stopped being surprised by everything and gazed around curiously. At least he had a foothold in the place, and no one seemed inclined to get rid of him. Sitting there quietly, it occurred to him that perhaps Cora and the Irishman were simply bored with each other.

Stephen said, 'I suppose you've had a chance to look around the town?'

'No, I came straight here.'

'There isn't a lot to see, I'm afraid. You won't die of excitement here, even at the height of summer, will he, Cora?'

Daniel took this to be a reference to Cora's first visit. She muttered something under her breath.

'Pardon?' Stephen said. He raised his eyebrows ironically.

She lifted her head. 'Oh, sod off!' She looked at him with blazing eyes, hands twitching.

Stephen seemed to derive great enjoyment from this reaction. He brightened up and smiled, becoming more alert and interested. Shooting glances at Daniel, then Cora, he said teasingly, in a stroking voice, 'Perhaps you'd like to be alone for a moment? I think this could be the point at which one goes and makes tea.' He strolled across the room, skirting Daniel's feet. 'Excuse me,' he murmured. Daniel drew back his legs as Stephen made for another door, one the visitor hadn't noticed, and disappeared.

'So that's the kitchen,' he said mildly.

'Daniel, what do you want?'

'Want? I had a home and a family. I want it back.'

Cora laughed abruptly. 'You really expect me to pack my case and come back with you, is that it?'

'Yes.'

'To what?'

'If not for me, then for Clare's sake.'

'Not that. I was waiting for that one.'

'It's true,' he lied. 'She keeps asking for you.'

'I don't believe you.'

'All right, don't.'

She put a cigarette in her mouth, dragging angrily at the matches, spilling some. He bent down to pick them up.

'Leave them. You can see this place is a pigsty.'

'Doesn't it ever get cleaned up?'

'Once in a blue moon. You have to threaten to leave, do something drastic.' She pointed at the refrigerator. 'See that thing? I don't advise you to open it. The most appalling stink comes out.'

'Why?'

'God only knows.'

As always when she pulled on a cigarette, her mouth seemed to be sneering. Her eyes watched him, and as if spitefully. He couldn't decide what to do or say. Here he was acting penitently, when it was Cora who was the wrongdoer. A voice told him to wait, do nothing, while something deeper, buried in a pit, was calling for violent action.

His voice seemed to issue from him of its own accord. 'Why not pack your things?'

Cora took the cigarette from her lips and stared pop-eyed. Then she flung back her head and blew smoke at the ceiling. 'Give me one good reason.'

179

'Not here. Come outside. Let's go for a walk.'

'I'm sick of walks.'

'Please, I've travelled all this way.'

'More fool you. Nobody asked you to.'

'Ten minutes.'

Cora was silent. She stared balefully at him. Finally she said, 'My back hurts.'

'What time's the next bus?'

'You get it. I'm not going anywhere with you.'

Bowing his head, he made a big effort to accept this humbly. He could hear clattering noises from the kitchen. Gripped with sorrow, he bent forward. In a low croaking voice he said, 'You don't understand. I want you back. I need you.'

'That's rich,' Cora said, with a strange glint in her eye. 'When was the last time you needed me?'

'It's true.'

'And how about me? Have you ever stopped thinking of yourself for one minute and spared a thought for me? I'm so lonely. God, I'm lonely!'

Stephen came in with a round lacquered tray. 'Here we are,' he said pleasantly. 'A nice cup of tea, as they say.'

Cora's hand flew to her mouth. She rushed from the room.

21

They went out shopping, the three of them. Before setting off, there was a brief discussion. Stephen drawled, 'Look, I can go, if you tell me what to get.'

'Oh, come on,' Cora said. 'I could do with some fresh air.'

'Would you like me to make out a little list?' Stephen asked. He was serious, but also being coy. His goal was always the same, to convert every activity into fun and games. Cora had seemed to find this a delightful trait in England. Now she said sourly, 'You mean a big list. The pantry's empty.'

'Is it really? I hadn't noticed.'

They set off, marching down into the town through dead streets, three abreast on the deserted pavements. Cora gazed straight ahead into the far distance with a frozen expression.

They crammed into the first shop entrance, and Cora rounded on the two men. 'There's no point in us all trooping in, surely?' Daniel went out again and hung around outside with Stephen.

At a bakery, Cora stopped, went in, then stuck her head out of the doorway. 'I need more money.'

'Yes, of course, sorry.' Stephen fumbled in his pockets and came out with a fiver. 'Keep the change,' he called out facetiously.

They climbed back out of the town. Daniel saw a glittering surface over to their left – he had forgotten there was a sea. Since arriving here he had gone round in circles like a man blindfolded, seeing nothing, working nonstop on his urgent problem. Maybe he should give up trying to solve the impossible, he thought, and concentrate on details. Even as this ran through his mind, his arm moved; he took hold of the shopping bag. 'Here, let me carry that.'

'With pleasure,' Cora said.

'How's the pain?'

'It comes and goes.'

'Have you got it now?'

'Yes.'

'What did the doctor say?'

'What they always say: it'll take time. The ribs have to knit together. I'm supposed to rest a lot.'

Stephen, who didn't appear to be listening, jerked his head round to say, 'How jolly!'

'For how long?' Daniel asked.

'Ask the doctor. I'm seeing him tomorrow afternoon. This itching drives me insane. I want to rip this strapping off and scratch and scratch till I draw blood.'

'I can imagine.'

They tramped on. Suddenly Cora cried out, turning her face up to the sky, 'Why doesn't anything good happen to me?'

Her unhappy face was suffused with rage. Toiling upwards, Daniel saw again how disgusting life had become. For the first time he realised what a joke was being played on them by fate. Stephen, to his right, was gazing round and humming quietly to himself.

Indoors, finding himself still clutching the shopping bag, Daniel took it into the kitchen to empty the contents. The floor in there was raised a few inches. About to lift his foot over the step, he froze where he stood. A large grey rat was waddling slowly across the linoleum. Staring, Daniel couldn't accept at first what his eyes witnessed. Then he backed out again. He felt sick.

'I just saw a rat – a fat one!'

Stephen raised his head. 'Did you really?'

'Yes, yes! It wasn't even running.'

'What was it doing?'

'I don't know – taking its time! Sauntering! It's probably still there, among the groceries. Haven't you seen it in there before?'

Stephen widened his eyes infuriatingly in what was supposed to be concern. It looked more like delight. Keeping a straight face he murmured, 'No, not lately. It's not very hygienic, I agree. Let me have a look, shall I?' He got up from his chair and peeped round the door. 'It's gone, I think.'

'It was there, I saw it.'

'Oh, I'm sure you did. That was our house rat. Irish, naturally. All the time in the world.'

Daniel still couldn't believe the evidence of his eyes. He appealed to Cora, 'Have you ever seen it?'

'No,' she said indifferently.

'If I make a lot of noise,' Stephen said, 'and leave the back door open, that usually works. It wanders off next door.'

He went into the kitchen and banged doors and saucepan lids, then busied himself making omelettes with mushrooms and tomatoes. Daniel was certain he wouldn't be able to swallow a morsel, until the cooking smells wafted in. He realised then how famished he was.

That night he slept in the box room where Stephen stored his collection of modern first editions. There was a narrow iron-frame cot, and lots of green-painted shelving punched with holes, the kind you find in warehousing. Nothing else. The steel racks loaded with a comprehensive selection of modern literature went up to the ceiling and covered the whole of the longest wall. Stephen poked his head round the door. In a perfectly serious voice, he said, 'I hope you've got everything you need.' He wished Daniel goodnight and left, shutting the door carefully behind him.

Thankful to be alone in the silence, Daniel stared around at his cubicle. It was cold; he could see his breath. At first it didn't occur to him to wonder where Cora was, or how they slept. As far as he knew the bungalow had only one bedroom, one living-room, a bathroom, kitchen – and this. What did he care? He was here, he had got this far. He told himself it was only necessary to survive the night, that next day things would look different. In years to come he would recall these events and burst out laughing, he told himself, but with little faith in his prediction. Feeling lonely, he went over for a book, wondering if he could ever stomach the sight of print. He got into bed and opened the book, a copy of Genet's *The Thief's Journal*. He supposed the title aroused his curiosity. The bungalow was silent, so quiet that he could have been the only person in it. He strained to listen, something he always did in a strange place. What did he expect to hear? From outside, near the window, came the feeble piping of a bird, made frail by the night. His heart ached as he heard these tiny sounds, which meant more to him than any words. Sitting propped up against the chilly plaster of the wall, he fell asleep.

In the morning there was a tap on the door, then another, even more discreet. He had been lying awake for at least an hour. He called, 'Hello?'

It was Stephen, with a plate of the thinnest brown bread he'd ever seen, and a cup of tea. 'I've brought your breakfast.'

'Thanks.'

'Did you sleep well?'

'I suppose so. I don't remember, so I must have done.'

'That's good.'

Left alone again, he ate the two triangular slices, swallowed the tea, then scrambled out and got dressed. The air was still frosty. He went into the living-room and found it deserted. He strained to hear sounds through the thin wall of the bedroom. Was Stephen in there – and Cora too? No, he came in from outside, smiled, asked after Daniel's health and went out again.

Cora got up late, as always. At home she would be rough-tempered in the mornings, and here was no exception. Daniel managed to hold his tongue. In the afternoon they set off together in a silent posse of three to the surgery, descending to the same shops. Threading through one or two narrow streets they approached a large stone house in its own grounds, the tousled front garden full of rhododendron, laurel, trees losing the last of their leaves.

They sat waiting in silence in an upper room among half a dozen others. At last it was Cora's turn. As the door closed behind her, Stephen leapt to his feet. He pulled out a chair at the oval polished table in the centre of the room, sat down, took a pile of magazines, *The Ladies Home Journal*, *Woman's Realm*, *Vogue*, *House and Home*, *Queen*, *The Lady*, and set to work systematically leafing through them at high speed. His eye darting over the pages as his fingers flicked, he sat with bent head eating up the pictures and ignoring everybody. Watching him put Daniel in a trance. He shook his head. He was watching Stephen, even himself, like a dream in which he looked on and also participated.

Finally Cora emerged, and Stephen was forced to stop.

'Well?' Daniel said, as they went downstairs. 'What's the verdict? What did he say?'

'Nothing much.'

'You were in there twenty minutes!'

'Stop raising your voice.'

'Twenty minutes,' he hissed.

'I know.'

After that she wouldn't answer.

He dreaded the return to the bungalow with its air of unreality, blank walls, squalor. He saw himself squatting in it hopelessly for ever, getting nowhere. Anxiety seethed through him as they entered the living room. He decided to force a scene before his nerves disintegrated. It was worth gambling everything for the sake of real contact, hard though it had become even to speak. Stephen didn't arouse active dislike in him for some reason, yet his whole being challenged and irritated Daniel. Whatever he did seemed provocative, though how much of it was calculated he would have been hard pressed to say.

Stephen sat in a torn armchair and crossed his legs, affecting neutrality with his eyes while his mouth expressed faint amusement. 'Surely if she doesn't want to come home with you, that's fair enough,' he said at one point, hardly bothering to conceal his distaste at the thought of couples.

'I wasn't talking to you.'

'As you know, you can stay here as long as you like,' Stephen said languidly to Cora.

'She's got a daughter waiting.'

Stephen looked at Daniel in mock astonishment. 'Really, I can't see what that's got to do with anything.'

Daniel jumped to his feet, about to start yelling something. Cora said in a lifeless voice, 'Oh stop it. Take the damn suitcase if you like. How can I carry anything in this state? Anyway, I'm not ready yet.'

Daniel stood limply, overwhelmed where he stood by this sudden capitulation. Though he no longer felt capable of grasping anything, her words told him the one thing he wanted to hear. Sooner or later, she'd come. Their normal life would resume, enhanced rather than diminished by all that was happening now. They would learn from it how to value each other and what they had, how to cherish their child, how to be united again as a family. Who knows, it may have all been engineered in some chamber of her brain and then urged into being by her unconscious, which is prepared to act, to take risks, so it's said, even when we are not. 'I'm not ready yet.' This could only mean that his hell was temporary. With such knowledge he could hang on, live in hope, he told himself.

Cora stayed on obstinately for another fortnight. One

186

morning a note scribbled on the back of a picture postcard told him to expect her in Bradford in a few days, but without giving an actual date. He began haunting the Interchange platform, waiting for arrivals like a train spotter. Another card arrived, this time naming the day, Thursday. He raced down in the morning and met train after train. She didn't get off. It was already evening when he saw her at last. She swung down the platform with her angry stride. As she drew close he saw that she was indeed in a foul temper, her eyes snapping. He allowed a day to elapse before starting to grill her about this and that.

She answered defiantly at first. Then her disillusion and bitter resentment took over. Daniel listened passively, not interrupting as she poured out the story of her misfortunes. The night in London on the way to Ireland had been a total fiasco. In the hotel where they had shared a double room, Stephen shrank from her and clung to the edge of the bed. He had a dread of being touched by a woman. Then during the day he drove her mad by drooling over teenage girls with long hair wherever he went, in shops, a travel agency, on trains, even the doctor's waiting-room after she fell down in the public toilet. It wasn't any particular person he fancied, simply that he had a craving for the long hair of girls. His cold disregard of her feelings made her want to commit murder, then to kill herself. Soon she was desolate, lonelier than ever. At this point she stopped, stamped her feet, her face became distorted, she wailed, 'You can't imagine what it's like,' and burst into hysterical sobs.

PART THREE

FIRES

22

Daniel's mother continued to watch him fearfully, but asked no questions. He went out, came back in, and nothing was said. Now and then, to amuse himself, he scrawled a few disconnected notes for a novel about a man who goes in search of his runaway wife, embarking on a sea voyage in pitch darkness and coming face to face with a silver-tongued, cold surrogate self who is in love with the mind's caprices and nothing else. 'Imagination is memory,' Joyce had said.

He suspected his mother of believing that an illness such as his was always there in the shadows, biding its time to reappear. It saddened him to see her struggling not to involve herself in his downfall, if that was what it was, while at the same time her poor mind, unable to rest, demanded some explanation.

'You aren't going back to her, are you?' she brought out one day. It wasn't so much a question as a demand for confirmation.

'No.'

'You can't, can you?'

'No.'

'Something's happened, that's why,' she said, speaking on his behalf, even using a sorrowful voice to be united with him.

He sensed her bafflement. They reached agreement in a dumb silence. Even her brown eyes were like his. He would gaze into them uneasily and be reminded of himself. In the outhouse bathroom he stared into his own eyes, to see if they were as anxious as hers. Since he was invariably worried by the possibility, they always were.

'Yes, something broke,' he agreed, wanting to speak gently but frustrated by her deafness.

Her hearing aid wasn't switched on, he noticed. Half to herself, she mumbled sadly, 'It's all different now.' She sighed. 'Not like in our day. Your father and me could have had serious fights. Everybody could. We always got over them somehow. You had to. It was how you were brought up.'

Her morbid conscience gave her no rest. She would never refuse to take him in, he knew that. All the same, peaceful though it was here, an instinct warned him that it was time to move, he had stayed long enough. He shelved his writing, stopped toying with the idea of contacting Bridget again and forced himself to concentrate on practical matters. The joint account was nearly empty. His wife, who now regarded her surname as a bitter joke, announced her intention of getting rid of it without delay. 'I want a divorce, and my self-respect back,' she wrote. In his mind he had already handed over the house – and with a strange eagerness. Soon, approaching fifty, he would be free, homeless, without direction.

He ordered a week's supply of the *Western Morning News*. In one edition, the description of a tiny Dartmoor cottage for sale, only thirty miles or so from the hospital, caught his eye. The advert was impossible to miss, appearing in several issues as if aimed at him personally. In order to secure the place he would have to ask Cora to sign over what was left of their building society money for a deposit. He wrote to enquire. She protested angrily, then gave in. An even more reluctant bank manager advanced a short-term loan to cover the outstanding ninety per cent.

Was he still floating in the clouds? To repay such a loan so soon, was, he knew, virtually impossible. Nothing deflected him for a moment: he was in the grip of yet another obsession. He had no desire to view the place – in his imagination he was already installed there. When he did call to inspect it, his mind was already made up. Two thousand eight hundred pounds over two years – he signed all the forms and surrendered the deeds to the bank.

The cottage was empty and he could move in whenever he wished. Now the property was his, he set out on another visit. It was possible to reach Devon and get back again in a day. According to the survey the place was sound. Basically it was two very small rooms with a short passage along one side called a galley kitchen. He went in: it had been left bare and clean. Upstairs the space had been partitioned to create a bathroom, a space so small that it was necessary to close the door in order to squat on the lavatory. He would be on the end of a row of four cottages, called Railway Terrace. The railway no longer existed. A family lived in the converted station down the road in the direction of the open moor. Standing on the little bridge he saw how the gap between the two platforms had been filled with earth and grassed over. Geese and ducks wandered back and forth on it.

The hamlet itself, lost between austere rocky hills, had such a remote air that it scared him, though he pretended it wasn't so. The previous owners, who lived at the other end of the terrace, sold him the abandoned piece of threadbare carpet in the bedroom for a pound. In the small square barn a few yards from his cottage was a rusty bike. He bought this for a fiver. The barn went with the property. It was a grimy, dark hole, which he thought might be useful one day if he could afford to have it renovated.

To move in, he needed a few items from Cora: his bed, a kitchen table, a chest of drawers, the folding iron-framed contraption called a Z-bed, a tea chest of books and papers. In order to transport these bits he had to enlist the help of friends. Barry and Judith lived in a gaunt warehouse down by the old harbour at Plymouth. Barry was a painter-printer. His wife, a potter, taught at the city art school. They owned a large van. Although he had only known them for a year they insisted on helping him. Too discreet to mention his troubles, they knew, he guessed, that his marriage was over. Who could have told them? He didn't know or care. When he tried to express his thanks they became embarrassed. 'Think nothing of it,' Barry told him. 'One trip ought to do it. The kids will enjoy a ride over Dartmoor, and there's a ruined lead mine I'd like to photograph.'

Daniel knocked at their door one Saturday evening to stay the night. The next day, Sunday, was removal day. Judith, normally silent, actually enquired after his health. So they've heard about that too, he said to himself. Judith wore a heavy fringe down over her forehead. Small talk gave her such problems, and she would avoid speaking to visitors unless cornered. Barry, a tall bashful man with a handsome profile, seemed of a similar temperament. Daniel assumed they recognised the same traits in him.

Without looking at him directly, Judith said, 'You can have a bath if you like.'

Startled, he couldn't manage a reply. 'Well . . .' he began to mumble.

'The water's hot.'

'All right.'

She had a near silent, snuffling laugh. 'You don't have to if you don't want to.'

'I do, yes. I need to relax.'

She turned to her son. 'Gabriel, fetch a bath towel from the cupboard by your bed. Have you finished your homework?'

'Nearly.'

'Fetch the towel, then finish it.'

Judith apologised in advance for the clutter around the bed Daniel was to use. Justin, the younger, used the spot as a playroom. It was more a cubbyhole than a room. Nothing in their home was conventional; in fact it still had the appearance of a warehouse, with great scars on the

193

walls and iron hooks in the ceiling joists. You passed a bath stranded out in the open on bare planks, opened a door of unpainted hardboard and there was the bed in the makeshift room.

On Sunday there was a thick sea fog. Daniel wiped the dust from the windowpane and peered out, high over a narrow street. The other side of the street was visible but ghostly.

He went down to the kitchen. Barry was seated at the table, eating a fried breakfast which smelled delicious. He nodded cheerfully and said in a low shy voice that he had some work to clear up, then they could go. It would be warm later, he predicted.

In the afternoon they climbed into a blue transit van and rolled primly through the quiet Sunday streets. The sun emerged. Inside the van it grew steadily hotter. The two boys squatted on a mattress in the rear, whispering urgently with their heads together. Daniel sat on the front bench seat, his hip pressed against Judith, who gazed into the far distance like a Red Indian. Suddenly she said, 'Is she expecting us?'

'Cora? Yes, I hope so.'

He needn't have worried: Cora had simplified everything. The front door was open. Inside, he spotted the loaded tea chest. He led Barry upstairs to his bedroom for the single bed, then down to the basement for the other stuff. They worked swiftly, like burglars. Where was Cora? Come to that, where was her mother? Had they made themselves scarce deliberately? Soon his few possessions were inside the van. Last of all was a roll of dusty pink bedroom carpet.

As they drove off again and headed for the city boundary, Daniel took note of Barry's large workman's hands lightly resting on the wheel, his bulky shoulders in the blue fisherman's jersey. He looked calm, capable, a man perfectly at ease in the world of action and facts. Why did Daniel always feel this same world to be inconceivable?

For all his confidence, Barry had the slightly surprised expression of a boxer who had no idea how he had come to be in the ring. It struck Daniel that the inner strength of the household came from Judith, who sat there in silence exuding it. He sneaked a glance at her. She appeared to be smiling faintly. When he looked again, closer, she wasn't.

Perhaps feeling his eyes on her, she said dryly, 'So far so good. I expect you're glad that part's over.' He had the impression she was also speaking for herself.

'I am.'

'The rest should be easy.'

Soon they were entering Tavistock. Leaving a tangle of streets at the base of a hill, the van climbed steeply for two miles, under the great round arches of a viaduct and up farther, until the market lay below and Daniel saw the glinting water of a river.

They drove into the depths of nowhere for several miles, along a deserted straight road, still climbing. When they wound down into the village and pulled up, he could scarcely recognise his surroundings. To want to live in such an uninhabited region now seemed to him insane. The cottage itself had shrunk pathetically. Everything to do with it spelled poverty. A front door of cracking wood panels was daubed crudely with cream paint. One of the tin numerals was crooked. Barry got out and bustled to and fro energetically, in a hurry to unroll the pink carpet over the split green lino. It was as though he was eager to prove that this papered cupboard-like space with its two tiny windows – one deep in the stone like a porthole, staring out over the butcher's field, the other overlooking the churchyard wall – was indeed a living room. He went ducking out through the low doorway to rummage in his tool box. Hurrying back in, he brandished a sharp hooked knife. He knelt down and sawed expertly at the carpet until it lay flat around the hearth. The factory-made fireplace, covered in beige mottled tiles, looked an exact replica of the one in Stephen Gonne's bungalow.

Daniel stood watching, trying not to feel ashamed of the cottage's meagre proportions. Judith came to see for herself, and gazed down impassively at the pink linty expanse. Barry was pressing flat the cut edges with his heavy climbing hoots. Forgetting the hacked-out lump he was still holding, he stepped back to inspect his handiwork. Judith relieved him of it. He jerked his head up in surprise. 'What?'

She held the piece in the air by one corner like a scalp, its hairy fibres dangling. 'Did you want it for anything?'

Bewildered, he shook his head. 'Good, right, that's it,' he said, suddenly decisive, and picking up his knife he clumped out like a workman knocking off.

They piled into the van again and drove on, out of the village and over a high treeless waste. Daniel was soon lost. He sat like a sack, pondering his awful mistake and thinking, can anything be more remote than this? How will I bear it? Barry seemed to know precisely where they were. Excited, he pulled off the road near the half-demolished chimney of some old mine workings. The boys jumped out and began scrambling on the slabby rocks and among lumps of rusted iron machinery and loose shale. Then they wandered away downhill on the sparse turf like little serious old men.

Judith unpacked a picnic basket while Barry got busy with his camera. Daniel struggled with a fear, growing all the time, of being left alone here. He hated it – it was like the edge of nothing. They sat on a sheep-nibbled hillock with the wind whipping at them and chewed at the neat sandwiches without speaking. It was full summer, yet the sun shining on his back felt feeble, lacking in essential warmth. All it did was make everything, stones and turf and sky, take on the brightly lit unreality of a mirage.

'Would you like an apple?' Judith asked.

Barry sat twisting about on the ground uneasily. 'I can't see the boys. I believe there's water down there.'

Judith shrugged. 'They'll be here soon enough when they're hungry.'

'I suppose they can't come to any harm,' Barry murmured. Nevertheless, his gentle eyes were troubled.

'Here they come now.'

Their heads appeared, then their diminutive trudging bodies. 'We're eating the last sandwich!' Barry shouted.

The boys came on at the same pace. When they squatted down and waited politely for something to eat and drink they hardly spoke. Daniel wondered at first whether they were self-conscious because of him. No, it was normal behaviour. Everyone in this family seemed peculiarly muted for some reason.

By the end of the afternoon they were back at the cottage. Daniel thanked them, said goodbye and went quickly inside. The strangely doll-like cluttered cottage seemed to have nothing whatsoever to do with him. For a moment he thought he was thankful to be alone with his feelings. A choking feeling of homesickness overcame him. The van engine noise died away. Now the silence was like an enormous boulder sealing him in.

He had closed the door behind him. Hastily, he opened it again. Out there, nothing was moving. No cars came through, no one walked by, he couldn't see a cow or even a dog. A mouse, a beetle would have been welcome. 'It's Sunday,' he told himself forlornly. Turning back into the room he saw everything as if for the first time: the one chair, the single divan, cheap wallpaper, mean dimensions. He took the four steps to his deal table and sat down at it. Truly he was alone and had nothing.

He let out a yell, because any kind of noise in this emptiness was a comfort. Then he thought he might as well lie down. The divan faced him, but he had draped a cover over it and was trying to see it as a couch. The night was several hours off and he already longed for it, thinking that when it came he would cease staring at these miserable sticks of furniture and be obliterated. This was such a seductive thought that he felt immediately weak, as if his body had been craving sleep for days. He got up and shuffled to the stairs.

197

Upstairs, jammed into the tiny room, there was the portable iron-framed bed, looking like a cross between a table and a sewing machine. It took several minutes for him to work out how to release the lever and then prise the two halves of the contraption apart. He had used it once and that was years ago, when Stephen Gonne had visited them. Instead of unpacking sheets and a blanket he unzipped a bright blue-and-orange sleeping bag and crawled into that on top of the bed. The gaudy blare of it struck him as so farcical that he nearly started to laugh. In reality he was close to tears. With his knees lifted he gave up hope, attempting to curl himself around the shame and misery he felt.

The daylight was still strong. The curtains, provided by his mother and hung on a length of stretch wire, were too thin to darken the room. When all else failed, he thought, you shrank inside to the size of an infant. That was what he did. Burrowing down out of sight he shut his eyes. Still it wasn't black enough. Putting his palms to his eyes was better. He lay thinking of his predicament, of the poky room below, beyond that the vast barren moor stretching away. His last thoughts were of being snug in his mother's cottage, and of the house he had relinquished in order to be unmarried again.

When he woke, he found he was curled into a ball, hands against his face as though to ward off something horrible. It was nearly dark. Like an alcoholic, he lay in a stupor trying to decide whether it was twilight or daybreak. It grew darker. He had never been more grateful for anything.

The next morning he lay awake watching filtered summer light, hearing birds and a brief shout or two. The invincible silence clamped down again. His own sighing, full of dismal truth, pinned him to the bed. He struggled to pull himself together and not hide from the light. Finally he managed it by inventing errands, telling himself there was

198

food to get in, various odds and ends needed from the shop.

Downstairs he felt nausea, which eased after a cup of tea. Such a warm tranquil light entered the humble room when he drew the curtains that he began to feel differently about its meanness. Hadn't he in fact simplified his life? Maybe it was a question of inner weather, he reasoned. The walls and exposed ceiling joists fitted around him cosily, like a small cave. In some dirty city streets he would have been oppressed by a sense of squalor. Here, on the edge of the moor with its raw slopes and grey blowy air, he felt himself to be a cleaner kind of animal. To his astonishment, the thought struck him that he might even get used to it. Cheered by his own audacity, he stuck his head through the outer doorway.

A battered car was parked outside, its dents showing up clearly in the strong light. Hearing a sudden commotion he looked again. He was in time to see a young man skip out of the next-door cottage. He was carrying a briefcase. Just as incongruously, the trousers of his dark suit were sharply creased. Daniel stood back a little to watch. The youngster bolted down his few yards of cement path and through the gap in the low crumbling wall, wrenched at his car door, shouted 'Morning' in Daniel's direction and then drove off. The engine sounded rough; blue smoke billowed from the exhaust. The car charged at the corner and disappeared. Daniel came in stupidly smiling, like his father before him. His response to strangers was sometimes his late father's naive eagerness, sometimes his mother's peasant suspicion.

The young man in a hurry was a Londoner, he learned later – he had recently married a Devon girl. In the village store and post office, owned by another Londoner, Daniel bought a few tins, salt, some bread. The man was friendly and obliging. From the living quarters in the rear Daniel heard a woman's voice call out, 'Kathy,' and a child answer rudely, 'What?' He left the shop and went back to his cave, telling himself he had made a shaky start, but a start.

Past his barn and a row of disused padlocked lavatories there was a gaunt yellow house with stucco walls, ugly as a public urinal. Joined on to this was a butcher's, owned by the farmer who grazed bullocks in the field behind Daniel's cottage. This man did his own slaughtering, someone had said – was it the person who had sold him the cottage? How else would he have known?

The stench inside the shop was fearsome. Instead of a counter there was a soaking wet block, all pits and deep fissures. Daniel bought liver and half a dozen eggs. The farmer sliced the liver pieces thinly as requested and managed to avoid meeting his customer's gaze, while a buck-toothed woman in a bloody pinafore – who could have been his wife – wrapped the offal in old newspaper and gave change out of a grimy saucer, keeping her head well down. Daniel purchased liver because at the hospital they had given him lots of it as part of their campaign to build him up physically. He intended to eat it for nourishment but was prompted by nostalgia.

An old man came in, chattering and laughing to himself. He talked a curious lingo which was beyond Daniel, his snowy hair wild, his collar twisted. The butcher's woman greeted him like a relative, presumably because he was a native. On the way out Daniel remembered onions. He returned to the store.

The youngish shopkeeper stood behind his counter, this time glancing up keenly in recognition. He made for the onion skip with such enthusiasm that Daniel felt obliged to buy more than the one or two he actually needed. This man is a foreigner, and so am I, he thought suddenly, and felt a little better about everything.

That evening he cycled into town, four and a half miles according to the signpost. A lane out of the village coiled up a never-ending hill in a spiral. He was soon forced to get off and push the machine. It was hot, with a pale clear sky. The rising lane reached a junction, merging with an empty road that was sizzling underfoot. Another formidable long hill stretched ahead of him. He kept walking, past the High Tor Arms on his right, an ancient chapel known to tourists perched on its round hill in the field opposite.

Another third of a mile of hard walking and he was able to climb back on the saddle. The tarred road ran now for three miles straight as a ruled line, dropping steadily all the time. He flew along, freewheeling blissfully, without seeing any sign of traffic. He noticed a woman in a wire pen beside her solitary house throwing handfuls of corn to chickens as he went racing past. Instead of being encouraged by the sight of a human being in this wilderness, he clamped his lips tight to stifle a groan. It was no use, he would never stick it. The trees and hedges had no connection with him. Even the grass looked strangely alien. How carefree he must have appeared, sailing along effortlessly with the cool air pouring into his wet shirt as it ballooned over his spine, and what a lie that was!

In Tavistock he propped his bike against the kerb and walked into an ironmonger's, his stance falsely confident, his hot face set in a lie. He opened his mouth and more lies ran out, as he bought household goods for a home that was no home, said they were what he wanted, walked out with them in his rucksack and felt himself lying with every step.

When the rucksack was full he pedalled round the streets in search of a café, bumping on his back a red plastic bowl, red plastic collander, a set of Hong Kong cycle spanners in a red plastic holder, a white plastic cycle pump. He told himself, lying, that he still wanted a frying pan.

Near the market entrance, in a cobbled alley, he discovered a small café, all its tables with green tablecloths. On the way in he noticed a sheet of paper cellotaped to the side window: someone was desperate for accommodation and 'would consider anything'. The announcement, hand-printed in that bold childish style favoured by students, had a fancy border in different coloured inks. Daniel read the appeal, and at once thought of his barn standing empty.

The idea took hold of him. He would have company out there. There and then he composed a reply in his head, went out, brought a letter card and came back. A chubby girl wrapped in a flowered housecoat walked over. He asked for a coffee and the use of a biro.

'A what did you say?'

'You know – a ball pen. Or a pencil.'

Coming over again, she put down his coffee and a pen she'd borrowed from the woman at the till. 'Here you are, sir.'

'Thank you.'

'Anything to eat, sir?'

'No, that's all.'

He would have ordered something but was without an appetite. He would have liked the waitress to return, say something else. Sometimes a Devon accent sounded wily to his city ears, close-fisted. Hers was the nicest he had heard. She had the untroubled smile of someone who looked no further than her eyes could see because there was no point. He sat watching her move to and fro. Her young body swelled against her clothes, incurably opti-mistic: she was all promise and fruitfulness. He watched, unable to feel anything. If she had brought the whole world and its secrets to his table, his answer would have been the same: 'No, that's all.' He had torn himself away from his family and now he belonged nowhere.

He got up and left. Heading out of town he posted his scribbled message in the slot of a pillar box, then forgot about it completely. His legs still ached painfully from the long initial walk, even though he had coasted for miles afterwards. He shoved hard at the pedals a few minutes more. The streets tilted sharply up. Getting out of here was even harder work than leaving the village. Walking now, he toiled on in battering heat under the towering stone viaduct arches. As he sweated he reminded himself that the miles of effortless freewheeling on the descent now had to be paid for, and with interest. Nothing came free. In spite of his weakness, something in him laughed.

He climbed up and around the steep hairpin bends, a wonderful view behind him if he cared to glance back. The ground rose endlessly. After a mile and a half he heaved on to the saddle and bent to his task. It was such agony that he was forced to stop. A bike here is worse than useless, he cursed in his thoughts. Not for the first time he fought off an urge to throw it in the nearest ditch.

Later, creeping along in the twittering hush with the whole road to himself, he wondered again what had possessed him to come here. The matchless blue sky flooding down yellow light only made the air of vacancy on every side more intolerable. The sun shone mercilessly, like a demon intent on illuminating everything in his spirit which had been laid waste.

He laboured on with a creaking chain, nose touching the handlebars, until the sinews of his thighs shrieked for him to stop. He got off and walked again, feeling that his body was dwindling. He kept asking himself how it was that he'd become so deplorably weak, but not really asking – he was too scared. Whatever it was that afflicted him had come out of the blue, from nowhere, to suck his blood. He felt attacked by something insidious that he couldn't see or smell and was powerless to fight. He foot-slogged, pedalled a bit more, toppled sideways and walked again, like a drained corpse that refused to lie down and disintegrate.

23

Two days full of crawling hours passed. Daniel tired himself out with long directionless walks, going once across the moor to another village and sitting in a pub. He became the lone spectator of a darts match, idly eavesdropping on the conversation. He grew bored and left, glad for once of his own company. Another day passed. On the fourth morning, in an attempt to shame himself into action, he unzipped the case of his second-hand Olivetti, then was reduced to staring blankly at the machine.

Someone knocked at the door. Who could want him? Who knew him? His first instinct was to back away and grab something heavy with which to defend himself.

His heart pounding, he went to see. A smiling youth with a brown fuzzy beard and lank hair down on his shoulders stood waiting meekly. Leaning on the gate behind him was another youth, smaller and darker, white at the gills as if bilious. This one examined the ground at his feet.

'I'm David,' the pleasant one said. 'I've come about the advert. Well, we have. That's Ray, my friend. I'm David Wilcox.'

Confused, Daniel asked, 'What did I advertise?'

'No, our advert. It was ours. You answered it.'

Of course – it had gone clean out of his head. Feeling idiotic, he asked them in. They stepped inside respectfully, one trailing the other. The smiling youth ducked his head but his companion was short. Up close he looked even weedier. Maybe he's really sick, Daniel thought. His black hair had been chopped short by an amateur.

Out of practice, and always at a loss with strangers, he began to stammer. 'That's right, the barn,' he got out. 'Yes, I remember. Here, sit down.'

He possessed a round wicker chair, worm-eaten, which squeaked loudly when sat upon, and a hard upright chair with a cushion for use at the table. If he had owned more furniture there wouldn't have been room for it.

David smiled winningly as he explained that they were broke. However, when Ray got his student grant through in the autumn and he, David, registered for dole, they would be solvent again. Daniel told them he wanted nothing for the use of the barn – if they could fix it up they were welcome to live there. It needed a little cash spending on it, but mainly work. 'Are you handy with tools?'

They exchanged doubtful looks. He saw that his idea was a non-starter. 'We'll have a dekko, anyway,' David said, 'if you don't mind.'

Daniel handed over the key to the padlock and they marched out to investigate. When Daniel decided to find out what was keeping them, he was surprised to see them out in the road, on the point of leaving.

'The key's in the lock,' David called. He gave his girlish smile, and Daniel noticed again his smooth forehead free of care and his pink cheeks and lips. His beard was so fine, it was possible to follow the line of his chin. The boy made a pleasant impression, so Daniel called, 'Not interested?'

'I reckon it's too small for us.'

'Yes, it's small.'

'We're both married, see. And Ray here's got a nipper.'

'Oh. Then it definitely is.'

'So long,' David said. 'Thanks very much.' They moved off.

Although Daniel felt certain they would have had next to nothing in common, still he was sad to let them go. But was it such a good idea? Having them so close, sharing the water supply, electricity and so on, could have brought problems. He regarded it now as a moment of weakness on his part. When people are desperate they seize on any solution, and the results are often disastrous; either that or they seek satisfaction in their own pride. He wondered if he still had any, or if he had reached the stage at which you were stripped of such luxuries.

An instinct warned him that to remain idle in solitude was asking for trouble. Though he had despised routines all his life, he began to hunger for one. What did he do now with his days? As soon as darkness fell he crept upstairs and closed his eyes like a dumb animal, staggering down at eight in the morning because the alternative was too frighteningly voluptuous. His lust for life had sunk so low, he could imagine himself dying of inanition between the sheets.

He would get himself out of bed by deliberately worrying about money, or rather the lack of it. Then, with the radio switched on and a pot of tea made, he forgot to follow up the worry. Nevertheless, after two weeks of guilty idleness, he had begun to make progress towards the creation of a routine which, though gaping with holes, worked after a fashion. As to the future, Judith had promised to find him a few hours of teaching in the liberal-studies department at her school of art in Looe Street, a few hundred yards from where she lived. But that was over a month away.

In the mornings he hammered out applications to foundations and charities for grants he guessed he had little chance of obtaining. Yet if he attempted to write simply to please himself, his stomach sickened. As a compromise he made random notes for a novel set in Ireland, to be called *The Disappearance*. If he had an aim of any kind it was to hit on a light humorous note. Whatever he wrote soon pulled him below the surface. Was it possible, he asked himself, to treat disintegration zestfully? He often felt he was rowing over water that was full of lurking monsters.

Also, he was conscious of grief, of the sorrow in him and in everyone who walks this earth. He remembered a saying from the eighteenth century he had come across once, in a ragbag of a novel by Saul Bellow, and he would remind himself of it: 'Grief, Sir, is a species of idleness.'

Each afternoon he strolled out to stretch his legs, ignoring the weather. Usually he felt ridiculous if he walked simply for exercise, but this was exercise in the prison yard to sort out his thoughts. He mooched around in a wide ring, circling the deserted village and arriving back, after half an hour, at his own front door.

Sometimes vivid memories would unwind themselves, gripping his heart, or he would create strange expectations within himself. Reaching his door one day he wanted to knock on it, imagining that Cora had paid him a visit and was sitting inside waiting to greet him.

He struggled to stay occupied. His mind wandering, he remained aware of himself as dangling in a summer which grew ever more listless, dark with omens, not knowing whether to rot or revive. The idea of winter stirred in him now and again like a lost energy source. One day, needing to break the monotony, he caught one of the few local buses and rode into Tavistock to join the library. This was only a large room knocked out of two, smelling strongly of wax polish. There wasn't much of a selection, but that suited him. He walked out with a biography of Hemingway by Carlos Baker. He was no admirer: what he needed was a true story which would serve as a long read for the evenings, to be rationed out a bit at a time. It mattered little that the tale was a familiar one. He found he was more impressed by the illustrations than the text; by, for instance, a photograph showing in close-up the suicide's famous elongated grin of sprung teeth, at which he stared repeatedly.

Another day, driven by the urge to seek out people and at least hear them converse, he tramped up to the High Tor

Arms for a snack and a drink. He was soon bored. On the way down again, he had reached the junction and was turning into the lane when he saw one of the hippies. It was David, standing on the corner by a farm fence, his arms full of groceries. Seeing Daniel, he waited, smiling his smile.

'How's things?' Daniel asked.

'Great.' David nodded in the direction of the farm behind him. 'This is where we live. We found a place.'

'In there?'

'Yeah, round the back, like. There's an annexe built on, that's where we are. We've got the whole annexe, not bad.'

Daniel said spontaneously, 'Well, I'm glad you're fixed up,' and was about to move off when the youngster said, 'Come in and have a look, unless you're in a hurry that is.'

Daniel laughed. 'Hardly.'

'Down this path and round the side of the house we are.'

They came to a side porch, which had a heap of muddy gumboots blocking the doorway. David kicked a path for himself, went through, and Daniel followed. They entered a small smelly room, the curtains partly drawn. What was the pungent odour? Focusing properly, Daniel saw a baby in a vest and grubby blue rompers, misshapen at the rear end, tugging at the spines of old paperbacks on some shelves improvised from planks and piled housebricks.

Passing through another opening they came to the kitchen, a large barren space with scabby distempered walls. There was a deep yellow sink of thick porcelain and an Aga cooker. A girl with long blonde hair sat at the table, shelling peas over a pastry bowl. David let his groceries slither down in front of her. 'Ali,' he said good-naturedly, 'I told you about this guy who's got a barn.'

Daniel thought at first how alike the two were, like blood relations. The girl laughed affably without replying.

David stood dreamily at her side. 'Can I do anything?'

'Just put the kettle on, love, eh?' Ali tossed her hair out

of her face and got up. Daniel was surprised to see that she looked no older than a schoolgirl.

Another girl came in, thick around the waist, with spiky black hair and a bony forehead. About the same age as Ali, she gave the impression of a certain maturity. Her sharp pasty face and broad hands spoke of hard experience. This time Daniel was struck by her resemblance to Ray. It was as if both youths had found their female counterparts. Jo, the baby's mother, asked him bluntly in Ray's accent if his barn was now occupied.

'No, it's empty.'

'I like barns.'

'Where are you from?'

'Dewsbury,' she said, then adding needlessly, 'so is Ray.'

Invited to sit down, he did so. They drank tea out of mugs, and David and Jo rolled cigarettes. After a while Ray came in. He acknowledged the visitor with an unsurprised nod and dumped himself down, in his dirty stained shirt and black waistcoat, staring down at nothing in a fuddled way. Jo went out and reappeared with the baby under one arm like a parcel. Both she and the baby, Daniel saw, had turned-up button noses. 'Good sleep?' she asked Ray.

He didn't glance in her direction; he merely looked disgusted. 'I doan remember,' he muttered. Then he said, ''Ello, where's me fag stuff?' and started patting his clothes. Jo pushed her makings across the table.

Daniel, for something to say, mentioned that he'd completed a teacher-training course. Ray, in the act of lighting a cigarette, coughed violently once or twice. He glanced over at Daniel civilly. He was in his second year, he said. It wasn't bad. If he got too bored he swallowed a tab. Daniel had to guess what this might mean, but kept his ignorance to himself. Ray went on, 'If it's raining I think, stuff it, and roll over. It could be worse, though. They have it in for you if you stay away a lot. Hurts their egos, like.

209

One lecturer last term said thank you once when I walked in late through the door. Cheeky bastard, I thought, and burst out laffin'.'

David asked, 'What did he say?' In anticipation of the answer he smiled agreeably.

'It worn' a he, it were a she. A real dried-up, moanin' little toffee-nosed twat. She went deaf, like.'

It was three weeks before Daniel saw them again, one Saturday night. He had been in to the city at the invitation of Judith and Barry. Staying later than he intended, he caught the last bus to Tavistock and then a taxi. Sitting in the dark as the cab burrowed rapidly through tunnels of trees, up that long straight haul he had once agonised over, he found himself wanting to delay his arrival home. As they swung round the farm corner he noticed windows ablaze at the rear of the building. 'Let me out here, please,' he told the driver hastily.

Daniel settled the fare, the man turned his taxi and the darkness swallowed it up. From inside the annexe came the sound of music and voices. Daniel hesitated, about to turn away. He wandered up and touched the bell, and was standing there doubtfully when Ali appeared. She called out, 'Hey, hello stranger – come and join the party!' Laughing gaily into the night she threw the door wide open in welcome.

Not wanting to seem churlish, Daniel stepped forward. 'What's it in aid of?' he asked rudely. 'Is it somebody's birthday?'

'Not as far as I know. Don't you like parties?' she asked, and laughed again. She had made up her face and was wearing a dress.

'Yes and no.' If he told the truth, he didn't understand them. Each time he had been trapped into going to one he had disliked it, yet for some mysterious reason the word created expectations in him. He imagined this to be normal.

Ali said over her shoulder as they went in, 'Where have you been keeping yourself?' He made no attempt to

210

answer. It was one of those meaningless remarks thrown out when one's mind was elsewhere. Ali, a nice open girl, eager to rejoin her friends, was the decent-hearted type of person who hears the doorbell and feels glad.

As often happens at parties, over a dozen people – many of them on the floor – were piled into the smallest room they could find. David acknowledged Daniel and picked his way across, smiling and vague as ever. 'Hang on, I'll find you a cushion,' he said in his pleasant boy's voice, standing up close and seeming concerned and serious, yet not making a move. Somehow his eyes looked peculiar.

'Don't worry.'

Daniel sat down on the grubby carpet, his back propped against the row of tatty science-fiction paperbacks. People were squashed convivially together around the walls. Music played on a tape, the same variations repeated again and again in an endless monotony, papering the room with blurred sound.

The sweet smell in his nostrils should have meant something, but it was so long ago that he'd forgotten. Cora had once wanted to try marijuana. One of her acquaintances, a young upholsterer, offered to initiate them. As Daniel didn't normally smoke he wasn't inhaling deeply enough. Cora filled her lungs with great determination. Nothing happened to her either. At one point she said hopefully, 'I think my palms are sweating.' A jam-jar of water on the table, to flush away the evidence later, was all he could remember in the way of excitement.

Sitting on the carpet and feeling foolish, he listened in on what conversation there was. As at all parties, nothing was being said that amounted to anything. Here, though, the snatches of talk didn't even make sense. He soon gave up trying to unscramble it. Ray, sitting in the murky gloom opposite him, seemed far gone, his chin drooping on his chest.

He caught a glimpse of the joint being passed from hand to hand. He saw it reach Ali, and noticed too her charming little gesture as she handed it on. It came to him, and without putting it to his lips he gave it to the man on his right, a hunched bearded fellow in his thirties. 'You don't partake?' the man said.

'I've got this instead.' Daniel had found a flagon of cider. Raising the bottle to his mouth he took a long drink.

'Is it that you don't approve?' the man asked, clownishly droll.

'Who am I to disapprove? Each to his own drug.'

'Right,' the man said. 'What's your name, by the way?'

Soon Daniel's backside was aching, his legs stiff. He drank more cider, still self-conscious about his age. Luckily he looked younger than his years. Before long he realised that it made no difference – no one was paying him the slightest attention. The man on his right had turned away and was engaged in a slow intricate conversation with someone lying down. The cider worked its gradual transformation of his character as he waited hopefully for any interesting developments. Finally he gave up and left.

Outside again, walking unsteadily down the winding and sinking lane, he concluded that the intimate scene he'd just witnessed was devoid of reality. Why then, he wondered, did it cling to his mind like a dream which nagged to be given a meaning? A vast sheet of stars hung over him. The night had begun to turn chilly.

Suddenly he craved to feel the bite of winter. All summer he had been idle as a snake. Waking up in the mornings, he liked to think of tasks waiting to be accomplished.

First of all he would go downstairs into the silence, like descending into a well. From being a feared thing, this was now his reward for a solitary life. He would seat himself at the table. The sound of the silence would put a trance on him. It was as if a gigantic bell had struck once, too far off for him to hear, and he sat there experiencing the vibrations. One autumn day was followed by another in hypnotic procession, coming to rest and ripening, each one golden and still, like ancient women.

24

When he began to teach at the art school on Fridays, this became the highlight of his week: not that he regarded it as work in any real sense of the word. No more than eight students would gather to resist his pronouncements. They would oppose him passively, usually dozing off with their eyes open. If they were anything, they were anti-lecturer. So was he, he mused, but they weren't aware of that.

Nothing he said was ever directly challenged. Perhaps when they knew him better they would find the nerve to confront him with their objections. He hoped so; it would lessen the boredom. Modern prose began with Hamsun, he told them. 'Who's heard of Knut Hamsun?'

They stared resentfully at him. One boy at the back grinned cockily. Being provocative in this situation was a waste of time, Daniel decided. Soon he was dissatisfied with saying whatever nonsense entered his head and read them short stories from an anthology, as if reading to children in a kindergarten. Someone would mutter at the end that they didn't think much of it. 'Can you say why?' 'No.' He learned the trick of never reading aloud from anything he felt passionate about – it was too upsetting.

For him the exciting part of the day was the journey in, for it meant breaking out dramatically from his fastness. He would relinquish the wilderness joyfully, then reclaim it with gratitude that same evening. John, his next-door neighbour, gave him a lift as far as his factory on the city boundary and then he carried on by foot through three miles of suburbs. Getting out of the car, he shivered with the thrill of being released, set free – it was such a marvellous prospect. He swung along in a wash of memories and with each stride he relished anew his state of independence. The road thundered with rush-hour traffic, thousands of people with grim faces hurrying to jobs they either detested or endured without question.

The more he dwelt on the strange course of his life, the more preoccupied he became with its complexities. The ordinary was extraordinary, as he had always suspected. His route took him down a last hill – from the crest of which he could catch a glimpse of the sea – and past the mouth of Cora's street. Whenever he reached this point he felt the goosepimples rise on his skin. What was she doing at this moment? Of course, she would be asleep. He felt a pang of grief, a mourning for something betrayed and lost for ever, and yet part of him rejoiced that it was over. He knew he would never go back. His recent agony was all deserved: the pain he'd inflicted on her was unforgivable. Between the two of them, things had finally come to a climax. When a woman tore off her veils and showed the face of a destroyer, that was the end. If you could move, you ran. Was he muttering aloud, or were these his thoughts? He shuddered again at the memory of that final picture, which dripped blood, and was the same the world over.

One of the art school lecturers, a woman, reminded him of someone from his past. Had it been at the hospital? Who could it be? Ah, he remembered, it was Miriam, a mature student in his English group at college. Maybe this lecturer's mouth bore a certain resemblance to Miriam's which he pictured as fleshy, sardonic, helplessly provocative. Even now, to recall it made him smile.

Miriam was also funny, with a down-to-earth funniness. Talking to her had been a refreshment. Her dry comments came thick and fast. She had a fruity chuckle, veering towards bawdy. She showed her uneven teeth a lot. Daniel would be buoyed up by their snatches of conversation, brief though they were. Whenever he poked his head into the noisy Common Room and failed to see her there he had been disappointed. The feeling had stayed with him to this day, even though he couldn't recall now what it was they talked about. He could see her yellow hair, her fringe, the impish twist to her mouth, and a mixture of slyness and innocence in the eyes as she expressed some opinion or other – often prompted by her scepticism concerning experts. She made a strong physical impression. After meeting her he would carry away sensations that remained active, like the vague sensual disturbances at the edge of his consciousness when he woke up on certain mornings.

One desperate Saturday, about to fall into a pit, he found himself snatching at these disconnected bits of her. Concentrating, he was rewarded with her lazy, wide-hipped walk, more of a saunter, which seemed, like her mouth, grave and insolent together, to be telling him things about her he should appreciate.

For someone like him, living alone, the weekends – when families were reunited – could be especially bleak. His few hours at the art school had forced on him an old awareness of Saturdays and Sundays. He felt himself sinking slowly and horribly. Picking up a handful of loose change he ran out of the door and up the road to the call box outside the butcher's. He thought as he ran that either his impulse or the void would win – which would it be? The operator would, he hoped, track down Miriam's phone number. Although the risk of defeat was great, didn't something worse hang over him? What did he have to lose that was worth bothering about?

Miriam lived in Exmouth, which meant that they had the same county in common. Her husband, if he remembered correctly, was a builder who worked for himself. They came originally from Leicester: he believed she once said that her parents had retired to Devon. He liked to

215

hear how a person landed up in a particular place – it was a short cut to discovering what tricks life had played on them. In Miriam's case, there had been no opportunity to follow the trail very far. When he asked her how she had come to follow her parents south, she replied, 'It's a long story. Are you sure you really want to know?'

Obtaining a number, he took a deep breath and dialled it.

'Hallo?'

He recognised the voice at once. In his relief and embarrassment he started to babble, Miriam listening patiently as he explained as briefly as possible what had happened to him since they had lost touch with each other. He paused to gulp down some air. 'Well, what a surprise to hear from you,' was her only comment. Her tone sounded as friendly as it had always been.

To his astonishment he heard himself blurt out, 'I thought I might pay you a visit.'

Without a second's hesitation, she said, 'Oh, good.'

'You'd like me to?'

'Yes, I think you'd better. Wait – excuse me a minute.' He heard her speak to someone across the room. 'Go on.'

'When would it be convenient?'

'I don't mind. I'm always here.'

'Are you sure it's all right?'

There was a small pause. He thought he heard a faint chuckle. 'Quite sure. It's not every day I get the chance to talk over old times.'

Hearing her indulgent tone made him want to laugh with pleasure. It was as if she were winking at him. Thanking her, promising to call again and propose a definite arrangement, Daniel hung up and walked back the few yards to the cottage, elated but in a conflict. Had he clambered out of one hole by digging another? That, as he knew from past experience, was a bad habit of his. Anxiety billowed up. What was he about to get into this time? Here he was, sometimes intensely lonely but with a life blessedly free of complications. Did he really want more entanglements? No, definitely not. This time, he vowed, it would be different; he'd act cynically from the outset.

On Sunday morning, the instant he woke up he thought, I'm no longer alone here. Someone's expecting me, thinking of me, perhaps at this very moment. Though fully conscious of Miriam's powers as a woman, he actually liked her – a new experience for him. Also he believed he saw her without idealism. How many men have said the same? She talked plainly and honestly and yet somehow, it seemed to him, managed to avoid confronting the truth about herself. Her funny twists and turns had intrigued him. She appeared to have no guile, no coy devices. In essence she was as naked as a pagan. What must she be like in a passion, setting aside her tonic qualities? Once or twice she had hinted at ecstasies, cravings. Lying in bed, he felt a rush of heat. If she was in chaos underneath, withholding knowledge from herself in order to survive, then he, too, another survivor, wanted to sink down in the mud with her, chaos and all.

Sunday afternoon was the time when he phoned his mother, out of duty and from shame at having deserted her so readily. These expected calls were acts of pity which he felt degraded them both. This Sunday, feeling guiltier than ever, he rang in the morning.

As usual, it was hopeless from the start. His mother pleaded with him to speak louder, and he was shouting already. Even before phoning the thought of his ordeal would cause him to sweat, but he knew how desperately she waited for his call. Sunday was her worst day, engulfing her in darkness, now that her simple faith had collapsed. The brutal truth was, he thought, she had made his father her god and her religion.

'Speak up, please,' she was imploring. 'It's no good, I can't hear you. Oh, now I can.'

'Is that better?' He stood cursing under his breath a contraption which seemed at times a miracle, at others an instrument of torture.

217

'It's a terrible faint line.'

'There, my mouth's closer to the mouthpiece. How about now?'

'Daniel . . .'

'What did you say?'

'I'm so lonely . . .'

'Yes.'

'Don't you ever get lonely, all by yourself there?'

It was a crucifixion. Propped upright, he glared savagely through the little frame close to his head where the pane of glass was missing. Black water rose in his chest. And this time his feet itched to be somewhere else, in Exmouth – another secret to be kept from her. He was rotten with secrets. Meanwhile, the ghastly plight of his mother wailed in his ear. He was horrified, and yet resented it bitterly, as if his heart had frozen. Words of comfort for her deaf ears jammed in his throat. He said, 'I'm thinking of going on a trip.' This admission led him on to say, 'Look, I'll have to go soon.'

'Why doesn't Anthony ever ring me?'

'You should ask him.'

'Sometimes I think I've only got one son.'

'Mum, listen . . . can you hear me? I'm going on a short trip. Soon.'

'Where are you going?'

'Exmouth. Not far from here.'

'Goodbye then, son.'

'No, I don't mean now, not this moment. Soon. A little later.'

He thought he heard pitiful sounds. Ashamed, his heart steely with ice, he dropped the phone.

It seemed to Daniel that he could still hear her. Certainly he could see her. Walking away numbly, he realised as he reached his door that she had suddenly heard him perfectly well, asking where he was going but taking care not to ask the reason. To suspect one's mother of jealousy was for him tantamount to having an obscene thought, like imagining her in a state of lust. Yet he knew she was capable of the first, if not the second. Not long after his father's death, when he was staying for a few days – really in order to see Bridget again – he happened to announce that he was going out for the evening.

'Where are you going?' It was the same phrase exactly. On that occasion too she couldn't bring herself to ask the person's name.

'For a drink. With Bridget and Jack.'

Daniel's involvement with Bridget had no doubt reached her in the form of rumour. His mother seemed to choke. Her face darkened and she clutched at the edge of the kitchen door and hung on, while a wave of violence distorted her. In a voice unlike her own, primitive and mad, she screamed, 'Go, then, if that's what you want! Don't bother to come back!'

Afterwards she sobbed brokenly and crouched against him, begging to be forgiven. While she clung to his coat Daniel was clinging to his resolve, with the blind obstinacy he used to detest in his father. He went out, promising not to be late.

He reached the pub. Bridget, who was accompanied by her husband, stared into his face and said, 'Aren't you feeling well? You look as if you've seen a ghost.'

'I've seen something,' he said. 'I think I need a brandy.' When he tried to laugh, it came out shaky.

25

Unsure of his intentions, he wrote to Miriam as a means of giving himself more time. He went on several trips to Exeter, to sit in the reference library there and engage in sporadic research for the Lawrence book. The agent had asked for what he called a precis. If by that he meant a programme or a new point of view, that was that, he thought – he'd be stumped. He simply hoped that by re-telling the somewhat hackneyed life story in his own words he would discover what he, personally, thought and felt.

In the meantime he wrote more notes for the Irish novel, called now *The Condemned Man Rejoices*. Once, long ago, he had written a poem with this title. Trying to recall it, he walked up and down, taking the few steps in each direction which the tiny room allowed. Stirred, he sat at the kitchen table to rattle off on the typewriter a line or two from memory:

> Nothing surprises him,
> locked in his pen for a long stretch,
> the blanket foul with knowledge,
> a surge of blossom at his thief's mouth ...

Out of doors, the air had become much colder. As autumn took hold, the moor seemed to raise itself, to show bones. It stood high over the village, a huge bulk rusting out. Then it began to burn dully to a brown waste. Another winter was in the offing. Wind and cloud shadow grew teeth and raked over the sapless bleached grasses. Whenever there was a lull, the moor's silence fell like a blow. Up on the bare rocks by the old chapel the world was all sky and minerals. Light splintered against his eyes with a roar.

Notes for his novel came thick and fast, prompted to some extent by the season. With the cold air came energy. It had been November when he had lifted up Cora's suitcase, a black cardboard monster, and made for the door with it. Staggering, he found he could hardly carry it, but by then it was too late to ring for a taxi, and he was eager to appear strong. He summoned up the strength by reminding himself that he was walking away with her dresses, shoes, books, and that now he had these in his possession she was bound to follow.

A bus took him to the dock gates at Dun Laoghaire. With the darkness, a foggy drizzle had descended. He started to hump the accursed case over the greasy cobbles for the final two hundred yards. Halfway there, when his back was running with sweat, an urchin who seemed no higher than his waist darted out of a dripping stone passage to his left. 'Mister, will you be letting me take that?'

Daniel ignored him because it seemed absurd, and went on. The small boy was shadowing him. Daniel dropped the case again with a gasp. The lad ran round from the rear and seized it. As if by magic he got it on to his back and was trotting beside Daniel, bent almost double.

The boat reared up. He was there. His helper pocketed Daniel's change and was gone, swallowed by the fog, before he had time to thank him.

Soon the night ferry was moving. As the gulf widened until he could no longer see the shore, a chorus of farewells rose up, strong at first, then fading. 'Bye, Paddy! So long! God bless you and keep you, son!' Daniel was held to the rail, transfixed, the sounds were so utterly forlorn. He heard one wailing cry, a female's: 'I love you, Pad!' He stood as if nailed to the deck by this cry of distress. The

221

ferry wallowed around and then ploughed away stumpily at the open sea, rising and falling to a slower, deeper, profoundly ancient rhythm. All at once he felt an impulse to laugh. Was there anyone on board who wasn't called Paddy, he wondered, apart from himself? And even the thought seemed Irish. He wanted to laugh into black night at the shame and sorrow, in spite of everything. The wooden rail was wet with drizzle. Gripping it with both hands he leaned out his shoulders and upper body to feel the sensation, hanging out in space over the churning water as far as he dared.

An old man appeared outside his cottage, lingering by the gate and scowling up at the roof. Was he selling, begging? He wanted to sweep the chimney. He said, 'This 'ere's a vacuum job,' pointing at something that looked like a washboiler on wheels.

'How do I know if it needs sweeping?'

The sweep stood raking his filthy cracked nails over his grey stubble and squinting. He grumbled, 'You could 'ave a bird's nest in it.'

'All right.'

'Best to be sure, I allus say.' He unlooped the black rubber flex. 'You get a proper job, boss. No mess with a vacuum, that's the beauty on it.'

On clear December nights, if it was a Friday and he'd stayed in town for drinks and maybe supper, he would turn himself out of the taxi by the farm and descend the lane from the empty main road beneath the stars. It was exposed up there. Sometimes the cold onslaught was so savage, he felt like an animal. Leaving the cab, he would reel back and stiffen, telling himself it was good, he liked it. The night sky bent down with a pure ferocity. He walked fast, hissing between his teeth, stepping warily on the greasy skin of frost, his flesh shuddering. The thick stars thrust forward, insanely bright, making his eyes ache. Dark earth banks rose on either side of him, stern as iron.

The lights below among scattered houses and farms winked on and off as though crackling with cold.

He realised now that he was anticipating the first snows, waiting for them to fall and bury the landscape overnight. He had heard some of the old tales: he had visions of being cut off for weeks, and didn't fully understand his disappointment when it failed to happen. Was he hoping for extremes so that he could surmount them, or did he hope for a transformation within himself which would match the weather?

One raw winter night he had a caller. It was after midnight. He had been sleeping badly lately, so he thought he would stay up as long as possible and exhaust himself. He sat hunched over the remains of a log fire. Emptily musing, he jumped nervously when someone knocked on the door.

'Who's there?' he called.

'It's me, Jo. From up the road. Can I come in?'

She was white-faced and startled. He made her welcome, though he had learnt that surprise visitors were often a disappointment. Living alone as he did, he sometimes dreamt of miraculous apparitions, thrilling beings. Jo wore her scruffy brown duffel coat, under it the usual shapeless sweater and patched jeans. Had she and Ray fallen out? Her short hair stood on end. She's like a pasty-faced boy who's interested in nothing, his thoughts ran. Yet he still hoped for some drama, maybe an account of a fight up there. Nothing emerged. Everything was unchanged. Her face remained blank.

'I felt like a walk,' was all she would say, listlessly.

They sat together in a sexless silence. Eventually, after he had made a chance remark, she volunteered to trim his hair. He thought of Stephen and Cora. He sat on a stool with a towel around his neck and she chopped away quite deftly, producing a fringe. It could have been an interesting experience, he told himself ruefully when it was done.

Suddenly she said, 'I'd better go now.'

223

She bundled herself up against the cold again. Any hint of a female disappeared. Yet she was a mother. Daniel gave up trying to puzzle it out.

At the door, she still didn't smile. 'Tarra.'

'Goodnight. Tarra!'

26

All at once he was swamped by a sentimental desire to see Ruby again. He wrote to her, and she sent a stiff little note accepting his invitation, saying, 'Joe Baker, one of the nurses, is a good friend of mine. He says he can fix it up. Thank you for asking me. Your truly, Ruby Martin.' For the first time he became acquainted with her surname.

The visit wasn't a success. They came in a transit van, with Ruby's chair folded and stowed inside. Joe Baker, it turned out, was the nurse who had injected Daniel with insulin. 'I ought to remember you but I don't,' he said. 'I've got a terrible memory for faces.' He was stocky, dark, with small quizzical eyes under straight eyebrows. He set about unloading the chair and transferring Ruby to it with professional jauntiness. 'There you go, love – watch out for the traffic. No speeding eh!' Daniel stood by with no part to play.

They walked down the lane together in the direction of the station that was now a home, and the bridge over tracks which now had to be imagined. So did the past which Ruby and Daniel had once shared. Joe doubled back for his cigarettes and Daniel pushed Ruby along in a glum silence neither of them seemed willing to break. How strange – Ruby was no longer Ruby to him, away from her usual habitat. As if reading his thoughts, she said, 'You've changed, Daniel.'

'Yes, I expect so. I'm normal now.'

'Is that what it is,' she muttered.

'I'm glad you could come.'

'Thank you for asking me.'

'It was only selfishness. I missed you.'

'Is that a fact,' she said dubiously.

'Don't you believe me?'

She was silent for a moment. Then she said, 'I feel funny.'

'Funny?'

'I shouldn't have come.'

'You don't like me much now, is that it?'

'I don't know you.'

'Aren't we friends any more?'

'If you like. Anything you like. Can we turn round?'

As he obeyed, his spirits lifted. All he wanted was to erase the stupid mistake he had made in deciding – if that was what he'd done – on this reunion. Did he ever really decide anything? He was so completely uncertain most of the time. Pushing her back the way they had come, he said, 'What do you think of it round here?'

'Think?'

'Yes.'

'Not a lot.'

'You mean it's dull? Dead?'

'Well, isn't it?'

'I suppose so. That's what I like about it.'

Joe was strolling up the lane towards them. 'I'd like to go now,' Ruby called, in an entirely different voice, light and friendly.

'You would?' Joe asked, startled.

'Yes, please!'

Daniel hovered nearby as Ruby was helped into the van and her chair folded and stowed inside. Again he was willing to help, but clearly he was redundant. The van backed and turned, he waved, they drove off. He may have looked sad, and perhaps he was, a little. Actually he was counting his losses and already feeling better as he walked back to the cottage which he had come, surprisingly, to like very much. He entered the room quickly, like someone late for an appointment.

Miriam urged him to continue writing to her, as often as he liked and as freely as he wished. She adored letters, she said. From this he assumed that she kept her mail to herself. He saw her now as some kind of romantic realist. As well as receiving letters, she enjoyed writing them too. He learnt to his surprise that she had a lover, Bobby, of whom she spoke critically. He was too near at hand for letter-writing, and anyway she met him on too regular a basis. If he did write, his letter would be crabby and stilted. 'Academics are all the same,' she wrote. 'Like married men.' Daniel smiled at the comparison.

Correspondence passed between them in spurts. Warming to the task, he would pick up his pen and scribble out flights of fancy, including whatever rubbish was floating about in his head at that moment. This delighted her. Her own letters were dashed off in a hectic looping hand, sometimes a barely legible wild scrawl. He would get a first impression of madness, which the deciphered words soon dispelled. Her messages were full of gumption. They came on an assortment of papers, often torn violently from jotters, badly folded and stuffed anyhow into the envelope as if she was living her last day on earth. Everything spoke of haste and disorder, yet his abiding impression was of a lethargic woman.

There was usually a graphic phrase or two to amuse him and liven up the morning. In one she wrote, 'I haven't seen Bobby for weeks. He keeps running off to London to attend conferences, or so he says. I'm so frustrated, I could accommodate the Household Cavalry and all the horses.' In another she said that the sight of a snowdrop had made her burst into tears.

She admitted that she didn't feel herself to be wholly in charge of her utterances. Life shook things out of her. Otherwise, barely alive at all, she oozed about like a slug.

She could make a penetrating remark and follow it with a shower of banalities that he nevertheless appreciated, since they were endowed with a spirit unique to her. He was always unprepared for her tender touches. She would use trite words and yet the sentiment rang true.

Daniel's mother was expecting him home for Christmas. This was not so much arranged as understood. When an invitation came from Miriam and he decided to accept, he wrote to his mother saying his plans had changed and he'd arrive a couple of days late. She replied submissively, accepting his poor excuse. These were the delaying tactics he had been forced to practise from time to time when he'd been seeing Bridget, but now he was a free agent with nothing to hide. Why did he still speak in such evasive terms? He wondered if deception had become habitual with him.

On Saturday he sat at his all-purpose table. The trance necessary for writing wouldn't come. Having risen later than usual this morning he was too restless to work. What else stopped him? he thought. Well, there was no doubt that he was obsessed. He set off on his circular walk, seeing nothing, hearing Miriam's throaty voice, wanting it to cease and to go to her at once in one and the same moment, cursing himself for a fool at the mercy of his fantasies, who was being used as a standby and that was all. A sexual obsession was more debilitating, more of a humiliation, he was thinking, than any other kind. How insulting to be ruled by another's moods and caprices.

Determined to make up for lost time and work, he came back almost at a trot. He had sat down and was just about to start banging on the keys in a fury when someone knocked on the door.

Through the window he saw the familiar red van parked near the churchyard wall. Is Miriam writing twice a day? was his first thought. He opened the door. A bearded postman, not the regular one, held out a small buff envelope. The man looked surprised, as if his face was

a mirror reflecting Daniel's consternation. 'Telegram, sir.'
His eyebrows shot up.

'For me?'

He tore open the envelope and read: YOUR MOTHER
ILL. SERIOUS. RING AT ONCE. DENISE. Denise Weeks
was a shy young countrywoman who had met his mother
at a painting class. She lived on a nearby council estate.

'Any reply, sir?'

'No, no reply.'

Daniel watched the red van pull away, then made for
the call box. Why did he feel such a surge of anger? Surely
he didn't suspect his mother of faking an illness?

She answered immediately, in an enfeebled voice. He
heard her say, 'Sorry.' When he asked how she was, she
couldn't hear him. Denise came on the line. 'Is that you,
Daniel? Look, I don't think your mother should be left
alone.'

'I see.'

'Are you coming soon?'

'Tomorrow. No, I'll come the day after.'

'She's very ill, you know.'

For some reason, he refused to believe it. His mother
had never been seriously ill in her life: she wouldn't allow
it to happen. This was some form of conspiracy. A desperate need to reach Miriam blinded him to everything else.
He would get there, even if he had to crawl.

Still in the call box he rang her number. 'Oh, hello,' her
voice said after a delay. 'Sorry to keep you waiting, but
I've just got out of the bath. I'm standing here dripping,
not wearing a stitch. Isn't that interesting?'

'Yes. I'm ringing to say I can't come on Monday. My
mother's ill.'

'Oh, I'm sorry. Is it serious?'

'Apparently, yes. I won't know till I get there.'

He put down the phone, staring at it. Then he stepped
out into the road. It was mid-morning, the village spell-
bound. Afterwards he would tell himself that it was at this

229

precise moment that his obsession ceased and he understood he was alone again.

He reached Somerset to find that his mother had been removed to hospital. Denise, shy and fresh-cheeked, was curt to him. She told him in a severe voice what had happened and then said she would have to leave, she had her husband's meal to prepare. There had been storms in the area lasting nearly a week. Flood water draining off the fields after two days and nights of heavy rain had poured into his mother's courtyard and begun to seep under her back door. Panic-stricken, she spent hours fighting it off with a broom, standing out in the downpour again later to unblock a drain, poking at it vainly with a stick. A bronchial infection became pneumonia, then this was followed by a thrombosis.

In the cottage hospital, a tiny twelve-bed affair, she sat propped up by fat pillows in her crocheted pink bed jacket. She breathed painfully, but suffered far more from the loss of privacy. Above all she was horrified to think that she was such a nuisance to everyone. Daniel told her, 'Stop worrying, it's their job.'

A nurse brought her a cup of tea and one for him. His mother blushed, thanked the nurse abjectly, then whispered in her son's ear as he bent down, 'It tastes horrible!'

He was informed later that she had a fair chance of recovery. But they didn't know what he knew, that in spite of her terror she wished to die. Next day she suffered a massive thrombosis and was dead within minutes.

The hospital called him with the news. It was early evening. He had just filled the kettle – her kettle – and switched it on to make tea. He went on making the tea, only blindly, emptied by the nullity that death brings, not knowing what else to do. Later he sat by the window and tried to think of her. Unsure to the very end of everyone – even of him, her son – she must have died, he thought, as she had lived, bright-eyed with fear like a defenceless animal.

He had given Miriam his mother's phone number. She called that same evening. He opened his mouth to answer and promptly gagged on the first words.

'Daniel, what is it, whatever's the matter?'

'I'll have to ring you back – later –'

An hour passed. He rang back unwillingly, afraid he would make another ass of himself. This time his voice held steady. He listened to Miriam speaking tenderly at the other end of the line as though he himself belonged with the dead, and thought abstractly how nice it was of her to make the effort. She passed on to other matters, which he seemed incapable of grasping. Had he missed a vital scrap of information? Nevertheless he heard her out without answering, merely grunting now and then. She asked twice if he was still there.

'Yes, I'm here.'

'Will you call me when you're feeling better?'

Not understanding the question, he said he would.

'Promise?'

'Promise.'

'You're not exactly convincing me.'

'I'm sorry.'

She let him go.

He sat for a while, shivering in the knowledge that he was now liberated from everyone. It got dark. The sky had been in a state of gloomy twilight all day. He threw another log on the fire, but it took some time to catch alight. He gazed at the room. He had never really considered that he might one day find himself alone in it. In this cottage where he had always been the son he was now the sole survivor, and an orphan.

What was Miriam doing at this moment, what was she thinking? Her life was very much her own affair. Daniel sat outside it, naked, a child of forty-eight, sitting on a doorstep asking what next, shamefully ignorant still of most things. What had he learnt? Only that he had no one but himself, he was alone inside his own skin, reaching out with his hands to a fire which burned uncertainly.

In bed that night he felt even smaller, and wanted to crawl on to his dead mother's lap, something he was unable to recall doing as a small child. He fell asleep trying to imagine it. In a dream towards daybreak he boarded an airport bus, his flight booked to America. A girl of seventeen who was a complete stranger, slight and virginal, sat unselfconsciously on his lap and told him her life story. She had brown marks on her temples, one on each side. 'They think it's cancer,' she said, naturally and easily. 'That's why I'm going, for a test.'

A thought suggested itself. 'Are you a typist?' As his mother had once been, he nearly added.

She nodded. 'Yes, that's right.' And she rested her head on his chest. Sweetness flowed in, behind the breast-bone.

He cried out, 'I knew it!'

His own loud voice deep in the dream woke him up.

It was late March. He began to notice changes. Because of the scarcity of trees it was nothing dramatic, but here and there on the long flanks of barren moorland he saw patches of sharp green appearing.

The funeral was over. He had come back. One night, sitting quietly like a ghost, he thought about the bare magnolia he had seen that time outside the hospital library, about to clothe itself in flowers just as his skin and bones were about to flower so inexplicably, like a great blessing. What a joy the ripening flesh was, what luscious blooms it put forth and how sweet they were. From black buried roots, in that wormy slime. Flowers of sugar and darkness raised up. For a year now the magnolia's ghost had haunted him. The hard way back was lit for him by its creamy torches. He thought of its flesh, its curves, hung like lanterns between sex and death. To think of their clean lift was to be set free. Through the flesh we could be enslaved or liberated. We could lose ourselves in someone else, forget fear, find love. The magnolia had been waiting there inside him like a promise. 'Who knows, it may wait always, like desire.' It had darted in through the eyes and dropped seeds. Now it stirred inside him, around the root of his sex, like passion.

He had reached another spring. Only northern races could appreciate what that meant. He was through another dark time – the song of the cold was over. Another death had given birth to him. He was without parents, he had broken with his wife, yet his mind and body, instead of warring as enemies, were back in tune. The solitude hadn't finished him off. On the contrary he had stuck it out. Now he was ready to boast of his newly discovered taste for it. Each time he shaved he poked his chin forward jauntily.

As a result of his mother's death he could now consider putting his own cottage up for sale and clearing off his debts. As it turned out he actually made a small profit. His mother's place stood empty, it was roomier than his own, and his brother – who owned a half share in it as provided in the will – wasn't interested in living there. Daniel negotiated a deal to purchase his brother's half share by a series of instalments.

Grief for the woman who had been his mother would catch him unawares, as he sat mutely at the table reminding himself of his good fortune. I'm alive, he thought. I am sitting here feeling happy for once. Then her stricken face would appear before him and he could read on it the hopeless anguish of her last years. At once the world drained from him, leaving the terrible bleak emptiness that life had become for her. Like his father she had expressed a wish to be cremated, so there wasn't even a grave for him to visit. She was blotted out without trace. He wanted to weep but couldn't shed any tears. He wondered whether his grief was for her or for himself, left alone with his thoughts of death.

They had never revealed themselves openly to each other without fear. Now it was too late. 'Maybe grief is for what might have been and now can't ever be.' These

233

thoughts came to his mind. He would sit lifelessly, a prisoner of melancholy, at the mercy of his mood. It passed. The dismal truth would lose its power. He jumped up, ran from the room and knew another truth, that there was only him, and for some mysterious reason he had been spared, granted another chance.

Spring had come, but the squalls and rough buffeting went on just the same. Once or twice on wild nights, hearing the sound of the wind and rain like a raging sea, he found himself wondering what had become of Stephen Gonne. Was he still taking those solitary night walks along the promenade? Or had he found another playmate to accompany him? Was he out there now, at this moment, with his 'blazing secrets'?

A year had gone by. Fourteen months ago another wind had torn at the building where he lay freezing, as winter rain poured down his window and he waited terrified at what might be in store for him, smelling of his own death. The whole of his craving flung him backwards, to when he had once been a man. What was he but a lie, a dead weight, a grey webby creature entangling others and finally himself? A bad husband, a loving but neglectful father, he had forfeited his right to a home and everything that was meant by the word – everything. Truly he no longer had an address. Now, all at once he had two.

One morning, there was young David at the door.

'How are things with you?' he said.

Daniel asked him in for a coffee. He came in smiling seraphically, this visiting angel. He bemused his host with his sweet light, so much so that for a moment Daniel mislaid the question. Then he wanted to answer, 'Oh, I'm in luck. I'm such a lucky man. A year ago I was lost and now I'm found,' but his mouth replied for him and said, 'Fine. I'm alone now, but aren't we all?'

234